LO\

By

KATHERINE CACHITORIE

AUSTIN BROOK PUBLISHING

*This novel is a work of fiction. All characters are
fictitious. Any similarities to anyone living or dead
are completely accidental. The specific mention of
known places or venues are not meant to be exact
replicas of those places, but are purposely
embellished or imagined for the story's sake.*

Visit
www.austinbrookpublishing.com
for more information on all titles.

**MORE INTERRACIAL ROMANCE
FROM BESTSELLING AUTHOR
MALLORY MONROE:**

**THE PRESIDENT'S GIRLFRIEND
SERIES IN ORDER:
THE PRESIDENT'S GIRLFRIEND**

**THE PRESIDENT'S GIRLFRIEND 2:
*HIS WOMEN AND HIS WIFE***

**DUTCH AND GINA:
*A SCANDAL IS BORN***

**DUTCH AND GINA:
*AFTER THE FALL***

**DUTCH AND GINA:
*THE POWER OF LOVE***

THE MOB BOSS SERIES
IN ORDER:

ROMANCING THE MOB BOSS

MOB BOSS 2:
THE HEART OF THE MATTER

MOB BOSS 3:
LOVE AND RETRIBUTION

ALSO:
ROMANCING MO RYAN
ROMANCING HER PROTECTOR
ROMANCING THE BULLDOG
IF YOU WANTED THE MOON

AND
MORE INTERRACIAL ROMANCE
FROM
BESTSELLING AUTHOR
KATHERINE CACHITORIE:

ROMANCING MO RYAN

LOVING THE HEAD MAN

SOME CAME DESPERATE:
A LOVE SAGA

WHEN WE GET MARRIED

3

KATHERINE CACHITORIE

ADDITIONAL BESTSELLING
INTERRACIAL ROMANCE:

A SPECIAL RELATIONSHIP
YVONNE THOMAS

AND

BACK TO HONOR:
*A REGGIE REYNOLDS
ROMANTIC MYSTERY*
JT WATSON

ALSO AFRICAN-AMERICAN
ROMANTIC FICTION
FROM
AWARD-WINNING
AND
BESTSELLING AUTHOR

TERESA MCCLAIN-WATSON:

DINO AND NIKKI:
AFTER REDEMPTION

LOVING HER SOUL MATE

AND

AFTER WHAT YOU DID

**COMING SOON FROM
MALLORY MONROE:**

**DUTCH AND GINA:
BOOK SIX**

MO AND NIKKI

AND

MOB BOSS 4

Visit
www.austinbrookpublishing.com
for updates
and
for more information
on all titles.

ONE

I didn't mean to hurt her. John Malone was certain that was going to be the excuse. It was such a common refrain that he didn't even put it in his police reports anymore. Because they did meant to hurt them. Because any man who would beat on a female as if she was his personal punching bag, meant to do exactly what he had done.

He knocked vigorously on the door of the modest yellow home. "Police, open up!" he yelled as he knocked. He wasn't just the police, but a
police captain who was second-in-command of the entire Brady, Alabama police force, a man who rarely handled these kinds of calls. But he was only a block away, on his way home, when the call came in.

The door was snatched open by a muscular, t-shirt wearing black male with a bloody cloth pressed against the side of his face. His eyes were beginning to show signs of puffiness and he had that regretful look many abusers often displayed after the fact. John immediately unbuckled his sidearm. If the perp looked this bad, he could only imagine what the victim looked like.

"She's crazy!" the man was yelling as soon as the

6

door flew open. "She's fucking crazy!"

"Step outside, sir."

"She's nuts. I'm telling you she's a nutcase!"

"Step outside, sir," John said again.

But the young man frowned. "Why are you asking me to step outside? Look what she did to me!"

As soon as the young man began to remove the cloth, revealing the full extent of his swollen face, John grabbed him, slung him outside, and threw him, face down, onto the porch.

"What are you doing?" the young man yelled in agony.

But John was not a patient man. He had told him twice to step outside. He wasn't telling him again. He placed a knee into the small of the younger man's back, wrestled control of his wrists, and then removed handcuffs from his waist belt.

"What are you doing?" the younger man yelled again. "I could be dying here! I need a doctor and you're arresting me? Seriously?"

"Where is she?" John asked as he cuffed and began frisking his perp. "Where's the victim?"

But the young man was too wrapped up in his own anger for any of the captain's words to register. "I'm an attorney, what are you doing, man? You can't arrest me!"

John could hear police sirens coming near and he suddenly could feel a presence even nearer. When he looked up, in the direction of the doorway, he saw a slender black woman standing there. She wore a pair of gray workout shorts and a cut-off sweat shirt that revealed the bellybutton of her gorgeously flat, toned stomach. She was right around the same age as the suspect, mid-twenties or so, and her huge, golden brown eyes sparkled with alertness. He stood to his feet.

"Looking for me?" she asked him.

Her longish, jet black hair was framed around her apple-shaped face in a layered bounciness that made her seem so familiar to John that it, at first, stumped him. *What the hell*, he said to himself. "Are you the victim?" he asked her.

"*Victim*?" the young man yelled. "You must be joking! I'm the one who called the cops! Don't you see what she did to me?

A patrol car arrived at the scene, causing the young woman to look away from John. She recognized the arriving officer as Wayne Peete, one of only two blacks on the Brady Police Force and a young man she once had dinner with. He stepped out of his car and hurried toward the front porch.

"A victim, no," she said as she looked back at John. "I'm no victim."

It was only then did John realize this woman didn't have a scratch on her. "Are you telling me that you were the instigator here?"

"He was the instigator."

"She's lying!" the cuffed man yelled.

8

"Shut the fuck up!" John yelled back, slamming his foot into the small of the young man's back. The woman winced.

"I didn't expect to see you here, Cap," Officer Peete said as he arrived at the porch. Then he looked at the woman in the doorway. "Shay?" he said when he recognized her.

"Get this character to the hospital," John ordered the officer, lifting the bloodied man by the catch of his collar and slinging him toward Peete. "Let Doc Harlin have a look at him."

"Yes, sir."

"And get a statement if he cares to give one."

"Yes, sir," Peete said and began moving the man down the steps.

"All I did was slap her," the young man said angrily. "I'll be the bigger person and admit I slapped her. Shouldn't have done it, but I did it. But that's all I did to that bitch. Look what she did to me!"

Peete glanced at the young woman again as he all but dragged the still complaining man to his patrol car.

The young woman looked once again at John. John was already staring at her. Usually she was uncomfortable when men assessed her, especially when the last thing on her mind was anything sexual. But for some reason this guy didn't turn her off that way. Maybe it was because he looked like he'd been through hell himself and could use some care and attention of his own. Maybe because he favored her favorite actor, Robert Downey, Jr., with his head full of chestnut-brown hair piled in no discernible style around his strong, unshaven face. His tired blue eyes were bloodshot and joyless. His sports jacket was slung over jeans and a sweat shirt as if by merely putting on a jacket he could project the image of a cool professional rather than the burned-out cop he appeared to be. He, in fact, looked the way she felt: scattered.

"What's your name?" he asked her.

"Shay Turner. Yours?"

"I'm asking the questions here. Is this your house, Miss Turner?"

"Yes."

"Lived here long?"

"Two weeks."

"You've lived here on Bluestone Road for two weeks, or here in Brady for two weeks?"

"Both," Shay said.

John nodded his head. He knew he'd never seen her around these parts before. He didn't see how he could forget a face like hers. Not just because she was pretty: pretty faces in Brady were a dime a dozen. But this woman had a sharpness about her that made him know not to even go there with her. She meant business. He could see it in her swagger, in the way she moved from side to side just standing there as if she had promises to keep and this was holding her up. He could see it in her smooth, oak-brown face dominated by her large, golden brown eyes that seemed laced with a small, almost hidden dose of vulnerability, and a massive dose of ice.

"That guy," John continued, "he's your husband?"

Shay wanted to say something harsh to drive home the point that there was no way under this sun that he was any husband of hers. Although, just a few hours ago, before the truth knocked her sideways, he had been a strong contender. "No," she said instead.

What's his name?"

"Lonnie Resden."

"And you're telling me he's the one who started the fight?"

"He hit me first. I call that starting a fight."

"Over what?"

If he wasn't burned out, Shay thought, then he was shell-shocked. She'd seen it before. Only this cop's demons didn't appear to be from some hard-fought war, but from life itself; that maybe his best days were behind him and he was just trying to stave off the coming night. He was surviving, she figured he wanted to live, but he wasn't thriving anymore.

"What was the fight about, Miss Turner?" John asked her again.

"It's hard for me to answer questions from a man who won't even tell me his name. I feel at a decided disadvantage here. The least you can do is answer that

11

one question."

Any other suspect and John would have answered her question, all right. Answered it with cuffs on the wrist and a swift ride to headquarters. But with this particular suspect, he couldn't go there. "John Malone," he said, answering her earlier question.

Shay's eyebrows lifted up into a quizzical arch. John Malone? This burned-out looking cop was Captain John Malone? The legendary cop who cracked some of the toughest cases in Brady's history? She'd only heard about him. This was their first face to face.

"Why would a man of your rank and position be handling a domestic like this?" she asked him.

John stared at her. Had they met before? He would not have forgotten that face. "You know me?" he asked her.

"I wouldn't call it knowledge," Shay replied. "I'm a reporter with the Brady Tribune. I know your reputation."

John almost asked which reputation was it: his legendary cop rep or his legendary lady man's rep. The former rep he was not worthy of; the latter rep he wore like a badge of shame. But then he caught himself and stood erect. What the hell was he going around the mulberry bush with her for? "Answer my question," he said instead. "What was the fight about?"

His reputation also included how gruff he was, Shay remembered. "His women," she finally replied. "The fight was about his women."

John nodded. He had already worked that part out. These domestics were usually always about one of two things: money or some other woman. Or *women* in this case. "So you found out he was cheating on you?"

The pain was still there. But Shay wasn't about to reveal that part of herself to this cop. "Yes."

"He put his hands on you first?"

"When I refused to ignore the facts, yes, he did."

"So he hit you and you fought back?"

"That's right."

"And let me guess," John went on, "you didn't mean to hurt him?"

"I meant to beat the shit out of him," Shay replied without batting an eye. "Of course I meant to hurt him."

John almost smiled, so much for his theory, but he kept it professional. "What did you hit him with?"

"The first thing I could get my hands on."

"Which was?"

"A lamp."

This surprised John. He had heard of weapons before. "A lamp?"

"It was the first thing I could get my hands on."

"Mind showing me this lamp?"

Shay was a reporter, so she knew the drill. It was just annoying and embarrassing that she had to be associated with the drill. But she was in it now. Thanks to that good-for-nothing Lonnie Resden.

She went inside her home, leaving the door open for

13

John to follow.

It was even smaller than it looked from the outside, with a boxy living room leading into an even smaller dining room. The kitchen was just around the corner, apparently, by the arch of the doorway that led in that direction, but Shay stopped just short, at the foot of the dining room, where a lamp lay on the floor. She didn't pick it up, however, knowing that it would be evidence.

"That it?" John asked as he moved in front of her.

"That's it," Shay replied.

John crouched down and looked at the decimated lamp, his expensive loafers sparkling against the white tiled floor. He pulled a pen out of the inside of his jacket and lifted the lamp shade that had sagged down against the base. There were blood stains on the base, with a crack in the base itself. She really let him have it, he thought, looking at the condition of the lamp.

He then stood again and looked around the area itself. Although books and papers were stacked on the kitchen table, and also on the living room's coffee table, there were no visible signs of any struggle of any kind.

Then he looked at her. She was staring at him with such intensity in her eyes that he suddenly felt exposed. As if she knew, like he knew, like nobody else bothered to know, that he was a burned out shell of the man he used to be.

"So the fight took place right here?" he asked her.

"Yes," she replied, "if you want to call it a fight."

14

"What do you call it?"

Her arms were folded now, as if just looking at that lamp again brought back the memories, and he was suddenly sorry she had to relive them on his account. But he had a job to do.

"What happened, Miss Turner?"

Shay exhaled. It was no use. She was in it now. "He slapped me across my face. I grabbed the lamp and knocked him upside his head. That's what happened."

"One lick apiece?"

"That's right."

"Only yours could have killed him."

Shay was offended. "He put his hands on me. What was I supposed to do? Let him? Then tomorrow it's a black eye. The next day it's a broken arm. Then the day after that it's me in a pine box. No, sir. He'll get in that box first."

Tough as nails, John thought, and he liked that she was that way. But why did he keep seeing an almost searing vulnerability in her eyes? "After you hit him with the lamp," he asked her, "did he hit you again?"

"No."

"Had he ever hit you before this incident?"

Shay hesitated. "No," she said, without looking John in the eye. "We hardly ever argued before."

"Until you found out about the girlfriends?"

A sadness appeared in Shay's eyes. "Yes."

John looked down, at that flat tummy of hers again,

15

and then back into those radiant eyes. Something she wasn't telling him, he could sense it.

"And it was just you and Resden in this house when the incident occurred?"

"That's correct."

"Are you here alone now?"

"Yes, Captain Malone, I'm alone. No-one's here. No one witnessed any of this but me and Lonnie. So I guess it's my word against his."

Maybe, John thought. Then he glanced over at the dining room table. "Let's sit down for a minute," he said to her, pulling out his notebook. "I need to get some background."

They moved over to the dining room table. John pulled out the side chair for Shay, oddly aware of her femininity and attractiveness. Usually, when he was investigating cases, he didn't give a damn. Then he moved next to her to the armed chair at the head of the table. But as soon as he sat down in that chair, he caught Shay grimacing painfully as she moved around in her seat. He also noticed she was sitting with a sideways slant to her small body.

"What's the matter?" he asked her as he sat his notebook on the table.

Shay looked him in his tired, blue eyes. And although her mouth told him nothing was wrong, her eyes told him something completely different.

And his heart pounded against his chest. Which

16

surprised him. He stared at her. "Come here," he said, reaching out his hand.

"I told you nothing's wrong."

"Come here," he said again, a frown on his face. There was more to this story, a lot more, he could feel it in his bones.

Shay didn't see the point, especially since she was beginning to wonder if Lonnie had been right and she had completely overreacted, but she took his hand and went to him anyway.

John was surprised at how small her hand felt in his. And again she seemed so contradictory to him: so tough, but so vulnerable too.

He opened his legs, lodging her between them, and moved to the edge of the chair. "Turn around," he said to her.

"Captain, I'm okay. For real, though. I told you nothing's wrong."

"I saw you grimace, Shay. So don't tell me nothing's wrong. I have to see the full extent of your injuries or that asshole may just walk and end up doing the same thing to another woman. Is that what you want?"

"Of course that's not what I want."

"Then turn around."

But that didn't stop her embarrassment. That didn't stop the shame she felt. A look of distress came over her face.

John felt her distress. He couldn't explain why but

17

he felt it as deeply as if it was his own distress. She stood there, barely taller than he was sitting, her troubled eyes piercing him. "You didn't do this, Shay," he felt compelled to say to her. "This was done to you. You understand me? He did this to you. And I'll be damned if you're going to stand up here in front of me and be ashamed of what somebody else did to you."

Shay was, at first, taken aback by his sternness. Who did he think he was talking to her that way? He didn't know her like that. But her umbrage gave way to the reality of what he'd said. Because he was right. She had nothing to be ashamed of. She didn't do this to herself. This was done to her.

She turned around.

John had been in law enforcement since getting out of college and he'd seen it all in his fifteen-year career. Viewing bruises on backsides was nothing new to him. But the fact that he was suddenly nervous about viewing her particular bruises was something entirely new to him.

"Where did he bruise you?" he asked her. "Right, left, or both?"

Shay closed her eyes. "Right," she said.

"I'm going to need to see it for myself. Do you give me permission to take a look?"

She exhaled. At least it was John Malone. At least she knew *of* him, even if she didn't know him personally at all. But he had a rep as an honest cop, no smears or corruption anywhere near his name. Besides, if he didn't take a look then some pimpled-faced evidence tech would, and those types loved to gawk. She preferred the captain. "Yes," she said.

John reached over the waist band of her shorts and panties and carefully slid them both down over the mounds of her naked butt. His cock began to throb as soon as he saw the fullness of her tight ass, and the velvety smoothness of her brown skin. She was so small and round and plump that he now knew why he felt as if this was not going to be an ordinary viewing. He was getting a severe hard-on just looking at the upper end of her ass.

But when he pulled her shorts and panties down further and looked at the deeply-ingrained, belt buckled bruises that littered her small right cheek, his jaw tightened. There were three of them in a row, all beginning to show signs of welting up, as if this young woman had been branded.

Then John couldn't hold back. "That bastard!," he said, and as soon as he did tears appeared in Shay's eyes.

John felt her tremble and was suddenly so concerned that he turned her around. When he saw the tears in her eyes, his heart pounded against his chest. It felt so odd to him, as if this was his woman that asshole had beaten, and this was his woman crying in front of him. It wasn't, he knew it wasn't, but it was affecting him as if it was. And he did something he'd never done with a

19

victim before in all of his years in law enforcement: he pulled her into his arms.

Shay should have been startled when this cop embraced her. Especially a cop with a rep like John Malone. She should have been downright shocked. But she wasn't. Because she needed a friendly hug. And that was all it was, she decided, a fellow human being showing a little compassion. And that would have been all it was, had it ended there. But it didn't end there.

When Shay stopped sobbing, and they stopped embracing, John turned her back around. And his heart pounded again. If Resden was still here John would probably strangle him lifeless with his bare hands. How dare he do this to her! He felt angry and he felt frustrated. But he felt disheartened, too, at just the thought of what this young woman had gone through. He'd always been known to be adroitly empathetic to victims of crime. That might explain why he was thirty-seven and already burned out. But his response to Shay and her injuries was beyond empathy. It felt personal to him. And he was stumped to know why.

He pulled back up her shorts, kept his hands on her slim hips. For a moment they just stood there. And then John spoke softly. "What happened here, Shay?" he asked her.

Shay paused again, and then walked back to her chair, where she sat back down in that sideways slant. It was obvious she didn't want to talk about it. It was also

20

obvious that she had to talk about it.

"Lonnie lives in Birmingham," she said. "That's where I met him. Since I moved here to Brady a couple weeks ago, we hadn't seen each other. He decided to come down and spend the weekend with me. When he got here he wanted to have sex. We were in a committed relationship so I didn't see where that was a problem. But then he started talking about how he wanted to be a dom one day and he wanted me to be his submissive and I'm going whoa, back it up. Since when have you been into shit like that? I'd only been gone two weeks. He said it's no big deal and that he thought we should try something new, something he'd just learned himself. I was game, I thought it would be fun. I don't have a problem with a little variety in the bedroom."

John's penis began throbbing at the thought of her, variety, and a bedroom.

"So we played around with different things. When he started tying my hands and my feet, I mean, I thought it would be something different. I wouldn't let any stranger do it to me, no, of course not. But I knew Lonnie, I'd known him for years. He was going to be my . . ." She cleared her throat. "But when he pulled out this weird strap and started beating my behind, that's when the fun ended for me."

"You don't enjoy sex spankings?" John asked her. And as soon as he asked it he began to redden. Why in the world did he ask her that? Those bruises weren't

21

some sex spanking and he knew it. He couldn't believe he asked her that!

But Shay, to John's relief, didn't blink. "What he was doing to me wasn't a spanking, Captain," she said. "That's what he tried to call it, too. But I felt like he was brutalizing me."

John nodded his head. "Understood," he said.

Shay paused, as if the thought of what Resden had actually done to her was still a bitter taste in her mouth, and then she folded her arms. "I was so angry at that joker that all I saw was red. I wanted to hurt him back. But I knew I had to play it right. My daddy always taught me to never fly off the handle because you may need that handle. So I told him to wait, that I had a better way for us to do it. I encouraged him to untie me so I could show him. He had the upper hand as long as I was tied down. But once I was freed, I grabbed the first thing I could get my hands on, that lamp, and tried to knock the shit out of him."

John frowned. "You guys were in the bedroom?"

"That's right."

"Then how did the lamp end up in here?"

"Because he ran up front and I chased him with it, that's how. I wanted to kill his crazy ass. Nobody was going to beat on me with some buckled strap like I wasn't a person anymore but an object! He didn't explain how that shit worked to me. He just started doing it."

John understood fully what she was saying, but he

also remembered what she had said. "Why did you tell me it was about other women?" he asked her. He didn't figure her to be a liar, but you could never tell these days.

"Because it's true. It was about other women. He admitted it. He said some woman introduced him to it, and then he met this other woman who was into it, too. Which was fine, to each his own. But Lonnie and I were supposed to be in a committed relationship. What the hell was he out chasing tail after I'd been gone for only a couple weeks? Come on, now. Those were the kind of questions I was asking him. Then he got bold about it and told me the truth."

"That he'd been fooling around with those women far longer than a couple weeks?"

Shay looked at John. "Right," she said. "He was proud of it, too," she went on. "He said it wasn't a big deal, that he even wanted me to meet one of them, the one he called his submissive. 'She wouldn't mind,' he said. I cussed his ass out, that's how I felt about such a meeting. And because I wouldn't leave it the hell alone and wouldn't shut up, he slapped me. And that's when I did the real damage to that lamp."

John almost smiled, but he was still too invested in her emotions to minimize it. "So when I showed up you decided to keep the first part of this sordid episode private?"

Shay hated that she wasn't completely honest with him. "Yes," she said.

23

John stared at her. She looked so vulnerable to him. "Do you still want to keep it private?"

Shay looked into his tired blue eyes. She didn't think she'd have a choice. "Yes," she said. "I consented to being tied up and maybe to being spanked too. But what he did to me crossed the line. Some people may get off on bruising, but I don't. And he should have known that. But . . ."

John could just feel her anguish. "But what, Shay?"

"But I don't know what to do about it." She looked at John with troubled eyes. "He slapped me, but I knocked the shit out of him, too. And as for that beating in the bedroom, I had consented to trying it. He went too far, but he stopped when I told him he was going too far. So I don't know. I'm more angry at him for cheating on me than anything else. But I'm angry at him for bruising me, too, and I don't want to give him a pass on that, either." She shook her head. And looked at John.

John smiled. "After what you did to him, my darling," he said, "trust me: the last thing you gave him was a pass."

Shay actually smiled too.

"So," John said, closing his notebook, "I don't see how the bedroom part is relevant."

Shay stared at him. He saw the hopefulness suddenly appear in her eyes. "Does that mean, are you saying that it won't be in your report?"

"Not unless Resden makes an issue out of it, which

I'm sure he won't."

"He won't," Shay assured him too.

"And since it started out as a consensual sex act by some wannabe who didn't know what the hell he was doing, and he stopped when you told him you didn't want to go that far, it won't need to be in my report."

Shay stared at John. *What a man*, she had a sudden need to say. But she wasn't about to say something that lame. "Thanks," she said instead.

John gave her a quick smile that didn't last two seconds. "Resden's already admitted that he slapped you first, so I'm determining him to be the primary aggressor."

"Even though he's the one who needed medical attention?"

"That's correct. You won't be charged."

Relief flushed over her. "Thanks," she said again.

John stood up, his notebook in hand. "He said he was a lawyer. Is that true?"

"It's true. He practices out of Birmingham."

"I see," John said, his eyes staring at her in that contemplative cop stare of his, as if he was thinking long-term. "Think he'll pull this stunt again?"

"Pull it again? Ah, no. He won't have the chance."

"Yeah, they all claim that. Until lover boy comes back, begging for forgiveness."

Shay didn't respond. She could show him better than she could tell him because she never, not ever, gave

25

second chances once she realized who she was dealing with.

For some reason John had hoped she would dispute his claim. He was slightly disappointed when she didn't bother. "Are you afraid of your boyfriend, Shay?" he asked her.

"My ex-boyfriend and no, Captain, I'm not afraid of Lonnie Resden in any way, shape, or form."

He was inwardly pleased. "Okay," he said, nodding his head and looking down at that tummy of hers again, remembering her tight, firm ass, imagining just how toned and gorgeous the rest of her body probably was. "I'll get his statement and arrest him on an assault warrant. But I have to be honest here. It's the prosecutor's discretion to file charges against him, and the chances of that happening are probably remote. More than likely the prosecutor won't bring charges at all and he'll be released as a lesson learned. But maybe getting arrested will make him explain his intentions better the next time he has a woman in his bed."

John looked for a reaction from Shay. Did she still have feelings for the guy? But her face didn't reveal a thing. "But I think he now understands that if he hits you again," John continued, "he may not be around to get a trip to the hospital."

Shay smiled that wonderful white smile John found mesmerizing. Then she stood up and extended her hand. "Thanks for your help, Captain Malone."

John shook her hand, and immediately a hollow feeling washed over him. It felt as if he was saying goodbye to somebody near and dear to him, when nothing could be further from the truth.

"Take care of yourself, Shay," he said. Then he added: "As I'm sure you will."

They both laughed, and then he left.

He stepped off of her porch, got into his truck, and looked once again at that little yellow house as she closed her front door. And then he exhaled. *Wow*, he thought. *What was that about*? He'd never had that kind of connection to any stranger before in his life. For more than a minute he even thought she might have belonged to him. Which was ridiculous, he thought as he cranked up. He hadn't been divorced a month, had just gotten out of the pan, how in the heck could he even consider jumping into some pot? It was funny, was what it was.

But he wasn't laughing. Because he had to have her. He had to have her in the worse way. He kept seeing that tight ass, kept inhaling her wonderful scent, kept wanting his dick in her pussy so bad that it was a physical need that felt like a gunshot wound. He needed to take care of this. He needed *her* to take care of him.

And without thinking about it, without attempting to rationalize something this irrational, he got back out of his truck and walked, in quiet desperation, back to her front door

TWO

Shay leaned against the door a few moments longer after John had left. She had to compose herself. Because she couldn't stop wondering what in the world was that all about. The way he held her, the way he made her feel, the way she felt a connection to that man, to a *cop* of all people, was baffling the hell out of her. She was literally just hours out of a major breakup, she wasn't even technically on the rebound yet, and already she was letting some man get a rise out of her? She smiled and shook her head. She didn't like drama and this day had way too much in every direction. She therefore left the door, went over to the shattered lamp, and began to pick up the pieces.

When the doorbell rang, she froze. It felt almost like a premonition. As if she was expecting it all along. As if she knew, even though she didn't know a damn thing. She moved away from the area of the lamp and walked over to her living room window. When she saw that the big Chevy Silverado was still on her driveway, her heart rammed against her chest. Because somehow she expected it. But that didn't make it any easier.

She moved slowly toward the door. And when she opened it, and saw that it was indeed John Malone standing there, she didn't say a word, and neither did he. She simply pushed open the screen door, and let him back in.

"Hey," he said.

"Hey," she said.

And then they just stood there.

John's heart was pounding as he stood in her living room. And when she walked away and went back to picking up the pieces of the broken lamp, as if she understood fully why he had come back, he began moving around the room. He picked up a book off of the coffee table and glanced at the writing on its spine. Stared briefly at an African print on her wall. But it was all camouflage and he knew it. Because it was Shay Turner that he wanted, and nothing less was going to do.

So he kept moving until he made his way to the dining area where she was just reaching for the base of the lamp. He stood behind her, and removed the base from her hand, sitting it on the dining room table. There was such a sense of inevitability about this moment that it stumped them both. And electrified them both.

John placed his hands on her small arms and began to rub. Shay closed her eyes and enjoyed his masculine touch. And when he sat down in the chair at the head of the table, moving her body with him until she was standing between his legs again, her ass in his face again, the anticipation of what he was going to do to her suddenly had her aching for his touch.

She turned and faced him. "Why did you come back?" she asked.

"I came back to be with you, Shay," he said. "I want

29

to see you, and feel you, and be with you. If that's okay with you?"

Shay was getting hot just from his presence alone, and he was asking if it was okay with her?

"Is it, Shay?" he asked again. "Is it okay," he asked as he slowly began to pull down her shorts and panties, "if I touch you?"

"It's okay," she said almost breathlessly as he slowly turned her back around. She felt his fingers slink her clothes down and completely expose her ass. Only this time he kept pulling until her shorts and panties were all the way down to her ankles.

And he touched her. Shay closed her eyes as soon as she felt his warm, opened hand cruise across her un-bruised cheek.

"I knew you would be soft," John said as he rubbed her, lust in his eyes. "I knew you would have the texture of velvet when I touched you."

Then he looked at her bruised cheek. His jaw tightened once again at just the thought of that asshole Resden beating on her without regard to her delicacy. He wanted to tell her how sorry he was that something like this had to happen to her, but he felt compelled to show her rather than tell her. He therefore pulled her closer, and kissed her on her bruises.

Shay was at first startled when she felt the wetness of his lips on her. Because she thought it would hurt. She even moved to turn around she was so startled, but he had her small body so enclosed in his big arms that she couldn't move at all. And then, as he continued to kiss her, as she continued to feel the impalement of his lips pressing into her, she didn't want to move at all. Because it felt comforting. Because his heat was taking the heat out of those bruises. His power was removing the power of the pain. She leaned into him.

He caressed her bruises with his tongue, licking over each welt, slowly and gently and expertly. His heart was pounding and his cock was throbbing. He'd never done anything like this in his life. Hell yeah it was crazy. Hell yeah it didn't make sense on any level! He'd only just met this woman and he was kissing her ass? If anyone would have told him when he took the call and came to this little yellow house on Bluestone Road that he'd be doing something remotely resembling what he was doing now, he would have kicked their ass, forget kissing it.

But he was kissing hers. And licking hers. And caressing every crevice of her tight, round bottom. He couldn't stop kissing her ass and licking her ass and caressing her. Then he moved down, to the top back of her thighs, licking and kissing and caressing her there.

"Open your legs," he told her. And Shay was so caught up in the passion of the moment, so in need of this kind of affection, that she did as he commanded. She opened her legs.

"Lean on the table, baby," he said to her as he got down on his knees. "I'm going to taste your pussy."

31

Shay felt the steam of his words to the roots of her hair. And when she leaned over and felt his tongue lick between her legs, her breath caught. And when he parted her cheeks and began to eat her, she felt her pussy jump.

"You taste so good," John said as he ate her. "I knew you would make me want to mouth-fuck you for hours."

And as his mouth did its work, his fingers began to join in. First one and then another one slid into her folds to feel the moisture that was now all over her. Shay kept bucking as he licked her and kissed her and fingered her. Her insides felt as if they were inflamed. She felt as if she could have an orgasm from his fingers and his tongue alone. What was happening to her? She never planned for anything like this to happen! She'd never, not ever allowed some guy she'd just met to so much as touch her. Why in the world was she allowing this man to bend her over her own dining room table and mouth and finger fuck the shit out of her?

But it felt so good. And it didn't feel wrong, not with him. Somehow it felt normal. Like it was supposed to be. With this guy, this cop, it felt normal. Which, she knew, was about as abnormal as it could get.

But the insanity continued, because the sloshing sounds of his fingers massaging her wetness, and his lips sucking and kissing on her pussy was all that could be heard in her quiet home.

Until he managed to speak again.

"Where's your bedroom?" he asked between kisses, his voice now sounding almost hoarse. "Do you want to do it here or in bed?"

It wasn't exactly a choice. From the way he said it they were going to do it, pointblank, just the location was the issue. And from the way Shay felt, she knew it too.

"Here," she said. She didn't think she could make it to any bedroom.

He sat back in the chair and turned her around, facing him. He removed his gun and holster, tossing them on the table. Then he removed his blazer and slung his shirt off over his head, revealing a tanned, six-pack stomach and a gold chain around his neck. Shay had already figured he was well-built. She didn't realize just how well-built until he removed his shirt.

And then he unzipped his pants.

"Do you want some cock, Shay?" he asked her as he looked deep into her eyes. He was looking forward to her reaction. He usually didn't give a damn how females reacted whenever he pulled it out, although they always reacted favorably. But this time was different. "Think you can handle some real cock, Shay?"

"Pull it out," she said, her voice with that edge of confidence he liked. "I'll let you know."

He pulled it out.

And as soon as he did, as soon as his hand reached into his pants and pulled out that beautiful, hard cock, her

KATHERINE CACHITORIE

eyes went from mild amusement to impassioned sensuality. She stared at it, not just the size of it, which was massive, but at the magnificence of this thick, pink rod that she knew would give her nothing but joy. She even licked her lips.

He loved her reaction. He would have smiled at her reaction, in fact, if he wasn't so fucked up horny that he could barely see straight. "Put it in your mouth, honey," he said to her. "I want to feel that sweet, little mouth of yours on me."

Shay didn't have to be asked twice. She crouched down and took him in her mouth. It was exactly what she wanted to do. She wanted that rod in her mouth. And she took him slowly, licking him as if she gave head every day of the week.

But he loved how she was doing him. She moved slowly and deliberately, as if she was licking her favorite ice cream cone. And then she took him whole, going all the way down on him, causing his flat, ripped abs to clench.

She was back up again, licking the eye of his penis in a wet, circular swerve, and then licking all the way down to his massive balls. He tasted salty and powerfully masculine. His masculine scent, in fact, was making her so ready to have this man inside of her that she no longer felt the pain of those bruises. It was as if all of that crazy shit Lonnie had tried to do to her, and the reason for those bruises, would be perfectly sane if John tried to do

34

it to her.

John slouched down in the chair, leaned his head back, and enjoyed every second of her mouth fuck. Shay looked up at him, at his ripped stomach that was moving in and out in heavy suctions, at his muscular arms that were pulsating, at the way his chestnut-brown hair slung down over the chair as he held his head back. When she first saw him she knew he was nice looking. But daamn, she thought. This man had it going on. The total package, was how she'd describe him.

John knew she had something extra going on too. Not just a pretty face or a nice bod. Other pretty females with nice bods never had him wanting them like this. And she knew how to fuck too. She knew how to do him right. And it wasn't just the act that was turning him on, but the woman doing the act. *She* was turning him on. He rubbed her soft hair and looked down at her as she went up and down on him, slow and fast, with just the right rhythms. It felt masterful to him. Master strokes this woman had. She knew how to do him.

And when she looked up at him, her innocent eyes so big and trusting and vulnerable, his breath caught. It felt as if he knew her. She was no stranger to him, although, in truth, she was. But it didn't feel like she was. It felt as if she was his woman, and had been his woman for a long, long time.

He couldn't help how he felt. He just couldn't help it. And it all just felt so good and so right to him. He leaned

35

his head back again, as her strokes increased.

As she continued to go down on him so wonderfully, he kept expanding in her mouth. His washboard abs started inhaling in a suction motion to the feel of her wonderful tongue, and then exhaling as she moved down on him. And then it was nearly unbearable. He knew he had to take care of them both, and he had to do it now.

He pulled a condom out of his pants pocket as she continued to give him head. "Do you want me to fill you up with this cock, Shay?" he asked as he unwrapped their protection.

"Yes," she said, pulling his rod out of her mouth, a stream of silkiness slipping out with it. "That's what I want."

"That's what I want too," John said as he quickly sheath his rod and then placed his arms just under her thighs, as if to protect her bruised cheek. He lifted her up and placed her down on the top tip of his erection.

"Can you take it all?" he asked her.

"I can take it all," she said, and then held onto his broad shoulders as he lifted her down, breaking through her tender folds, until she could feel his balls against her ass.

"Oh yes," she said as he continued to ease her down, "it's so full."

"And you're so tight," John said. "Just the way I like it."

And his control nearly broke, as soon as he moved

36

up and down in her. When she winced, he knew he had to slow it down again. Her body was still getting accustomed to his massiveness. Which was odd, she knew, since Lonnie wasn't exactly small himself.

But John had a strength behind his size that made her folds tighten around him as if they were being sucked to him. And that tightness, that oneness, caused them both to let out sighs of delight as soon as they got into their rhythm.

She rode up and down on him in perfect harmony with his upward thrusts. He was breathing hard now as his erection could barely handle the tightness. He had to fight against coming right away, it felt just that fantastic. And the look on her face as he fucked her, that satisfied look, made him all the more ready to come.

But he held on. For her. Because she needed this release. Somehow he knew they both needed it. He lifted her t-shirt over her head, a move that revealed her taut breasts. He immediately started kissing them and licking his tongue over her nipples. She threw her head back as he kissed and licked and squeezed her breasts in a way that made the feelings deep inside of her intensify.

He pulled her body against his, lying her head on his shoulder, wrapping her into his big arms, as he fucked her with ever increasing thrusts. The thrusts were so intense that Shay felt as if she was on fire from inside out.

He looked at her, and she looked at him, and they kissed on the mouth. At first they both thought it would

37

be a simple kiss. Just a thank-you from one to the other. But it became such a sensual, passionate kiss, that for a moment all movement stopped. He wrapped her into his arms, and kissed her long and hard.

Shay felt as if she was in a different place when he kissed her. His lips, his tongue, his warmth caused her to close her eyes and want to just remain right in his arms. And John felt the same way. It was a kiss that wasn't supposed to feel this incredible. But it did. And he couldn't stop kissing her. They remained there, wrapped into each other's arms, and they just couldn't stop kissing.

Until his cock demanded attention too and his strokes began again. They kept kissing, but it slowly began to take a backseat to what was happening to them below. And he kept thrashing into her, gliding up and down along her tight walls, until neither one of them could control it.

It happened. Shay tried to lift off of his cock as the intensity was too powerful, but he wouldn't let her go. He kept her down, as his entire rob throbbed and stretched to the fierceness of the feeling. And he kept thrashing into her. She yelled out her elation, and he grunted out his. Until there was no more gas, not a drop, in either one of their tanks. They were empty. They were emptied out.

For more than a few seconds they just stayed in that chair in that small dining room. Although Shay had never had a one-night stand, John had had plenty of them, and

38

he feared that this encounter more than likely would be yet another one. Why he feared it, he couldn't even say. Because everything about it was wrong, yet everything about it was right too. He had never had this kind of connection with another human being in his life before, not ever. And it was disturbing him.

And the unprofessionalism of it. He was a *got*damn police officer on a call for crying out loud, and he was fucking the victim? He'd never done anything like this in his entire career! But he'd done it now. He wanted her just that powerfully. And, to his everlasting shame, he still wanted her.

Shay, too, was baffled. She'd never had a one-night stand, let alone something so riddled with emotion as whatever this was. It had been as if John Malone was no more a stranger to her than her own parents, and it made no sense. And now, after the fact, after the act, the hard, cold truth was setting in: this man, despite that outburst of passion they'd just experienced, was, indeed, a stranger to her.

She moved to leave as reality set back in, but he pulled her back against him. John wrapped her in his arms. He didn't want her to go. He should let her go, but he couldn't. His muscular chest and ripped abs were now pouring with sweat. It was late. He was exhausted. But this wasn't some slip-up with him. He wasn't the kind of man that had slip-ups. This meant something. It had to. He had been around long enough to know that this was far more than some sex-charged, momentary lapse.

"You okay?" he asked her as he held her.

"Yes," she replied. And then added: "But I think you'd better leave."

John knew it too. He should have never come back. He was just divorced and she was just literally in the midst of a break-up. What in the world were they thinking?

But that damn feeling would not let John go. "Believe it or not," he said, suddenly feeling a need to redeem himself, "but I've never done anything like this before."

Shay looked at him. "And you think I have?"

"Oh, no," John immediately moved to clarify. But when he looked at her and realized she was smiling, he smiled too. "I'm just sayin'," he said.

And they laughed. But then, like an elephant in the room ready to knock them down: reality came around.

And he released his grip on Shay.

Three days later, on a bright Monday morning, Shay drove her dark blue VW Beetle convertible into the parking lot of the Brady Tribune newspaper building. She stepped out into the warm, Alabama sun, her dark shades covering her sensitive eyes, and retrieved her shoulder bag and briefcase from the passenger seat. Although she was dressed for success in her short, pastel-colored skirt, her bright orange sleeveless silk blouse, and her short, white jacket that reached down to her waist, she still felt nervous. She had only been in town two weeks, but it hadn't been going great for her.

The editor appointed a fellow reporter to be her team leader, for one thing. And that would have been completely fine if she was some rookie who didn't know squat about journalism. But she'd been a reporter for four years, and had been a top reporter at the Birmingham Union-Star, one of the most prestigious newspapers in the state. The idea that she would need somebody shadowing her, overseeing her work, making sure she wasn't incompetent was a tad insulting. But then again, she thought as she locked/alarmed her car, she needed this job badly. So she dismissed her complaints, and headed for the entrance.

As soon as she walked into the newsroom, Ronnie Burk, that chubby, blond-haired team leader of hers, was standing at his desk, grabbing his suit coat and keys, preparing to leave.

"Let's go, Shay," he said to her.

Shay stood there, her briefcase in one hand, her shoulder bag in the other, and frowned. "Go where?"

"City Hall," he said, heading for the exit. "They're having a presser on background."

"Oh," Shay said, following her team leader. "The mayor's having it?"

"The police. It's about that big drug bust they scored over the weekend. Nearly half a million bucks in dope,

41

can you believe it, headed straight for these quiet streets of Brady."

"Quiet my ass," Shay said and Ronnie laughed.

They hopped on the same elevator Shay had just a minute ago hopped off of.

"Just remember," Ronnie said as he pressed the first floor button, "you can't ask any questions on background, and when you write your story you can't quote the source."

Shay wanted to roll her eyes. "Ronnie, I know. I've done this job before, remember?"

Ronnie smiled. "Point taken. But this ain't Birmingham is what I'm saying. We do things differently around here."

The elevator doors dinged open at the first floor.

"Who's going to be our source at the press conference?" she asked, expecting it to be, as it usually was, Sergeant Riley, the police spokesman.

"It won't be Riley," Ronnie said as they stepped off. "This was one of the biggest drug busts in city history. They bring out the big guns for the big busts. John Malone is our source on this one."

Shay didn't miss a beat, as they hurried out of the revolving doors of the newspaper building, but her heart seemed to skip many beats.

And it didn't let up when she arrived at the City Hall Press Room. She knew she would have to meet him again. They had kind of decided to go their separate ways after Friday's encounter, and she had dismissed it as just some crazy emotion of the moment. But she never dreamed she'd be face to face with him this soon.

But she was, as soon as they walked into the Press Room. The presser had already begun, with John Malone, his suit coat off, his white dress shirt topped off with a pair of expensive suspenders. He looked so sexy that Shay almost stumbled as she walked. But she didn't. She held it together as she made her way to the back of the room. She wanted to hide because she was sure she was blushing. Because as soon as she saw him the memories flooded back. She remembered him so tanned, so ripped, so naked. She remembered him holding her, pounding her, tasting her. She remembered it so vividly that she was already getting wet.

Ronnie felt that they could have squeezed in for a closer seat, but he nonetheless followed Shay to the back of the room. He liked Shay Turner. He liked her friendliness and her meekness and the fact that she was easy to work with. He looked at her as she stared at John. She was everything, he felt, a young lady should be.

John commanded the room as he spoke on background. And although Shay would never know it, his heart began hammering as soon as she walked through that press room door. She looked so radiant, he thought, as soon as he saw her, so beautiful. He was busy all weekend, caught up in the drug bust of the century as far as Brady's history went, and he didn't have time to even consider phoning her.

But he had wanted to phone her. Especially when, late at night, he finally made it to bed. He'd think about her smile and her sharp sense of humor, and her intellect. And he'd think about the way she tasted, and the way that sultry mouth of hers came down on him so hard. He got a hard-on just thinking about her. Late last night, after another long day, he got in bed and couldn't stop thinking about how tight her pussy was and how intense she made him feel. It got so bad on him that he actually pulled out his rod, and fondled it until it spilled.

But he didn't call her. Now, as he looked at her walking toward the back of the room, her short skirt flapping around her shapely brown legs, her face taking on that confident look he adored, he wished he had.

That was why, after the press conference, as some of the reporters gathered around John to see if he would answer questions they knew he wouldn't, he called her out. She and Ronnie were heading for the back exit, and she was more than happy to make a clean getaway. He looked beyond the crowd.

"Turner!" he yelled out.

Shay's heart dropped.

"Shay," Ronnie said, tapping her on the shoulder, his face surprised. "I think he's calling you."

It was only then did Shay look in John's direction.

"I need to see you in my office," he said, and then

44

returned his attention to the press of reporters surrounding him.

Shay and Ronnie headed out of the press room altogether. Ronnie was staring at her. "What would Captain Malone need to see you about?" he asked her.

"How should I know?" she replied, although she had a darn good idea.

John's office was on the fifth floor of the Police Memorial Building and his secretary, a young, pretty brunette, told Shay to have a seat against the wall. It was an uncomfortable wait. Not just because of having to deal with John again and therefore having to acknowledge that they actually went there Friday night, but that secretary of his kept taking peeps at her as if she was big-time suspicious. It was as if she either knew, by virtue of the fact that Shay was there at all, that something sexual had happened between her boss and Shay, or she suspected something had happened. But either way, she didn't seem to like it.

And that was why Shay was antsy. She'd only been in town a couple weeks, but even she had heard how John Malone had a reputation with the ladies. She knew, if word ever got out that she'd also been with him, that she'd be categorized too. She'd be considered yet another one of these silly women around here who too easily gave their bodies to a good looking man, only to be dumped on as he moved on. But it was a fact: she had given her body to John.

John arrived after about fifteen minutes of Shay just sitting there. He was still in his shirtsleeves and suspenders. Still gorgeous personified. And that cologne he favored still whiffed into the air like a sweet aroma as soon as he entered the room. Shay suddenly felt small when his large presence entered. To remedy such an odd feeling, she stood to her feet.

"Chief wants to see you, sir," the secretary said to him.

"In a minute," he replied, and then looked at Shay. "Right this way, Miss Turner," he said.

Shay followed him through his office door and closed it behind them, the secretary still staring as the door shut her out. Shay suddenly felt suffocated, especially since John remained at the closed door, directly in front of her.

"I know we both don't have much time, but I wanted to say hello to you properly," he said to her.

"Okay," she said.

"You were going to leave without speaking to me?"

"Ronnie Burk, he's one of my colleagues---"

"Yeah, I know Ronnie."

"He wanted me to go with him to check out the Hopson trial over at the courthouse."

"It would have only taken a moment, Shay."

Shay didn't know what to say to that. She was going to leave without speaking, it was a fact. She didn't know what else she could say.

46

John looked down, at that body he'd been dreaming about, and then back into her face. "How have you been?" he asked her.

"I've been good. And you?"

"Busy."

"Yeah, I've heard. Congratulations on that drug bust."

"It was a long time coming, I'll tell you that," he said as he ran his hand through his thick, brown hair. "We've been on to those guys for months on end now. So I'm grateful."

"I'll bet."

"I don't know if you know this, but the prosecutor's office declined to file charges against your boyfriend Resden."

"My ex-boyfriend. Yes, I know."

"You okay with that?"

Shay thought about it. "I'm okay with it. When I finished with him I felt like justice had been served."

John laughed. Looked at her small ears and the curve of her small neck. "Oh, fuck it," he said and moved up closer to her. "I need to see you again, Shay," he said. "To be with you again."

But Shay was shaking her head. "No, John."

"Why not, babe?" He said this and leaned over and kissed her on the side of her face.

"Because I can't---"

He kissed her on her neck.

"I can't just---"

"You can't just what sweetheart?" John asked as he kissed her ear.

"I can't---"

Then he captured her mouth with his and pressed down hard. Shay immediately felt the fire of his tongue as he coursed around hers in a sweet assault. He pulled her into his arms, and she wrapped her arms around him. And just like that they were at it again. Shay could hardly believe it. Was this all it took? She had been certain that she would never allow anything like this to happen ever again, and just three days later and she was not only allowing it, but enjoying it!

And she was really enjoying it, as he deepened his kiss, as he pressed his rock hard body into hers as if he wanted to make certain she understood just how much he was enjoying it too. He reached beneath her skirt and placed his hand inside of her panties. He began tinkling her clit, rubbing it and pulling on it in such an expert way that it made Shay moan. And he kept on kissing her. He kept on searing her with his lips.

When his hand moved down further, between her legs and his finger entered what was already a wet passage, her entire body tightened with anticipation. John knew his way around pussy, it was obvious, because he was handling hers to perfection. He eased his finger in, moving it ever so gently from side to side, capturing the moisture and rolling around in it.

"You're so wet, babe," he said as he fingered her. "I love to feel your wetness."

Shay loved how he felt it, too, but she wasn't about to verbalize it. She was still upset with herself for allowing this to begin again. But if felt so damn good!

It wasn't until John whispered in her ear, "I want to fuck you again, Shay," did she realize what she was doing. And she immediately pulled back from him. His finger at first resisted her pull, remaining lodged in her pussy, but then he slowly, reluctantly pulled out.

"I can't do this," she said.

John understood her anguish. He understood she didn't want some physical relationship without any commitments. But he also understood his need. "We're two consenting adults, Shay. I'm not asking you to marry me."

"Right," she said. "You're just asking me to fuck you. Just like you ask woman after woman after woman to fuck you. Despite what happened Friday night, John, which I still can't explain, I'm not one of those women."

John's heart plummeted. That wasn't what he meant at all. "Of course you aren't!" he said as if that was self-explanatory. "I don't want you to be."

"Then why are you bothering with me? Why did you call me to your office? Why are you trying to get into my panties when you've got a wealth of women whose panties are readily open to you? It's a dead end street. You don't want to make any commitment to me and I'm

49

not ready to commit to you or anybody else. I just broke up with Lonnie. It's too damn early. What happened Friday night was just an aberration, it was just an outpouring of passion. Nothing more. You know it and I know it."

Although she was right, John still didn't see their relationship as only physical. They made an emotional connection too, although neither one of them seemed to want to admit it.

"Who says we have to commit to each other?" he tried again. "Maybe we can just take it slow and see where this leads." He didn't know why he was so hell bent on having her in his life. Yes, her sex was great, and yes, he loved being with her like that. But damn. He didn't really know her, did he? And that emotional connection they did make kind of necessitated that it would require some kind of commitment eventually. When he knew, like she knew, neither one of them were ready for that.

"I'd better get to the courthouse," she said, turning to leave. "Ronnie's waiting."

But John grabbed her by the arm. Shay looked at him. Why, she wondered, was he trying so hard to beat this dead horse?

The look on her face, of a kind of bewildered distress, gave John pause. The last thing he needed was a hot and heavy affair with a woman who turned him on the way Shay did. And the last thing Shay needed was him.

He reluctantly, but necessarily let her go.

THREE

Three months later

John Malone woke up in a bed he quickly realized was not his own and with a hangover that caused his sleepy blue eyes to squint. He looked to his left and saw a woman lying there, some bleached blonde with her big pink breasts uncovered and her eyes, were they blue, brown, or green he couldn't say, closed. Kate or Kim or some such name. Something with a K. He remembered a K. He remembered talking with her at the bar last night, laughing about stamina and studs or some other filler talk, and then following her to her house. Had a few drinks, he remembered drinking with her, and kind of, sort of remembered screwing her.

He did something with her at any rate. She was screaming in excitement and wiggling underneath him, and he remembered thinking at the time how he wished she would shut the hell up.

Now it was another five a.m. and he was crawling out of another woman's bed with yet another overused, limp dick that gave him nothing more than memories so unremarkable that he wasn't even interested in the details. He just wanted out.

She began to stir as he stood up, causing him to glance back at her. The harsh glare of the morning light revealed lines of age around her eyes that the darkness of the bar never would have. But she remained asleep as he moved lightly. He was hoping she wouldn't wake up. Because he wasn't interested. He was never interested the morning after, no matter who the female was. If she woke up she might want to exchange numbers. She might want to make plans to meet up again when he knew meeting up again with some female he met in some bar wasn't going to happen.

He just wanted out.

He grabbed his jeans and jersey from various spots around the room, and began dressing quietly but quickly. He glanced in the wastebasket by the bed. Saw two freshly-used condoms, one at the bottom and another that barely made it and was hanging on the wastebasket's rim. *Damn*, he thought as he dressed. He fucked her twice? *Her*? When he didn't remember anything worth remembering about their hookup, just her screams of excitement and wiggles, and how her excitement irritated him.

He shook his head as he zipped his jeans and slipped into his shoes. She was probably a decent woman. Was probably just lonely and out for a good time. Maybe was even hoping against hope that she'd find something different out there this time. Then he came along, some big-dick Willie who promised nothing but had to know, if somebody's desperate enough, that nothing was a promise too.

The thought of her vulnerability caused him to pause, and look at her again. Was she hopeful? Did she fall asleep last night thinking she'd finally found Mister Right? Did she think that all of her false starts were finally over? He sure hoped not. For her sake he prayed she wasn't that naïve. She was old enough to know better, but that didn't mean she did. Hell, he was pushing forty and still sleeping around like some teenager in heat. He should know better too. But what could he do about it? He always told them up front to expect nothing from him. Was it his fault if they didn't believe him?

After dressing and then tossing those condoms into her bathroom toilet, he headed for the exit, glancing back at Kate or Kim or whatever her name happened to be. It was as if in watching her he could will her to remain at peace, to remain asleep, so that he, like the bastard he knew he was, could silently get away.

Shay locked the door of her small, two-bedroom house on Bluestone Road and hurried to her Volkswagen Beetle. She wore an ocean blue flair-leg pantsuit with a sheer, white blouse that crisscrossed at her ample breasts, a red scarf around her neck, and a pair of apple red stilettos that gave her the kind of height she enjoyed. She wasn't normally a matchy-matchy type of dresser, but today her wardrobe just fell into place.

She cranked up her Beetle, sat her shoulder bag and briefcase on the passenger seat, and drove off. Her neighborhood was older and quiet, with rows and rows of small cottages made along the same style as her small, rented house, but she loved it there. The neighbors, many of them seniors, treated her as if she was a long lost daughter. And one elderly woman who lived across town, a woman everybody called Aunt Rae, was slowly becoming her closest friend.

Aunt Rae's home was on the north side of town in an area they called Dodge. It was the poorest part of town, but it also housed many older people who bought homes there decades ago when the area was safe and clean. And they, like Rae, wasn't about to move.

Shay drove across to Rae's small, frame styled house and pulled quickly into the driveway. She never had to blow her horn because Rae was always ready. And sure enough, as soon as Shay's VW turned into that driveway, the front door crept opened and Rae Braxton came burrowing out. With the array of plastic bags she carried with her, from her crocheting needles and balls, to her bags of medicines and ointments, she could easily be mistook for a bag lady. Even Shay, who first met her at the local drugstore, thought she was perhaps homeless or very nearly. But it wasn't the case. Rae used to be one of the most respected schoolteachers in town, a woman who brook no mediocrity. And although she'd been retired for nearly twenty years now, and was certainly eccentric, she still possessed an excellent mind.

She was also ornery as hell and some often

wondered why Shay even bothered with her. Nobody else did. But Shay could see beyond Rae's gruff exterior. When Shay looked into the old woman's eyes, she didn't see gruff. She saw somebody terrified of being alone, but just as terrified of settling for less. In other words, Shay saw a lot of herself in Aunt Rae.

Rae locked the door of her home and hurried across her lawn to Shay's passenger side door, gripping her bags as if they were her security blanket. Shay moved her shoulder bag to the back seat and smiled as the short, dumpy woman with the warm but stern face, stepped in.

"Good morning," Shay said.

"You took your pretty time getting here," replied Rae. "I don't play that late game."

"You won't be late, Aunt Rae. Have I ever gotten you there late one time?"

"I'm just saying. I don't play that late thing."

"Yes, ma'am," Shay said with a chuckle as she backed out of the driveway.

Rae, as was her way, gave Shay her routine look-over. Then, as was also her way, she shook her head.

Shay smiled. "What is it this time, Auntie? I'm matching this time."

"It's a waste, that's what time it is. Girl with your brains and beauty and yet you're all alone."

"Here we go," Shay said as she turned the corner off of Liberty Street.

"Not in my day," Rae continued. "They didn't play that in my day." Shay laughed at Rae's use of popular vernacular. "In my day," Rae went on, "women had a career, but they also managed to find themselves a good man too, raise a family, and be as happy as larks. I was like you back then, stubborn just like you. Expecting too much from these men and nobody could tell me a thing. And it all passed me by. No husband, no children, nothing. Just memories of a career long gone and old students who don't know me anymore, and all these new students who don't care to know me. I don't want that to happen to you."

Shay didn't respond to that. Because she would love to have herself a good man and raise a family, too. Only the good man part had pretty much eluded her so far.

The ride became a silent one as both women looked at the road ahead of them rather than each other.

Finally, a red light. Rae looked at Shay.

"You heard from that Lonnie Resden fellow?"

Shay looked at the school kids as they crossed the intersection. "Nope," she eventually replied.

"You should call him."

Shay could not believe it. "I should?"

"Yes, I think so."

"Think again, Aunt Rae, I'm not calling him. Look, I know you think Lonnie was a good choice for me. Hell, I used to love the guy, I thought he was a good choice too.

But after what he did, after fucking everything in a skirt and then slapping me because I refuse to go along with his bullshit, no way. He'll be the last human being on earth I'll call."

"But---"

"But what?"

Aunt Rae held up her fingers. "He's an attorney, number one. He's great looking, number two. He's great in bed, and don't you dare tell me he's not. You can look at that brother and tell he is, number three. He's a great provider, number four. He'll give you some beautiful babies, number five. He's got a lot going for himself, young lady."

The light turned green and Shay drove on. She couldn't disagree with anything Rae had said. "Yeah, you're right," she admitted. "He's all of that you mentioned, but he's so much more. Because he's also a cheater, he'll hit a woman if he gets riled up enough, he's not the kind of man I could trust as far as I could throw. So no, thank-you, Aunt Rae. I'll never get that desperate. He's one person I can do without in my life."

Rae stared at her and then smiled. "Good," she said, nodding her head. "I was just testing you."

Shay looked at Rae, realized she was smiling, and smiled too. "Let me get you out of my car," she said, and they both laughed.

They arrived at the Brady Senior Center where vans were unloading the less-mobile seniors and some members of the staff were helping with the unload. Rae grabbed up her bags and pocketbook, staring at the Center. Then, as was her way, she shook her head.

"This place is filthy," she said. "And that staff are the laziest young folks I've ever seen in my life. When I was their age I was working eighty hour weeks without giving it a second thought. They can barely pull forty. And look at the grass. Brown already."

"Why do you do that?" Shay asked her elder. "Why do you sit in my car every morning and complain about this place? Then you turn around and show up here every single day. You never miss a day. I don't get it. Why do you come if you hate this place so much?"

"I don't hate it," Rae said, still staring at it. "I just hate the fact that it's all I have."

Shay's heart dropped. "Auntie, I didn't mean--"

Rae looked at Shay, saw the concern in her beautiful eyes, and smiled. "I know you didn't, dear," she said, squeezing her hand. "We've only known each other for less than three months but already I know you could never harm a flea. Unless that flea is a two-timing man."

Shay laughed. But Rae's look lingered. "Well?" Shay asked, knowing something more was coming. When Rae just sat there, Shay smiled. "Okay, let me have it. What's your pearl of wisdom for me today?"

"Name your price," Rae said, pointing at Shay. "And if you can live with it, stick to it. But make sure you can live with the price you set. Name your price."

Shay knew what Aunt Rae had just told her had absolutely nothing to do with money, but she didn't ask for an explanation. She never did. Because every little pearl of wisdom she had given Shay ultimately was understood in time. Just never at the time it was given.

"Have a good day," Shay said as Rae got out of the VW and, in her always brisk manner, made her way toward the Senior Center's entrance as if her life depended on her quickness, all of her bags in tow. Shay stared at the old woman, wondered how it must feel to get up every morning to do something she didn't want to do and to go someplace she didn't want to go. But loneliness was a bitch. It could be so crippling that, for some people, bad company was preferable to no company at all. Shay, however, wasn't one of those people. Then again, she thought as Aunt Rae disappeared inside the Center, Rae wasn't either, once upon a time.

But Shay couldn't think about that right now. Because she had an appointment of her own to get to. She drove above speed limit along the bustling streets of Brady, Alabama. She never dreamed she'd end up living anywhere other than Birmingham. She went to school there, the University of Alabama at Birmingham, and, after graduation she got her dream job there: a reporter for the Birmingham Union-Star. Her career was on the upswing. Until a new editor came along, hired his niece as the new crime reporter, and started relegating Shay, a woman with, by that time, three years of experience under her belt, as second string to his fresh-out-of-college-niece.

When she didn't go quietly into that good night of earning a paycheck without making waves, and protested the nothing assignments the editor was continually tossing her way, her life became a living hell. He began to badmouth her around the newsroom, decimating her hard earned reputation as a strong reporter. And when the decision was made to lay off some staff in a cost-cutting move, her name was at the top of the list. She fought it, she even made it all the way to arbitration, but she lost in the end. There was no malice aforethought, the arbitrator concluded. They had a right to get rid of their dead weight. *Dead weight*, they called her, because of the nothing assignments she was forced to work. And the fact that she had taken on her mighty boss at all became the death knell for any bright future in Birmingham. No newspaper would hire her after that.

That was why, when she was offered a job with the smaller Brady Tribune some two-hundred miles away, she took it. It was a major step-down from her glory days in Birmingham, but she was nobody's fool. She had to eat and pay her bills. Her parents, who had moved to Philadelphia before she graduated college, were school teachers barely able to pay their own bills. And her only sibling, a sister in California, had her own life to live. Her ex Lonnie Resden offered to help her, but she turned him down. No way, she had thought at the time, was she allowing herself to be that dependent on some man. She gladly accepted the Brady job.

Now she was twenty-six years old and felt as if she was starting over; as if she still had so many points to prove. Sometimes she even felt like the untalented rookie her former boss tried to make her out to be. Mainly because her new employer seemed to have heard those Birmingham rumors and was treating her as if she wasn't quite up to their standards either. They even had another reporter as her team leader, as if a woman with her years of experience still needed some strong man to guide her along the way. But she didn't complain. She needed the Brady Tribune far more than they needed her.

She turned into the parking lot of the City Hall complex refusing to relive all of that past pain. This was a beautiful new day, she thought as she found an empty spot and killed the engine, and she was embracing the day.

"Thank you, Lord, for this day that You have made," she took a moment and said. "I will rejoice and be glad in it."

And then, with only seconds to spare, she got out of her vehicle quickly and raced up the steps of the huge building. Ronnie was waiting at the top of the steps.

"It's about time," he said as his round, cherubim face looked like an orange pumpkin against the Alabama sun.

"I'm not late," Shay said as she made her way to the

top. She lifted her shades off of her face and placed them on the top of her head. "I'm exactly forty-one seconds early."

Ronnie grinned. "My bad," he said and she grinned too. "Ready?" he then asked her, his small, green eyes trailing down the length of her low-cut white blouse that contrasted gorgeously with her dark skin, and the very feminine, sheer scarf she wore around her small neck.

"Yes, I think so," Shay replied. Although she still didn't feel she needed a team leader, she had to deal with the fact that she had one. And sometimes he was great, giving her pointers on local history and how to handle the deep racial tensions that always seemed to bubble just below the surface in Brady. Other times, however, she felt leery of him, as if his geeky, golly-gee persona hid a darker side where something was off; where something just wasn't quite right.

"Remember what I said," Ronnie said. "Keep your mouth shut and I mean shut tight. If you go on and on all you're going to do is alienate the veteran reporters, and anger the brass. Just keep it zipped and you'll be fine."

"Ronnie, this isn't exactly my first press conference," Shay politely reminded her leader. "I've been a reporter for over four years. I've been to a ton of these press conferences."

"I understand that. But this is your first press conference with the chief of police here in Brady. You don't know that guy like I know him, Shay. If you ask questions he doesn't want to answer, it'll be hell to pay. Keep your mouth shut I'm telling you."

Shay nodded as if she agreed, although she didn't see how she could. A reporter was supposed to ask questions, not just stand back and let the chief of police or anybody else recite their talking points unchallenged. But she had to keep it together. She wasn't there to ruffle feathers.

Besides, she was reasonably certain that John Malone, as the Chief's right hand man, would be at the presser too. And seeing him again, after three months of avoiding seeing him at all, was going to be a challenge.

Ronnie, however, was completely in the dark about her concern. He was looking down at her outfit again. "You look real pretty," he said.

"Thanks," Shay said with a smile, but was uncomfortable when his look lingered. "Ready?" she found herself asking him.

"I was born ready," Ronnie said with a grin, his green eyes moving back up to her brown ones. And then they hurried through the revolving doors.

After rushing home to shower, shave, and brush his teeth, John Malone also ended up at City Hall. He walked through the revolving doors smoothing back his thick brown hair, buttoning his smartly tailored suit, stepping hard and fast in his tasseled leather loafers. Looking, to the average eye in his average southern town, as if he'd just stepped off of the pages of a glam magazine rather than out of the bed of a strange woman whose name he still couldn't recall. Last night he was Hit-and-Run John: drinking too much, sexing too much, not living right by even his own barometer. Today he was Captain John Malone, senior investigative officer for the Brady, Alabama Police Department, and the department's Mister Fix-it.

By now his hangover wasn't excruciating anymore, except in the sun when even his shades didn't stop his head from throbbing. But he was out of the glare of the morning sun. He took off his shades to prove that point. And as he walked into the City Hall press room, he walked, instead, into the glare of the media. And even in that media's glare, where a battle-weary, jaded cop like John Malone had seen it all, he didn't see Shay Turner coming.

He had been standing beside the podium for nearly twenty minutes. He stood with his legs spread eagle and his muscular arms akimbo as he held fort beside his boss, the chief of police Walt McNamara. They were answering the usual questions by the usual reporters about the usual cases. Until Shay raised her hand.

John hadn't seen her in three months and the last time he saw her they had agreed to go their separate ways. He had wanted a sexual relationship with her, but she wasn't having it. Which, in truth, he was glad to know. He would have been mighty disappointed if Shay, like so many other women in his life, would have given him that kind of leverage.

He still vividly remembered his first encounter with her, when he was deciding whether to haul her ass in on a DV. More than seeing that backside of hers, or even hugging her and fucking her, he remembered the emotions she invoked in him. It was so unnerving that he still couldn't work out what was that really all about. And that body of hers, and the way she so perfectly went down on him, had at one time given him wet dreams more befitting an adolescent than a man his age.

This time, however, it wasn't about them. It was all business with her. She, in fact, stood up and asked the chief of police, a well-respected and feared man with twenty-eight years of experience, if he was a racist.

The shock reverberated around the press room and took on a life of its own. Reporters, seasoned veteran journalists, looked at this newbie as if she had just grown fangs. Did she just ask Chief McNamara if he was a racist? Seriously, did she really? Nobody spoke to the great Walt McNamara that way. Even Ronnie Burk looked embarrassed.

But, to the kid's credit, John thought, she did not back down.

"I ask the question," she said, a slight nervous quiver in her voice, "because of the number of murders in Dodge the past few months and the fact that you and your department seem to be the only human beings on earth who refuse to see a connection."

McNamara frowned, his hands outstretched. "Who the hell are you?"

Some of the reporters laughed. But again, John thought, she held her ground.

"I'm Shanay Turner, crime reporter with the Brady Tribune. Three women, sir, have been brutally murdered in the last few months. All three were African-American, all three were prostitutes, all three were found in very close proximity, mere blocks, from each other. Yet you keep insisting that those deaths aren't related."

"That's because they aren't related!" McNamara shot back with anger in his voice.

John looked at his boss. He usually handled tough questions with his beloved smile, as if no question could possibly unhinge him. But Shay, John knew even if nobody else in the room did, had hit a nerve.

And Shay wasn't about to let up. "But the backgrounds of all three women are so similar, sir," she went on.

"Three murders on the north side of town is bad news, yes, I'll grant you it's a horrible statistic," McNamara pointed out. "But our town is growing, young lady. Lots of outside agitators coming in. We've had eleven murders in total this year, which considering our growing population, is a very good statistic. Two of those deaths were white victims from the south side of town. But that doesn't mean I'm connecting those murders to the same perp, either. Crime is crime, and unfortunately the bulk of the crimes always occur in depressed areas. That's not unusual and that does not denote any racial animus or underhanded dealings by my police force. It simply denotes the facts of the matter. How long have you been a reporter, Miss Turner?"

It was the old trick: turn the tables on the questioner. Make her the issue, rather than her question. Every reporter John had ever known usually slithered away once that happened. Nobody wanted McNamara's glare on them. John stared at Shay, wondering if she would slink away too.

She was a fighter, John knew that much about her already, a woman who had to scratch and claw for everything she ever earned. And today was no exception. Only now she seemed more of a reluctant fighter to John, a woman, this early in her career, already well acquainted with taking blows.

He wondered how long she could endure McNamara's legendary punches.

Shay wasn't exactly immune to the fact that she could become the chief's punching bag. But what was the point of being a reporter, she reasoned, if she wasn't going to ask the tough questions that needed to be asked? She had waited for some other seasoned journalist to ask it, and was astounded when nobody would even broach the subject. It was as if this was some exclusive club and all of the reporters in the room were careful not to lose their membership.

"I've been a reporter for four years, sir," she proudly answered the chief, "and with the Tribune for three-and-a-half months."

"Three months," McNamara said snidely and reporters laughed again, making Shay feel like the lone wolf she always managed to become. And McNamara, pleased to pit new reporter against the old school vets, kept the fun going. "Three long months," he continued with a sneer in his voice. "Just got on the stage and she's already demanding the mike."

John noticed how his boss overlooked the fact that she'd been on that so-called stage for four years prior to her stint here in Brady. But he also knew that such a fact was beside the point these days. McNamara, a man John used to respect, no longer cared about the facts of the matter. In this election year sideshow what the chief cared about was the appearance of the matter. And making that snide remark about her experience was for appearances sake. It was all about making her seem small to further elevate himself. Which, in John's eyes, made McNamara the small one.

"But in answer to your insulting question, Miss Turner," McNamara continued, "no, I'm not a racist, never was and never will be, and I'm offended that you would suggest such a thing. But that's what unprepared, incompetent reporters do. They play the race card. They take a few murders and just because the victims were of the same race and from the same side of town, they automatically scream *Connection! Cover-up! Racism!* What I suggest you do is learn more and speak less, like your colleague Ronnie Burk has always been prone to do. You can learn a thing or two from him. But you have a long way to go, Miss Turner, to be half the reporter Ronald is. And with an attitude like yours I'll be damned surprised if you make it."

Then he looked away from her, certain that he had put her back in her place. "Next question?" he asked.

Hands shot up, but the kid, to John's admiration, refused to back down.

"The fact still remains, sir," Shay yelled out, to the room's shock and growing annoyance, "that all three of the victims were poor, African-American prostitutes, and all three of the murders took place in Dodge. Not just on the north side of town as you suggest, but specifically in the poorest of poor neighborhoods known as Dodge. All of the victims were tied by the wrists, had duct tape over their mouths, and all were attacked late at night. Yet instead of sounding the alarm that a serial killer might be on the loose and citizens fitting the victim profile should be more vigilant, you and your force shrug it off as a coincidence. As *three* coincidences."

"We don't shrug off any murder, Miss Turner."

"But there's been such lax investigations, sir-," she started to say, but could feel Ronnie Burk's hand touch her on the elbow. Because she was new and still on probation, Ronnie was a team leader with the power to recommend termination. But knew she was only doing her job.

She jerked her elbow away from him and continued to address the chief. "If other prostitutes understood the risk, sir, then they might take more precautions at night. They might---"

"They might all become nuns and live happily ever after," McNamara said to laughter from the room. "Now if you interrupt this press conference one more time, Miss Turner, you'll be barred from coming back. Get a handle on her, Ronnie, or I'll lock out your entire newspaper."

"Yes, sir, and I apologize, sir," Ronnie Burk said with some degree of his own anger and this time not only took Shay by the elbow, but escorted her from the press room altogether.

He sat her on a bench in the corridor outside of the room and began to rip into her for ignoring his advice. Shay leaned her head against the wall and listened, but she wasn't buying it. It was the job of a journalist to be confrontational.

Journalists were supposed to seek the truth from city officials, not their favor.

But Ronnie went on and on, for nearly ten minutes he lectured her. And she listened, but she still wasn't buying it.

As the press conference ended and other reporters began to peel out of the room, Shay noticed that Ronnie's voice became even more animated. It was as if her refusal to go along to get along had put his reputation on the line and he wanted his colleagues to know how definitively he disapproved. Shay understood the game, so she let him have his say.

And then John Malone came out of the press room, and began heading toward the exit doors, which meant he had to walk pass them. Ronnie, seeing this as his opportunity, Shay supposed, immediately rose to his feet.

"Sorry about that, Captain Malone," he said as John approached. "It won't happen again."

John looked past Ronnie and at Shay instead, who remained seated on the bench. He was so proud of the way she comported herself in that press room, despite McNamara's bullying, that he wanted to kiss her. But his face revealed nothing.

"Keep up the good work, Turner," he said and kept on walking.

Shay looked as John walked on by. Although she was floored by his vote of approval, she couldn't help but smile.

Ronnie, however, frowned. He was dumbstruck. "What good work?" he wanted to know.

FOUR

That same afternoon, within the busy Brady Tribune newsroom, Ed Barrington, Shay's boss, walked over to her cluttered desk. He was a tall man with pasty skin in bad need of some sun, a receding hairline, and always wore clothes so rumpled and stained they looked as if he had slept in them. Often he forgot what day of the week it was, sometimes he forgot what month. But he was one of the best instinct editors in the business.

"I understand you showed your ass this morning at the chief's press conference," he said to her in his usual blunt style.

Shay looked at him, her big eyes filled with consternation. "I asked him tough questions, yes, sir."

Ed nodded. "Good," he said, causing Shay to inwardly sigh relief. "Good for you. Too many of these reporters around here are booty wipes for City Hall anyway. But watch yourself. There's a thin line between hard-hitting journalism and unfairness. Make sure you stay on the hard-hitting side."

Shay smiled. "Yes, sir," she said with that sincere look in those huge eyes of hers that Ed found most attractive.

"However," he continued, which Shay knew meant something less gratifying was about to be unloaded. "I'm pulling you off of the Dodge story." He avoided looking

73

directly into Shay's now troubled eyes.

"Pulling me off? But, sir---," she started.

"No, but," he interrupted. "Ronnie will handle the story going forward. And that's final. I want you to focus on these." He tossed a small stack of papers onto her desk.

Shay looked at the papers now strewn on her desk. "What is it?"

"Info on those string of burglaries over in Queen's Ridge. Not glamorous, granted, but it'll keep you employed and out of trouble."

This, for Shay, smacked of the same bullshit they pulled on her in Birmingham. Give the big stories to everybody else. Give her the crap. "But I thought Lance was handling those burglaries," she said halfheartedly.

"They're yours now. You're going to handle them now."

Shay's heart grew faint. She was only doing her job and this was the thanks she got. But it wasn't as if she had a choice. She had to eat. "Yes, sir," she said unenthusiastically.

"Don't look so depressing, Turner, geez."

Shay looked at him. "I don't see where I did anything wrong."

"Did I say you did something wrong? I said I'm pulling you off the case. That's all I said." Then he exhaled. "Just stop your griping and get to work," he ordered, glanced down at her breasts as he always did to remind her that he could make her life a whole lot easier, and then walked away.

Within a week of her hire he called her into his office and propositioned her. He said one way a female reporter could ensure success in such a male-dominated profession was to have an inside man on her side. Spend the night with him, he had blatantly said, and he'll be her inside man. He'll move her career right along.

She remembered standing there amazed that her boss would be so blunt. And it saddened her to know that it was going to be this kind of ride. But she made herself equally clear.

"If sleeping with you is the only way for me to get ahead," she said with more bravado than she felt, "then I won't be getting ahead."

And she left his office. Walked right out. She halfway expected to be fired that same day. She was on probation and could therefore be fired summarily, without cause. But remarkably there was no blowback. She didn't find that he tried to sabotage her with bad assignments, or to pull her off of big ones.

Until today.

Ronnie Burk waited until Ed was back in his office before he left his desk near the front of the newsroom and hurried back to Shay's desk near the back.

"He kicked you off the story, didn't he?" he asked as soon as he walked up to her.

"Yes, Ronnie, he kicked me off," Shay said.

"What did I tell you? Didn't I tell you that would happen? You have to keep your big mouth shut in this town, Shay. That's how you make it in this town. Speak less. That's how you get ahead."

Shay looked at Ronnie. He was one of those fat-faced know-it-alls with an obnoxiousness he couldn't seem to help. He, in fact, so eagerly took her under his wings when he became her team leader that it felt suffocating. She saw him, however, as one of the good guys. "It's done now," she said, resigning herself to the fact of the matter.

"I can talk to him," Ronnie said, his green eyes blazing with that eagerness. "You want me to talk to him?"

"No," Shay said with a sternest she didn't mean to display. But she didn't want to owe any man anything. She knew where that would lead. "But thanks for asking," she added with a smile.

Ronnie hesitated, as he usually did, and then walked away.

Shay always got the impression that something was bothering him and he wanted to address it with her, but he never could get up the nerve to do so. But just as she was about to call him back, to ask him if there was something on his mind, her desk phone buzzed. She pressed the blinking extension and picked up the phone.

"Shay Turner, may I help you?"

John Malone was seated in his black and gray truck,

a big Chevy Silverado, at the red light intersection of Dale Avenue and Hodges Boulevard. He took his cell phone off of speaker and put it to his ear. "This is John Malone, but don't say my name," he said.

Shay's heart pounded. "Okay," she said.

"I need to talk to you."

The last time they talked he wanted her to be his sex partner. She therefore proceeded cautiously. "What is it that you need to talk to me about?"

"Dodge," he said as the light changed to green and his truck began moving again.

Shay looked around the newsroom, realized no-one was watching her. "The Dodge murders?" she asked in a lowered voice.

"Right."

"So you agree they're related?"

"We won't be discussing it over the phone. I can move a few things around and get with you tonight. If you're still interested in the truth."

Shay didn't want to tell him that she was no longer working the case. What rational reporter would turn down an opportunity to get inside information from an inside source like John Malone? But she was no liar, no devious person, and wasn't about to become one now. Not even for her career. "You'll need to talk with Ronnie," she said with some degree of bitterness. "I've been removed from the story."

"Of course you were removed," John snapped.

"What did you expect calling out the chief on his own turf? McNamara had a conversation with your publisher as soon as that press conference was over. Nobody's going to stand up to him the way you did and expect no retribution."

Shay was taken aback by his snappiness. "Then why do you want to meet with me?"

"Because you stood up to him," John said. *And never backed down the way those other so-called veteran reporters would have,* he wanted to add. But added instead: "You did understand you would be pulled off of the case when you went that far, didn't you?" He was suddenly praying that she did get it; that she wasn't so naïve as to be surprised by the move.

Shay sighed. Of course she should have expected a penalty for going toe-to-toe with the chief of police. But that was what she thought journalists were supposed to do. "I just didn't think about that," she replied honestly. "All I could think about was another female in Dodge, going out at night, thinking nothing's wrong. And then she ends up butchered too."

John stopped at another red light and leaned his head back. He understood what she meant. He was thinking about the next victim too. "Are you still interested?" he asked her.

"I'm interested," she said, grabbing a pen. "Where do you want to meet?"

"You still live alone, don't you?"

"Alone?" Shay asked, oddly taken aback by the question. But she quickly regrouped. "Yes," she said. "I still live alone."

"Okay. I'll try to get over there at nine or around that time. And Turner," John added, "this is strictly confidential, you hear me? Not even Ronnie Burk or Ed Barrington are to be told about our little get together. Understood?"

"Yes, yes of course," Shay said. "I'll see you tonight."

John killed the call and then tossed his cell phone onto the passenger seat. He ran his hand through his thick, already rumpled pile of hair and shook his head. Why he didn't just leave it the hell alone like the rest of his colleagues were doing, and just let the little investigating he'd been able to do play itself out, was a mystery to him.

And why confide in her? Yes, she showed some spunk this morning at the press conference, and yes he viewed her as a tough kid. But so what? That didn't mean he should be risking his entire career by putting this kind of information in the hands of some new-to-Brady outsider like her. Besides, she wasn't even on the case anymore. She may not even know how to handle this level of information.

Then he wondered if it was more her body than her spunk that was driving this move. Wondered if he was really more interested in fucking her again than schooling

79

her about this ass-backwards case that should have been exposed a long time ago. Although he just discovered what was really going on himself, he knew for a fact that Chief McNamara and others on the force knew all along.

But he had to get this just right or it could blow up in his face. And of all the reporters he could have gone to, he decided to take a chance on this fresh young thang with those large and terrified, but adorable eyes.

But to hell with it, he thought as he blew through another intersection. It's done now. She was the only reporter he felt would possess enough backbone to see this through, so he was going with her. For good or ill, he was going with her.

His cell phone began ringing. He grabbed it from the seat. "Malone," he said. To his disappointment, it was Blair Malone, his ex-wife, reminding him that the mortgage needed to be paid.

"What are you reminding me for?" he asked her, an angry scowl on his face. "It's not even due yet. Do I ever forget?"

"Yes!" she said emphatically. "But not this time, John. Parker and I are going to our Timeshare in Hilton Head and we don't want any problems."

John frowned. What in the world does her going to South Carolina with some boyfriend of hers have to do with his paying the mortgage on a condo he doesn't even own? But knowing Blair as he did, the point of this call wasn't about the mortgage payment at all, but all about making sure he personally got the word of the trip itself. As if she could possibly make him jealous or cause him to feel any kind of emotion toward her, except unbridled anger. Sometimes maybe even hatred.

Although their divorce was final nearly four months ago, he agreed in the divorce settlement to pay the mortgage on a condo she jumped up and purchased just before the divorce. In exchange for him getting to keep the house, he agreed to pay the condo's mortgage for one year only. Until, as her lawyers put it, she can regroup and get back on her feet. John had snorted even then. The only time that bitch was ever off her feet was when she was fucking another one of those young muscle heads she loved to screw. And she loved to rub it in while she was doing it too, hoping he'd get jealous. When he didn't, and he never did, she'd call him late at night crying about how much she loved him and still wanted to be with him.

He'd hang up in her face.

But whenever she truly needed him, and it wasn't bullshit-related, John would be there. When her mother died and it looked as if she would go to pieces, he was right by her side, helping her get through it. When she had her gall bladder surgery, he was right there. He couldn't even verbalize why he hadn't severed all ties with Blair. It certainly wasn't because of any love he still held for her. Before he filed for divorce, and they were still trying to work out their differences, he found out she was fooling around with yet another body building brainless turd. That pretty much killed the love as far as he was concerned.

But he did love her once, and cared deeply for her. But they should have never gotten married. Neither one of them were the commitment types. Things happened, tragic things that were ultimately his fault, but she started behaving as if it gave her a license to do whatever the hell she wanted to do. In less than half a year after their honeymoon, she was sleeping around. And not long after that he couldn't seem to keep his dick in his pants, either. It was a nightmare. They kept trying, though, year after year, recommitting and recommitting until even the idea of either one of them ever committing to each other was beginning to seem absurd to John. The final straw was when he finally agreed to get marriage counseling with their church pastor. Something he never, in a million years, would have envisioned doing. Then to find out she was still sleeping around even after they had begun the sessions. That was the outside of enough for John. He filed for divorce.

"Well?" Blair asked. "Are you going to pay it now or what?"

"I'm going to pay it when it's due, Blair."

"Which is right now. Or at least in a couple days. But I don't want to go out of town without knowing if you've taken care of it."

John shook his head. Sometimes he truly believed

his wife was certifiable. What in the world did her going out of town have to do with his paying the mortgage on that crappy condo? Especially when the mortgage wasn't even due yet!

But she kept on. "Why can't you just step up to the plate like a man and take care of it, John? Why do you have to always wait until the last second to do everything? I'm so sick and tired of your nastiness towards me, I declare sometimes I want to throw my hands in the air and have nothing more to do with you. All I've ever tried to be was a good wife to you, and now a good ex-wife, and this is the thanks I get. I love you, and you know I love you, but it's getting harder and harder for me, John. You've got to show me some signs. All I'm asking you to do is pay the mortgage now, that's all I'm asking, and you can't even do that for me."

"I will pay it when it's due, Blair, and not a second before."

"But why can't you just pay it now? I want it paid now!"

"Then pay it yourself," John shot back, finding the entire conversation insane. But he could barely recall a phone conversation he'd had with Blair that didn't border on sheer lunacy.

She, however, took offense to his snide remark. "What did you say to me?" she said to him.

"I said if you want it paid so quickly then pay it your *got*damn self," John said even clearer. "Or better still get that muscle-headed boyfriend of yours to pay it!" John said this and killed the call, and then slung the phone back onto the passenger seat. He hit his hand against the steering wheel as he drove. She seemed to relish in unnerving him. And after being married for nearly six years to a bitch like her they wonder why he bounced from woman to woman now? He smiled a tight, bitter smile, shook his head, and then blew through another intersection.

Shay sat at her desk still stunned by the call. The idea that the cop who was considered Chief McNamara's right hand man would want to give intel to an outsider like her, especially since he already knew she was off of the case, was kind of weird to her. Then she began to get suspicious. Just why, she wondered, would he single her out? She wasn't even considered a good reporter, not by her boss back in Birmingham, not by her boss here in Brady.

She leaned back in her chair. Was this get together all about the Dodge murders as he had said, or would it be yet another attempt by him to get in her pants once again? She was beginning to feel a kind of nervousness, a kind of queasy hesitation she always felt whenever a man tried to crack her shell.

But was she reading too much into this? Was he really interested in cracking her shell, or cracking his case? Then she smiled and shook her head.

"Get a grip," she silently said to herself, and then got

84

back to work.

FIVE

As soon as John walked into Shay's small house, he once again knew he was dealing with a different kind of lady. He had expected her home to be immaculate when he arrived. Expected to smell that just-cleaned scent and see fresh bouquet of roses and trays of potpourri all over the place. Expected her to pull out all the stops. That was usually the case whenever he had a scheduled visit with a female, even on an official capacity. They seemed to enjoy impressing him.

But when he stepped across the threshold of Shay Turner's home, he quickly realized that she had no interest whatsoever in impressing him. Her home, in fact, had that *take it or leave it because impressing you is not what I do* vibe all over it. Which made John smile. He had decided to give his info to young Shay based on instinct alone. He didn't even consider their previous relationship because this was business. She seemed to him to be a person who wasn't an ass-kisser and wouldn't fall for the okey-doke McNamara and his boys were sure to throw her way. And now, as he looked around her home and realized she wasn't trying to kiss up to him, either, he believed his instinct was dead on.

Just as it was the first time he entered her home, it was a clean house, but it was an untidy one. Books and newspapers littered the place, from the sofa to the coffee table to the dining table at the back of the room. Shay, in fact, answered the door with reading glasses on her face and a book in her hand. And she didn't try to remove the glasses when she saw him, either. Didn't try to smooth down her long hair that she wore in a gorgeously rumpled ponytail, or put on any makeup. Vanity didn't seem to be on this chick's radar screen. And the clothes she wore, a well-worn UAB Blazers t-shirt and a pair of loose-fitting athletic shorts, was even more evidence to John that unlike those other females who went to great lengths to please him, she wasn't jumping through any hoops whatsoever on his behalf.

It was downright refreshing to him.

As he entered her small home, filling it with his larger-than-life presence as soon as he walked in, Shay could feel the mood of the room shift and take on an almost sexual charge. He had changed out of the suit he wore at the press conference that morning, and into a pair of jeans and a tucked-in white polo shirt. He was all biceps and thighs as he walked in. And the mere scent of him, that fresh, cologne scent that met her nostrils, was enough to make his masculinity become as much a presence in her home as he was. This was supposed to be a normal meeting with a source, but it was already feeling like something completely different.

And as she closed the door and escorted him to the sofa further into her living room, moving ahead to clear the books and papers that covered the seat, she knew she had to get it together. Because if she didn't, she would be behaving as if she was the lousy reporter some at the Tribune and even Chief McNamara predicted she was going to be. She knew she had to forget the fact that the guy was gorgeous. Forget the fact that virility and sensuality cloaked him like a strait jacket, and just do her job.

John knew he had a job to do, too, but that didn't stop him from checking out her long dark neck, her straight back, her smooth, curvy legs as she led him to her sofa. And when she bent over to remove stacks of books and papers that clogged the seat, and he got an unobstructed view of that same firm bottom he could still visualize, his penis began to throb.

She turned him on. He, in fact, was turned on the first time he saw her. At first it was all physical for John. It was her nice, curvy figure, her style, the innocence in her pretty eyes. And although he knew he could find a woman with a better looking body and a nicer looking face any day of the week around Brady, there was something about *her* face, and *her* body that made him almost anxious to get her naked and in his bed.

But most striking to John was his emotional reaction to her that day three months ago, and the way she stared at him with such intensity that day. She stared as if she could see right through his bullshit. That look of hers was so fine-tuned, so precision dead-on that she made him feel exposed. He was a burned-out, shell of a man, not the tough-as-nails hero the newspapers always made him out to be, and she knew it, that look said to him. It spoke so loudly, in fact, that after their second encounter in his office, he avoided her gaze ever since. He would ask about her, whenever he ran into Ronnie Burk, and Ronnie even chided John once about how he never inquired about any of the male reporters they had on staff.

But John, for a minute, had been a little smitten with Shay Turner. Found something remarkably different about her. But time was a powerful antidote and he soon moved on, to cases that required his undivided attention, to women who gave him what he needed without any demands or expectations. And he no longer gave much thought about the young black reporter with the expressive golden brown eyes. Until he saw her again this morning, at Chief McNamara's press conference.

"You aren't exactly little Miss Martha Stewart are you?" he asked as he sat down on her sofa.

Shay was at first surprised by his honesty. Then decided that she liked it. "I do my housecleaning on the weekends," she said with a smile.

"Yeah, right," John said snidely. "Me too." And they both laughed.

"Would you care for something to drink, Captain?" Shay asked before sitting down.

"John," John said. "And no, but thanks, I'm good."

Shay sat down, placing her feet beneath her butt. John was leaned back on the sofa, his legs crossed, his body turned slightly toward Shay's. As he looked around the books-and-newspaper-dominated room, she took a quick look at him. He was obviously an attractive man, but it was his midsection that she found her eyes drifting to. She knew he was packing a large bundle of joy inside that zipper, and it was beginning to excite her again. She even found herself imagining what it would feel like to have that big, thick joystick inside of her again.

And then she caught herself and smiled. She hadn't thought about having sex since she left John's office three months ago, and now he showed up and she was behaving as if all she thought about was having sex! *Get a grip*, she told herself.

"You read all of this stuff?" John asked her, picking up a book off of the coffee table.

Shay knew her need to read didn't endear her to most men, but decided she could live with that. "I do," she said truthfully.

"You know you could have a lot less mess with a Kindle or a Nook."

"I know. But I'm still relatively new to Brady so I'm trying to learn the town's history and culture. You won't find these books as eBooks."

"Understood," he said, tossing the book back on the table. "So you want to add that local flavor to your reports?"

"Exactly."

What a thoughtful young lady, John thought. "Well

that's a good thing," he said.

His acceptance of her hobby surprised her. "Really?" she asked. "So you don't find the fact that a twenty-six year old is immersing herself in old newspaper articles and local history books odd? Everybody else does."

"Everybody?" John asked as he looked intensely at her. "As in your new boyfriend?"

Shay was puzzled. "What new boyfriend?"

"I assumed, after Resden, you'd find yourself another guy."

"Oh. No. I meant everybody as in Aunt Rae, actually. Although she's not really my aunt, but just this elderly lady who took a shine to me when I helped her get her prescriptions straight at the drugstore. We've been friends ever since."

"And this Aunt Rae has a problem with your reading habits?"

"She does. She says I need to get a life."

John laughed.

"I kid you not. A seventy-seven year old woman told me to get a life."

"That's a shame, Shay."

"Ain't it a shame? I told her I have a life, thank-you. But she figures all you have to do is look around this place to know that's not quite true."

A quietness came over the room when Shay made that statement. John could feel the change.

"Where are you from originally?" he asked her. Seeing her again sparked his interest in her again. And he suddenly wanted to know all there was to know about her.

"I'm from right here in Alabama," she replied. "Birmingham born and raised. My parents moved to Philadelphia when I was still in college, but I didn't go with them. I love this state."

"And by your UAB t-shirt," John said, looking at her sizeable chest, at the fact that she appeared to be braless, "you attended college in Birmingham, majored in journalism or communications or some such major, and decided to plant your career flag in this state that you love."

"That's right," she said with a proud smile. "What about you? You're a 'Bama man?"

"Bite your tongue, young lady. I'm an LSU man. I'm originally from Baton Rouge."

Shay smiled. "I see. Your family still in Baton Rouge?"

"Yeah, but we aren't close or anything like that. My mother's no longer with us, and my dad's an asshole, so I don't spend too much time over there. But back to you. What happened after college?" he asked her, finding any discussion of his father not worth the breath it took to mention him.

Shay hunched her shoulder. "I got a job. Got my dream job with the Birmingham Union-Star, one of the most prestigious newspapers in this state. I worked my way up from their nobody roving reporter to one of their top crime reporters. I was on my way." A faintness came into Shay's eyes. John stared into those eyes.

"What happened?" he asked her.

"I loved that job. Loved it. Worked my ass off with every assignment too. Would have stayed there forever if they would have let me."

"But they wouldn't let you?"

Shay sighed and then nodded, a kind of stark sadness suddenly coming over her entire demeanor. "They wouldn't let me," she admitted. "My forever ended up being only four years. After that, after they let me go, I had to grab whatever I could get."

"And I take it our Brady Tribune was what you could get?"

"Yeah, it was. But I'm grateful to have it."

"Yeah, but come on, Shay. You went from the biggest newspaper in the entire state to one of the smallest. That had to feel like a considerable step backwards."

"Oh, absolutely," Shay admitted. "It was a major letdown. But a girl's gotta eat."

John smiled. He was beginning to see why he immediately liked this particular girl the first time he saw her. "But if you were working your ass off, doing such a great job, why were you let go?"

Shay exhaled, and that sadness reappeared. Could

93

he handle the truth, she wondered, or would he declare, like everybody else she'd ever told it to, that she had it coming? "They said I was becoming dead weight." She said this and looked at him with an expectation of disapproval that broke his heart.

"They said *you* were dead weight? No way."

Shay stared at him. "How could you be so sure?"

"Doesn't take a rocket scientist to know that you're a very hardworking girl, Shay. You wouldn't allow yourself to be anybody's dead weight. It doesn't take a rocket scientist to figure that much out."

"Apparently it did take more than that because they weren't trying to hear my objections. They just wanted me out of there."

"So you loaded up the truck and moved to Brady?"

Shay laughed. "Something like that."

"And according to Aunt Rae you need to get out more."

"That's what she says. But right now I'm just trying to get settled in at the Trib."

"How's that working out for you?"

"It's been challenging, I can't even front," Shay said with a smile. "They either treat me like I'm some idiot who doesn't know squat, or some kid who needs to be led all over the place by some male reporter. It's infuriating really."

John glanced at Shay's mouth, the way it curved at the tip. "Has Ed Barrington tried to hit on you?" he asked

94

her.

Shay looked at John. Why would he know anything about that? "Ed?" she asked, her eyes wide with hesitation.

"Don't worry," John assured her, "it goes no further than here. I just happen to know Ed and I know he hits on everything in a skirt." *Especially somebody with your attributes in that skirt*, John wanted to add.

"It was no big deal."

"You sure?"

"Yeah. I handled it. It's over."

"What did you do?" John asked with a smile. "Tell boyfriend and boyfriend gave old Ronnie a little visit?" Why he was so obsessed with her telling him if she had a new boyfriend or not disturbed him. But it was a fact: he needed to know.

Shay was a little disappointed that he would hold such a chauvinistic view. "No, remarkably, no boyfriend had to get involved. I was able to tell Ed myself."

John immediately realized his blunder. "I'm sorry. I'm an asshole, right? I didn't mean to suggest that you weren't capable-"

"Oh, I know. That's just a sore spot with me. Single ladies are always expected to have some man in their life ready to fight their battles at the drop of a hat, when many of us don't even have a man period."

Don't have a man, John thought. A smart, thoughtful kid like her? Were these young guys out here crazy? Or was it more to it than that? "Do you single ladies want a man?" he decided to ask her.

Shay smiled. "Some do, some don't," she said.

John began rubbing his forehead as he looked at her. And he couldn't stop wishing that his life had been different. If he was younger and wasn't so messed up, then maybe he could have been worthy of a woman like this. Maybe he could have been more than happy to commit to her and her alone. "What about you?" he asked her. "Do you or don't you?"

Shay hesitated. This wasn't exactly the conversation she expected to be having with John Malone of all people. But it was an oddly relaxing conversation for her. "I do," she admitted. "I would love to have a companion. But it's just not the easiest thing in the world to find that right person. Most guys just want sex nowadays."

John felt a twinge of embarrassment when she said that. "What about Aunt Rae? I'll bet she has an opinion on the matter."

Shay smiled weakly. "She does. She says I expect too much from these men out here. She's an old spinster-"

"Never married?"

"Never. That's why she says she knows what she's talking about. She wanted a good man too, wanted one desperately. Only to discover, she said, that it's all relative and nobody's good. Not even her." Then Shay frowned. "But she found out too late."

John and Shay exchanged a lingering look that caught them both short. There was something about his eyes that startled Shay. She saw such compassion there, such understanding. *Where did that come from*, she wondered.

John, too, was caught off guard when their eyes met. He saw a sweetness in Shay's eyes, and a deep vulnerability that made his heart squeeze with a need he didn't recognize. All along, from their very first encounter to now, his reaction to her had been a stark one. It was as if he saw in her something so unique, and so refreshing that he knew a man like him hooking up with someone that decent would be obscene.

But when he looked into her eyes just now, and felt that surge of protectiveness overtake him, he wondered for the first time if it could really be true. He wondered if somebody like Shay Turner could view somebody like him as even a possibility.

Then he quickly decided not. They were just too different. She was young and ambitious and still filled with those high hopes for life and her fellow man that he continued to lose every time he saw another dead body in the street. He was a thirty-seven year old, commitment-phobic rake still hopping in and out of women's beds as if he was still some kid in heat. And he didn't even have enough courage to sever all ties with a marriage that, for all intents and purposes, ended years ago. They were just too different.

He therefore uncrossed his legs and leaned forward. Decided to make light of their sweet, ephemeral moment. "Don't listen to that old biddy," he said as he pulled a small stack of folded papers out of his back jean pocket. "There's still good men out there waiting to snatch up a good girl like you. Not everybody's as hopeless a catch as I am."

"You aren't hopeless," Shay found herself blurting out and John looked at her. She didn't mean to say it, she didn't mean for a second to be that obvious, but she knew she couldn't take it back. John saw that war in her eyes: that hopefulness and apprehensiveness all at once.

And it was Shay's turn to press ahead. "What do you have there?" she asked as she moved to the edge of her seat and looked at the papers in his hand. "Is it info on those Dodge murders?"

John was still thrown by her defense of him, something he wasn't accustomed to. Most people, especially women, would agree without hesitation that he was a hopeless case. But not Shay.

She smiled that sweet white smile of hers that he was beginning to adore. "You're staring, Malone," she said without looking back up at him. "It's rude to stare."

"You don't think I'm hopeless, Shay?" he asked her, his heart pounding at the possibility.

Shay didn't mean her comment to be some defining moment, and she didn't quite know how to take his response. She looked at him and he could see, even with those glasses on, how her eyes just sparkled. "No, I don't think you're hopeless," she admitted.

But it wouldn't work, John decided. She deserved far better than some jaded joker like him. It couldn't work. And he had to make her know it, too. "My ex-wife would disagree with you," he decided to say.

If the effect was to throw Shay, it worked. She was thrown. This wife might have been his ex, but apparently he still had feelings for her or he would not have mentioned her.

"I certainly wasn't implying---," she began, but then decided it didn't matter and shook it off. This was business. They shouldn't have gotten personal anyway. She looked at the papers in his hand.

"What do you have?" she asked.

He felt like a jackass going there, especially since his ex-wife was really a woman he couldn't stomach, but he knew he was doing her a big favor in the long run. He couldn't be committed to one woman if his life depended on it, and he knew it. And he also knew that a woman like Shay would demand that commitment. He therefore took the papers and spread them out onto her tabletop.

"Take a look," he said to her.

Shay moved closer to the coffee table's edge and stared at the photocopies in front of her. "These are crime scene photos."

John nodded. "That's right."

Shay began perusing each one. "So there is a connection then?" she asked absently as she stared at the photos. John leaned back and stared at her. Ronnie had said she was all about career, didn't have time for any man, and for some reason this suddenly concerned John. Why wouldn't she have a life beyond her work, a smart, sharp, sweet girl like her? Did that Resden character burn her that badly, he wondered.

She looked at him, as if she could feel his stare. A stare, given his comment about his ex-wife, that was beginning to annoy her. "Well, Captain, is there a connection?"

"Yes."

"So you believe we have a serial killer on the loose and all three of these women were his victims?"

"Not three, Shay," John said. "Thirteen."

Shay's eyes blinked, as if she didn't hear him correctly, and then stared at him. She had that same intensity he remembered from their first encounter. "Thirteen?" she asked, astounded. "What do you mean thirteen?" When it dawned, her already large eyes stretched even larger, and she pushed her glasses up further on her nose. "Are you saying that there's been *thirteen* similar murders in the last three months?"

"Over the past twelve months, yes. The pattern started out sketchy early on, so it was easy to miss, but now it's clear."

"And all the victims were black?"

"All African-American, female prostitutes, all murdered in Dodge, all duct-taped, all strangled and then raped. Same, same, same."

Shay frowned. "But how could that be? How could thirteen people end up killed, and murdered the same way, with nobody making any connections? With no alarm bells being sounded?"

John ran his hand through his hair. "You remember the press conference this morning?"

How could she forget it? She felt as if it was her against the world. "Yes."

"Remember when you asked McNamara if he was a racist?"

"And he responded that he was offended by my question, yes, of course I remember."

"You remember what else he said?"

Shay had to think about this. John leaned back and watched her think. She was sharp, he saw it the first time he met her. But he wondered if her way of thinking was nuanced enough. Most smart people had great book sense, but streetwise sense was different, and required more insightfulness. He stared at her.

"He said I was playing the race card," she said, thinking about it, "and that I was unprepared and incompetent and that's why I was screaming that there was a connection and a cover-up and racism." Then Shay looked at John, a look of understanding beginning to pierce through the thoughtfulness in her eyes. "But I

101

didn't say anything about a cover-up."

John exhaled. She got it. "No, Shay, you didn't."

"He said cover-up when I never mentioned anything about a cover-up. But there is one?"

John nodded. "At first, no. Three murders in a month in Dodge is no big deal. Not these days. The fact that they were poor, no biggie either. But by month two and yet another victim was found, and then three in a two-week span, and then another in month four, and things changed. It was coming into the new election cycle and the mayor, Chief McNamara's boss, was up for reelection. Admitting that they had a serial killer on their hands, which they knew they did, would be exactly the kind of bad news the mayor's opponent could exploit."

"So they hid the similarities between the victims?"

"Yes. They stopped releasing certain information. Started fabricating the crime scene, moving victims, not reporting the stats. They started claiming this murder was drug-related, or this one was a DV. And Shay they started doing body dumps."

"Body dumps? Is that when they move bodies to change the crime scene location?"

"Right," John said. "They would move the bodies to other counties so that those murders wouldn't be reported as a Brady murder. Eventually, of course, it may trace back to Brady, but probably not before the election."

Shay shook her head. "I never really believed in conspiracy theories, never. But . . ." She looked at

102

John. "But if what you're telling me is true-"

"Then it's a cover-up, Shay. It's a cover-up at the highest levels, and it runs shit deep."

Shay stared at John, back at the crime scene photos, and then at John again. "But how do you know all of this? How long have you known about this?" she asked him.

"I looked into it a couple days ago. I should have done so a lot earlier, it was obvious that something was being mishandled, but I was the drugs guy. I was working on drug smuggling cases with the DEA and McNamara was running all murder cases. But cops that were loyal to me started making comments to me, and some of them were working those murder cases. They gave me what they could, which is what you have there."

"Will those cops be willing to go on record?"

"In a trial or grand jury, yes. To a reporter, no."

Shay shook her head. "How could they allow this to go on, John? Is it because the murder of prostitutes were never seen as a big deal?"

"That's right," John said. "And don't look at me that way. It's a fact." Then he leaned forward. "In the back of that stack of photos are all of the actual information on each one of those crimes, versus what the public was told. It'll be easy to pinpoint the problems."

Shay looked at the back of the photos. "Why are you telling me this?" she asked him.

"Because what happened is a damn shame.

Because the families of those poor victims deserve better than what we've hashed out to them. Because somebody needs to sound the alarm, as you so eloquently put it." John wanted to add that he was telling her because for some crazy reason he trusted her and knew she'd do the right thing. But he didn't go there.

Shay still couldn't believe it. "But McNamara says we've only had eleven murders in total in Brady. And now you're telling me we've had thirteen in Dodge alone? How could McNamara fix his mouth to tell such a lie?"

"McNamara's full of shit," John said. "They're covering up the number until after the election. Then they'll do what they call an updated assessment. Then the alarm bells will be sounded and the public will know that a serial killer is on the loose. After the election."

"And how many more women would have to die first?"

John closed his eyes in burdensome culpability. Opened them again. "Exactly."

Shay stared at him. "What do you want me to do?"

"Write the story and give it to Ed Barrington. Nobody else. You show him those photos. You tell the truth. Before another woman dies."

"But doesn't the police oversight committee investigate all homicides?"

John snorted angrily. "Give me a break, Shay. Those guys are nothing but patsies for McNamara. Hand-picked and family-owned. They will report that the chief handled everything perfectly fine."

"The public will be outraged by this, you know that?"

"I know."

"They'll demand McNamara's resignation."

"I know that too. They'll demand mine too." John exhaled, ran his hand across his face. "But that's beside the point now. You've got to go public before another woman dies. I just got wind of what was going on and I can't remain silent. Going to McNamara or his cronies on the oversight committee would be like a convict complaining about the warden. They'll just plant evidence on me or declare I'm insane or do something to discredit me. But they will never admit the truth."

"Unless the truth is revealed before they know a damn thing."

John smiled. He loved how quick she was. "That's right, Shay. That's exactly right."

Her doorbell rang and both of them looked surprised. Shay stood up and walked over to her bay window. Saw Ronnie Burk standing on her porch.

"It's Ronnie," she said.

John gathered up the photos. "Put these away," he said. "I don't want Burk's paws on any of this. He'll just take it straight to McNamara."

This was news to Shay. "You think Ronnie would do that? Really?"

"Really," John said as Shay walked over and accepted the photos. Their hands touched. John didn't remove his hand. "And I'd better go."

Shay nodded. "Okay," she said.

John stared into those wondrously big, bright eyes of hers. Leaving was the last thing he wanted to do, but fate had spoken. Ronnie had arrived. "Take care of yourself, Shay," he said.

"I will. And thanks for the information. I won't name you at all in my story."

"You do so if you have to. Don't protect me at the expense of this story getting out, you hear me? You get the story out, no matter what. Even if Ronnie mentions the fact that he saw me at your place tonight, and he gets word to McNamara, you get that story out. I'm depending on you, Shay."

Shay felt a swell of respect for this man. This move by him would more than likely cost him his job, but he was still willing to do it. She nodded. "I'll get the story out," she assured him.

John was certain now that he had made the right decision. He clasped her hand tighter as his heart swelled, too, with feelings for this woman. And he leaned to her, to kiss her on the lip, he needed to feel her soft lips on his. He wanted just a small, sweet kiss from her. But she looked at him.

"I'm sure your ex-wife wouldn't approve," she said.

Before John could respond, the doorbell rang again.

They continued to look into the other's eyes. Both were experiencing that kind of *what could have been* regret that always came along at the worst possible time.

"I'd better hide these," Shay said of the papers and made her way to her bedroom.

John exhaled, amazed that he was beginning to have the kind of feelings for Shay he hadn't had for any female since he was a young man in love. But that so-called love only got him heartache after heartache and then a train wreck of a marriage. So much for love, he thought as he made his way to the front door.

Ronnie Burk walked into Shay's home with a silly smirk on his face, as if he was certain he'd just interrupted some hot n' heavy sexual workout. When, in truth, John hadn't been able to get a kiss out of Shay. Not a chaste little kiss. Not that it wasn't his fault. It was. He was the one who threw up that sorry-ass ex-wife of his like some roadblock against Shay's real or imagined interest. A strong lady like her wasn't going to just overlook that fact and let him slobber all over her anyway.

But Ronnie, here, on the other hand, he thought, was single. She would have no problem with his chaste, sweet kisses. But then he dismissed that idea. Shay had better taste than that.

"Captain Malone, hi," Ronnie said as he entered, his hand extended. "Funny to find you here."

"I was just leaving," John said, shaking his extended hand.

"Not on my account, I hope."

John never did like this guy. "You flatter yourself,

Burk," he said as he stepped past Ronnie to get out of the door.

Ronnie laughed. "Oh, but I speak truth to power, my friend." John glared at him. And then kept going. "And I still need to talk to you about the Broadman case, Cap. You promised me an exclusive."

"Come by my office tomorrow," John yelled without looking back. "We can discuss it then."

"Sure thing, Cap," Ronnie said, still smiling, as he watched John Malone leave. Then he closed the front door.

And his smile disappeared.

SIX

"Burk! Turner! In my office!" Ed Barrington stood at his office door and yelled across the Brady Tribune newsroom. Ronnie immediately jumped from his desk and hurried into the office. Shay finished the last of the sentence she was typing on her desk computer, grabbed a pad, pen, and her secure-lid cup of coffee, and hurried to the office.

When she walked in, Ronnie was already seated in front of the desk and Ed was seated behind it.

"What's up?" she asked as she took the seat beside Ronnie's.

"The shit has hit the fan," Ed said, "and McNamara's talking about libel suits and defamation of character, he's hot."

"We told the truth," Shay said.

"But you told the truth with no sourcing," Ronnie said in his know-it-all voice. "Nobody was willing to go on record. That's always a weak story, Shay, you have to know that. McNamara may just have a serious point here. I don't think we should have ran with the story to begin with. If I would have been informed prior to the running of the story, if you would have asked my advice, which you or nobody else did, I would have said to not run it."

"We did the right thing," Ed said and Ronnie frowned.

Shay inwardly sighed relief. Ed knew how it worked around these southern towns. Nobody was going to talk on the record, not this early in the game, anyway.

"There's a press conference at noon," Ed continued.

"McNamara?" Shay asked.

"That's right. And he's going to put on the righteous indignation performance of the year so be prepared for it. But the mayor's going to be there too."

Ronnie was impressed. *Wow*, he mouthed but did not say.

"Wow is right," Ed said, reading his lips. "And get this guys: he's not going to be on stage with McNamara, but in the audience with the press."

Shay shook her head. "He wants to separate himself from his now embattled police chief," she said.

"That's exactly right. So you know McNamara's coming out with both barrels blazing. I just want you to be prepared for the incoming, Shay."

"Me?" Shay asked, surprised.

"That's right. It's your baby now. You're the one who got the evidence and got us that front page exclusive. I want you to represent the Tribune at that press conference."

Shay smiled. "Thank-you, sir," she said. And if John Malone was there, she'd be thanking him too. Because of his decision to trust her with this big breaking news story, there may just be a victim spared tonight or tomorrow night or whenever the killer had hoped to strike again. And, to a far lesser degree, her career just might begin to get off of life support.

"I'll go with her," Ronnie said as he stood to his feet. "To keep her in line." He said this with a smile, although it stung Shay.

"No need for that," Ed said. "Shay can handle it. You take over the story about those Queen's Ridge burglaries."

Shay wanted to smile and tell Ronnie that that was what he got for keeping his mouth shut, but she didn't go there. She, instead, kept her own mouth shut, hurried out of the office, and began to prepare herself for her very first Brady, Alabama close-up.

The City Hall press room was jam-packed with reporters, from print reporters to television and radio anchors to bloggers, and Shay took her seat in the middle of the pack. She was so nervous she could barely breathe comfortably. The story broke this morning, headline news, and her phone hadn't stopped ringing from local news channels who wanted more information. Now the mayor was standing against the side wall, a big, burly man with a scowl on his face. A scowl that became even more animated when Chief Walt McNamara and Captain John Malone stepped into the press room.

John wore his customary press conference get-up: a

tailored, double-breasted suit that made him look hunky and gorgeous as usual, and his expression was decidedly stoic. He, in fact, fit in so well with McNamara and the entire cop culture that Shay almost had a difficult time reconciling the man standing there with the man who put his entire career on the line to expose a miscarriage of justice. He put his entire career on the line for victims who many in society would conclude wasn't worth the price. But he was still willing to pay it.

And McNamara had the look of a man ready for a fight.

"The reason I called this press conference," the chief began, "is because of that weird story that appeared in the Brady Tribune this morning. It was the headline story, it was. Written by some cub reporter, some Shay Turner, who frankly wouldn't know her ass from her head. But I digress."

There was a smattering of laughter throughout the room. Shay, however, didn't crack a smile. There was nothing funny about her report, or McNamara's reaction to that report.

"This nobody reporter," McNamara went on, "decided to defame my good name, folks. And she probably did it as payback for the way I put her in her place the last time she was here. You remember, when she called me a racist? But I digress." Some laughter again.

"In this nonsensical article she wrote, an article that
112

LOVING HER SOUL MATE

inexplicably made the headline of this morning's paper, I guess it was a slow news day, I don't know. But this nobody reporter accused me of participating in body dumps and cooking books and refusing to alert the public of some so-called serial killer. I don't know. She might have even accused me of committing the murders themselves!"

Real laughter from the crowd this time. It took all Shay had not to lash back. John remained stoic, staring at no-one.

McNamara went on. "She claims there were fourteen, no excuse me, thirteen murders in Dodge, not three as we've reported it. Thirteen, folks. That's what this girl wrote. That's what this Shay Turner nobody reporter wrote. Well I will tell you, ladies and gentlemen, Shay Turner is a damn liar!"

An audible gasp went up into the rafters of the room. All eyes suddenly turned to Shay, as if she was going to challenge McNamara right here and right now. Shay's heart was pounding, but her expression remained unchanged. John, however, was now staring at his boss.

And McNamara could just feel the stare, and he wondered why John suddenly seemed so hostile, but he went on. "She'll write anything to jump-start her failing career," he said. "That's why they got rid of her in Birmingham, because she wasn't worth a damn. Yeah, I said it. If you don't believe me check it out for yourselves. They got rid of her in Birmingham too. She's never been a good reporter. She just goes around defaming people's good names."

He hesitated, as if he needed to calm himself down. Shay looked at John. He looked as if he was this close to harming his boss. She looked back at his boss.

"So this slip of a girl," McNamara continues, his voice now rising, "decides to write this nonsensical, libelous nonsense, and I won't stand for it. She's a liar and what she wrote is a dirty lie! And yes, folks, I'm angry about it. I've been an officer of the law for dang near thirty years and I have never been accused of the lies this child accused me of! Not ever! It's not my problem that she's some frustrated female who can't find herself a man! It's not my fault that she's one of those incompetent journalist whores who can't---"

"Knock it off, Walt," John interrupted his boss so forcefully that everybody in the room immediately looked at him.

"Eh-what?" McNamara asked, astounded by the interruption. He turned toward John. "What did you say to me?"

"I said knock it off," John said, not backing down.

"What's the matter, John?" a reporter decided to yell out. "You disagree with Chief McNamara?"

"Yeah, John, tell us what you think!" another reporter yelled out.

John moved up to the podium. At first McNamara stood his ground, and then he slowly stepped aside. He knew John Malone was a hero in Brady, a man who was far more popular for his fairness than McNamara or even the mayor ever was.

"I think what Chief McNamara is doing is wrong and I will not stand up here and allow him to denigrate a fine journalist."

McNamara frowned. "Denigrate *her*? She's denigrating *me*, what are you talking about?"

John looked at the assembled press. "Everything Miss Turner wrote in that article was the truth. She did not lie about any of it. And I should know because I'm the one who told her what was going on in this police department. I'm the source of her article."

The murmurings and gasps and camera clicks were like a sudden bolt of lightning in the room. They were enjoying this. Their readers and viewers were going to enjoy this. John Malone, McNamara's right hand man, wasn't going along with his arrogant boss any longer. And they loved it.

Shay, however, was terrified for John.

But John kept going. "Chief is upset, and I can understand his anger. But he's pointing his fingers in the wrong direction. This nobody reporter, as he calls Miss Turner, is a young lady with more backbone and guts than all of these back-scratching, ass-kissing, so-called veteran journalists combined! I stand by every word she wrote, because she wrote the truth. I know it, McNamara knows it, and all of you would know it too if you took your faces out of his butt crack long enough to see this department for what it really is."

"And what is it, John?" yet another reporter yelled.

"It's a cesspool of corruption, that's what it is," he said. And then he stepped aside.

The amazement in the room was palpable. McNamara, stunned witless, looked over to the mayor for help. But the mayor wanted no parts of this. McNamara therefore stepped back up to the podium and attempted to smile it off.

"What a card," he said smilingly. "You know John. Always kidding around."

Only this time nobody, not even the chief's most ardent butt-kissers, bothered to laugh.

Shay wrapped her bathrobe around her just-dried body and hurried from the master bath. She glanced at the clock on the nightstand as she hurried. When she saw that it was nearing eleven at night, however, she became worried. Who, she wondered, would be ringing her bell this time of night? But when she made her way up the hall and into her living room, and was able to look out of the window onto her driveway, she sighed relief. John's big Chevy Silverado sat quietly on that driveway. She quickly opened the door.

John walked in looking so drained that Shay was immediately concerned. Just as she had been after that press conference. But John, to Shay's pleasant surprise, was more worried about her. As soon as she closed the door, he placed his hand on her robe-clad arm.

"You okay?" he asked her.

"Me? What about you? Did they fire you yet?"

He smiled weakly. "Not yet," he said. "Although I suspect it's coming. McNamara has been suspended pending the mayor's investigation and now the mayor has me and my guys going through reports to prove my allegations. He says he wants me to prove it. That's what I've been doing until a few minutes ago, when I sent my guys home and called it a night."

Shay stood there, her face a mask of concern.

"What's the matter?" he asked her, rubbing her arm. "You did nothing wrong, Shay, you hear me? You may have even saved a life by asking questions, by digging deeper. By writing that story."

"And you may lose your job."

John exhaled. "I know that. But that's just the price I'll have to pay. I should have been on this story from day one, and I wasn't. That's just the price I have to pay."

Shay had never met a man quite like John Malone. She realized, standing there, that she respected him. She just didn't know too many men who would give a damn, especially since the victims were prostitutes, especially since the victims were of a different race than he was and poor as dirt. But that didn't even seem to enter his mind. He just did what he knew was the right thing to do.

"Thank-you," she said.

John smiled. He was really fond of this lady. "Come here, you," he said and opened his arms to her.

Shay smiled, wrapped her arms around his neck, and allowed her body to fall against his. Her robe, however, which had been held together by her hands, gaped opened and it was her naked, freshly scrubbed body that fell against his.

And they both immediately realized the difference.

Shay's big eyes stretched bigger as she felt her nakedness against John's rock hard body. She, at first, wanted to say oops and play it off, perhaps even pull back from him. But his arms felt so good around her that she didn't immediately make a move.

John, too, felt her nakedness against him and it was such a wonderful feeling that he closed his eyes and pulled her closer. And when she attempted to move out of his embrace, as if she was now realizing the error, he held her tighter. He didn't want to let her go.

It was a fool's game he was playing at, and he knew it was. Because it wouldn't work. Because he was a man who abhorred commitment, but yet he was holding onto a woman who required it if he had any illusions about being with her. But he couldn't let her go. She was unlike any woman he'd ever met. She had spunk and integrity and a quiet strength he loved. If he was fire, she was ice. He somehow knew instinctively that she'd know how to handle him.

He pulled back only slightly, so that he could look into her magnificent eyes. And his heart swelled with emotion. She was so much younger than he was, over a decade younger, and he was well aware that he was everything she didn't need. But he was so exhausted, and so weak at this very moment in his life that his need to have her in that life of his overrode his need to protect her from a man like him. He lifted her chin, looked down at her gorgeous brown, African lips, and kissed her.

If Helen of Troy had the face that launched a thousand ships, Shay Turner had the lips that launched John's heart into overdrive. He couldn't stop kissing her. He moved his head right, then left, then dead on kissing her. She tasted like pure honey to him. He never kissed the women he fooled around with. Never pretended that he wanted to do anything with them but fuck them.

But with Shay, kissing her alone was giving him that same high. He moved his arms inside of her robe as he kissed her, to feel what he knew would be her soft, brown flesh. But as his arms encircled her bare body, as his hands moved around her waist and rested on her tight ass, squeezing the life out of her, she was softer than he had even remembered her being. He closed his eyes, to fully experience her, as he pulled her tighter against his body.

Shay could feel his hard-on against her. She could feel his erection growing with every pulsating second. And it was a strange, intoxicating, wonderful feeling. This

119

was the legendary John Malone, the man she'd grown to respect and admire. And if his kissing was any indication, she knew she was in for a fantastic roll in the hay.

But it was slightly terrifying feeling too. Because this was the legendary ladies' man John Malone, a man who once mentioned his ex-wife as if he might very well still be in love with her. What was she getting herself into here? Could she expect anything from this man except one more night of sex? Would rumors start flying about her romantic interlude with him, just as the rumors were flying about his romantic nights with other females in Brady? Was she about to get on what some around town called John's hit list?

But as his mouth finally left hers and began kissing her down her neck, toward her breasts, she ran her hands through his wonderfully rumpled hair. How in the world was she going to resist this? She knew she should. She knew she was nothing to this man but yet another willing bed partner; yet another warm body in his arms.

It saddened Shay to think that this could more than likely end what could have become a pretty good friendship. Because it was so soon. Because neither one of them had the kind of investment in the other that would make for an alliance beyond the sheets. But as his mouth found her breasts, and he began to suck on them with the expertise of a well-honed lover, she knew it was hopeless. Because she wanted this night with him. Even if it meant she would be nothing more than another notch on his belt tomorrow morning, she needed this night with him.

And John delayed no longer. He didn't think he could. He lifted this prized woman into his arms and carried her down the hall to the back bedroom, still kissing and sucking her breasts as he carried her. This was going to be a long night of passion, he could feel it in his bones, and he could only hope that he'd be able to hold out for the entire ride. He was determined to give her a thrill because somehow he knew his weakness for her body, for her sweet, passionate love, was going to eventually kick his ass.

SEVEN

He sat his gun and holster on her nightstand, and then sat on the edge of her bed. He lifted his polo shirt over his head, revealing those tanned, ripped abs and that thick gold chain around his neck that Shay remembered so vividly. He tossed the shirt across the room, to a chair, and then he opened his legs and pulled her standing body between them.

"You'll never know," he said as he opened her robe and removed it from her body, revealing her sexily flat stomach and plump brown breasts, "how much you turn me on." And to prove his point, as soon as he feasted his eyes on her breasts, his dick jounced upward in an almost salute-styled erection.

"*Oh, geez*!" he said and pulled her closer. He began kissing on those breasts, squeezing them and kissing them and taking those hard nipples into his mouth and licking around their dark hub. He wanted her. He needed her. His need to have her was building with every touch, with every squeeze, with every kiss against her tender skin.

Shay felt the touch, too, as the pressure of his lips kissing and then sucking her breasts made her lean her chest forward for more. She needed more.

And John gave her more. He placed her nipples between his thumb and finger and lifted them, rolled them

122

around, and then placed one and then both in his mouth and feasted on them. Shay was already getting wet and moist. She was already feeling the tingle as she coursed her hands through his hair. Her vagina folds reacted to his kisses so intensely that she thought she was going to injure his scalp. And when he lifted her legs, gaped open, and sat her face-front on his lap, causing his dick to ram against the crack of her ass, she shrieked in pleasure. That was when he wrapped her in his arms and kissed her.

She closed her eyes and relaxed in his kiss. His lips were so expert, as they kissed her hard and deep. And then he found those already marked breasts of hers and feast there again. She loved it when he squeezed her. She loved the way his lips licked her. But when he lifted her legs over his shoulders, her pussy in full view of him, and he began to lick her there, she let out an even louder shriek of pleasure that caused her entire body to buckle.

John didn't drop her, as she buckled and fought against the intensity of the feeling. "*Oooh*, John!" she yelled as she fought. But he, instead, increased the intensity. He began eating her pussy as if he was eating a steak. She was bucking him now, as the feelings rippled so deep inside of her that she didn't think she could take another wave. His tongue sliced into her, zigzagged into her. It flicked around her clit, saturating it, and then it ploughed in deeper, sucking up her wetness with a hunger that thrilled her.

Shay was so caught up in the feeling that she didn't even realize, while he was eating her, he was also unbuckling and unzipping his pants. And when he pulled out that rod, and Shay saw it in all of its stiffness, she had to have it in her mouth.

John was thrilled when she got off of him and then knelt down between his legs. He lifted up slightly and she pulled his pants and briefs down around his ankles. He was so anticipating her mouth that his penis was already beginning to drip. And when she took him, when her sultry lips clamped down on his rock-hard dick and began to move up and down in that slow, prodding way of hers, he fell back on the bed.

"That's how I like it," he said to her as she mouth-fucked him. "Yes, baby, that's how I like it!"

He placed his forearm over his forehead and closed his eyes as the intensity increased. Her tongue licked down and back up and then encircled his tip. Over and over. Down, up, circle. It was her rhythm that he loved. She knew when to speed up and when to back off. She knew when to hover and then move again. She did him right. She made him feel like his dick was being bathe and pampered. And then she took him whole, all the way to the back of her throat. She didn't gag, because she knew what she was doing. She did it right. No woman did him the way she did him.

"That's so good, Shay," he said as he moaned. "That feels so good!"

124

Shay knew it did, because she was getting turned up to the point of no return herself. And just as she thought he was going to come in her mouth, and she was going to climax from the reaction of his dick alone, he sat up, lifted her up, and then placed her on the bed. He stepped out of his pants.

Shay lay on her back watching him as he reached down into his pants pocket, pulled out a condom, and began to cover up. It wasn't just that he was so well-hung and handsome, although he was. But his thighs, his biceps, his washboard abs were all so rock solid, so tanned, so masculine in every way that she knew trying to compete for this man's affections was going to be like competing to win the lottery: a million-to-one longshot at best.

But she was feeling differently about him this time. When they first had sex she was too overwhelmed with all kinds of emotions that she didn't know what she was feeling. Now she knew exactly what she was feeling. She was feeling that she wanted to be with John. That of all the men she'd ever been with, her feelings for John were the most intense.

But that only made her feel even more wary of him. This man was the grand prize, and all those other women who'd slept with him knew it too. If Shay, who didn't play the field, wanted John this intensely, she could only imagine how intensely the others wanted him.

Shay looked into his face. This was bound to end

badly, there was too much drama swirling around this man. Why didn't she just go with the flow, having a great night of sex with him and forget about it in the morning? But that, for a woman like Shay, would be like forgetting about an arm she lost, or a leg. Or, in this case, a heart.

John was so remarkably in tune with this woman that he immediately saw the change in her eyes, a change so subtle that most men would have missed it. But he saw it.

"Baby, what's wrong?" he asked as he got in bed beside her.

"I'm okay," Shay said, wrapping her fingers around his gold chain. "I'm just enjoying you."

John smiled and began to rub his hand between her legs. "There's no way," he said, "that you could be enjoying me more than I'm enjoying you."

Shay smiled too. "Wanna bet?" she said.

John shoved his finger into her pussy, causing her to arch in pleasure and scream out "ooh!"

"Yes," he said, as he wiggled it inside of her, putting two fingers in as if he were shoveling inside of her. "I wanna bet." She kept arching as her wetness covered his fingers and made his movement even more flexible.

But he couldn't hold out much longer. That was why, just before she felt as if she was going to come, he moved on top of her and replaced his finger with his massive rod. And if his fingers had her arching, his dick had her electrified. She felt every inch of that rod as he moved into her in a painfully slow glide, so slow that she began to crave more speed. But he knew exactly what he was doing because by the time he had cleared her delicate entryway, and was halfway in, he shoved on in.

It was the shove that lifted her body. He began to thrash into her. "Yes!" she began yelling. "Yes!"

For the longest time it became a rhythm. The bed was bouncing as he fucked her. The sounds of her screams and his grunts made for a music all its own. And they made love in a way that made John astounded. This woman had him drunk with passion. All he wanted to do was to please her, to take care of her, to see that sensuality in her beautiful, smoky eyes and grind on her until a part of him was a part of her. He'd never felt this way before, that was for damn sure. But he felt this way with Shay.

He laid down on top of her as he fucked her. He closed his eyes as the warmth of her body, as the smell of her sweet, feminine scent, as the knowledge that he had in his arms the one woman who melted his heart, gave him a feeling so full and deep that he had to blink back tears.

And he couldn't understand it. Why was the connection so deep with this woman? He didn't feel this way about his other women. After the first few months of his marriage, he didn't even feel this way about his wife. But he felt connected to Shay Turner. And it wasn't just a physical connection either, although, right at this moment, that was a major part of it. Because he thrashed into her saturated pussy one time too many, and had to release.

He came with a hard drain-out. She was already climaxing by the time he came, her small body was already convulsing against his big, pulsating rod, and his release was so powerful that it lifted them into that realm of pleasure that was equal parts thrilling, and chilling.

Afterwards, while Shay slept, John did as he always did after waking up from sex with a female. He quietly got out of bed and began putting back on his clothes. His goal, as always, was to slip away undetected, to avoid any anger or resentment or, that word again, commitment.

But when he glanced over at the sleeping Shay, to ensure that she was still asleep, something gripped him. He found himself just standing there, staring at her. She looked so sweet to him, so precious, that he wondered what in the world was he thinking. How was he going to just tip out on her? How could he even think of doing such a thing? She wasn't some whore he met in a bar. This was Shay. A woman he respected. A woman who seemed to actually respect him.

So instead of tipping out as he never failed to do the hours after any love making session, even one as wonderful as this one had been, he moved to her and sat on the edge of the bed. He smiled at the way she was lying on the pillow, with both of her small, soft hands tucked underneath the side of her face. Like an angel.

She, in fact, looked so angelic, and so serene to him, that tears threatened to come into his eyes again. He should have been stronger. He should have never dreamed of taking her down this one-way, dead-end street with some burned out shell of a man like him. She deserved a younger man, somebody in their twenties too, who didn't have the baggage he carried. And it wasn't right. He knew it wasn't right. But he was so weak for this woman that it stunned him.

He looked down, at those lips he had kissed so passionately. He looked at her exposed, up-tilted breasts that still contained his suck marks all over them. And he knew he was cooked. He couldn't just walk away. He would do her a favor if he walked away. But he couldn't.

He placed his hand on the side of her pretty face. He smiled at the way she warmed to his touch. She even moved her body as if his hand alone was turning her on. And then she opened those devastatingly beautiful eyes. And he was a goner.

"Hey," she said, when she saw his face.

He smiled again. "Good morning."

She stared at him, at the spider-like lines on the side of his soft blue eyes. "What time is it?"

"Early. Three a.m.."

"Three o'clock?" Then she saw that he was dressed and ready to go. And her fear, that she would mean nothing more to him than another notch on his belt, was being realized. But she had to accept it. We are bound, she knew, by the decisions we make. And she had decided, of her own free will, to go down this path with him.

"You're leaving me?" she asked in such a vulnerable way that John's heart dropped. Leaving her? How could he leave her? And it suddenly seemed almost insulting to him.

"Leave you?" he asked. "Why would you say that?"

But they both knew why, and that was why Shay didn't respond. She just stared at him and placed the ball squarely where it belonged: in his court.

He exhaled and stared deep into her now troubled eyes. "No," he said. "I'm not leaving you." And then he stood up.

He removed the jeans he had put on, snatched his shirt back over his head, rendering himself naked again. And then he got back in bed with her.

Although Shay didn't resist moving over to allow him back in, her heart was still unsure. If the end result was going to be another hit and run, she would have preferred a quick hit and run rather than this lingering one. Because the longer he stayed in her presence, the harder it was going to be on her. She knew it. And as he pulled her into his arms, and they stared into each other's eyes, she knew he knew it too. And they both just laid there.

Then he spoke.

"I have a confession to make," he said.

Shay's heart pounded. "What is it?"

"I'm usually out of here by now," he admitted, and then looked at Shay, to make certain she understood.

She did. Her intelligent eyes always did. "That's why you were dressed?"

"Yes."

"You were going to leave without saying goodbye?"

"That's usually the way I do it, yes."

Shay frowned. "Why?"

"Because I'm a bastard, Shay. Because I'm thirty-seven years old and still commitment phobic. Because I'm the last human being on earth a girl like you should have given the time of day. I'm not worth it."

Shay just stared at him with such sincerity in her eyes that it broke John's heart. He wanted her, there was no doubt in his mind that he wanted this woman to stay by his side, but he knew he didn't deserve her.

Shay, however, didn't know what she wanted at this point in time. She respected John, admired him even, but a hot and heavy romance with a man with his reputation was such a risk. And this was a small town. The talk could get outrageous.

"You're hopeless, is that what you're saying?" she asked him. "Or are you saying a committed relationship with me is probably hopeless?"

Physical pain shot through John's body. "A little of both," he said.

"Bull," Shay replied.

131

John looked at her.

"That's bullshit, John," she said again. "Good men are good men because they choose to be good. Bad men are bad because they choose to be assholes. It's a choice. It's not a sickness or a disease. It's a choice. And if our trying to make something work is hopeless, it's because we didn't try to make it work. It's our call. It's up to us."

John's heart wanted to soar. He stared at Shay. Could she really take him on? Was she really the one who could do it?

"I'm gruffy and scruffy and can be very ill-tempered," he said, still staring at her.

Shay was staring right back at him. "Same here," she replied.

"I don't suffer fools well, even if it hurts their feelings."

Shay could be that way, too. "Same here."

"The kind of sex we had tonight is the kind I enjoy having. I sometimes like it rough."

Shay didn't even have to think about that one. She wasn't sure if she would enjoy sex the way John had laid it on her, but it nearly blew her mind it was so intense. "Same here," she said.

John's heart could barely contain his joy. He therefore went for broke. He was going to be completely honest with her. "I'm not a weakling, Shay," he said. "I handle my woman. Not the other way around."

Shay smiled. "And I handle my man. Not the other way around."

John laughed uproariously. "Child, please," he said in a vernacular that caused her to laugh. "You truly think you can handle a man like me?"

"Yup. Watch me."

John shook his head. This kid had that cockiness in spades. His instincts about her were being proven absolutely right. "Come here, you," he said as his smile began to dissolve.

Shay moved closer and he pulled her on top of him. They were face to face. He wrapped her into his big arms. Then he rubbed his hand slowly down her soft, bare back, and then onto her butt, giving it a nice, hard squeeze. Which was fine by Shay, since her bruises were now completely gone. And then John spread her legs, just enough so that his penis could rest in between.

"What can I do, Shay," he said like a man grasping for life again, "to make this work? What can I do to be the kind of man you would want to be with?"

Shay swallowed hard. This was do or die time for her. He either was going to be all in with her, or they needed to get out now. While her heart could still take it.

"No bullshit," she said. "No lies," she added. "And especially no other females." She said this and looked at him. He saw that troubled look of doubt in her eyes.

"Before I met you, the last part, about the other females, would have been out of the question for me."

Shay's heart began to pound. Was this when he told her she either allow him room to roam or forget about it? She would have to forget it if he did go down that road, but that wouldn't lessen her pain.

He kept on. "I liked variety and I had to have variety. But now," he said, staring deep into her eyes, "it feels almost as if it's the opposite. It almost feels as if it's out of the question to think that I would want any other female."

Shay knew it was always out of the question early on. Until the routine of being with the same woman day in and day out set in. She looked at his chain, and rubbed it. "So it's as easy as that?" she asked him. She then looked, once again, into his big, blue eyes.

John shook his head, pulled her closer. "No, babe, it's not going to be easy at all," he admitted, rubbing her hair. "I know it won't be easy. Not for a man with my kind of appetites. But I guess what I'm trying to say is that I'm willing to try it. And that alone, for a man like me, is progress."

Shay smiled. Her heart didn't quite relax, but it did stop pounding.

"What about you?" John asked her.

"What about me?" When he didn't respond, just continued to stare at her, she got the message. "I don't know," she said. "It's kind of scary, to be honest with you." Then she scrunched up her face. "If that makes sense."

John chuckled. "It makes perfect sense, my darling. Taking me on isn't going to be as simple as taking me on. You'll be taking on a lot of baggage too."

His last statement particularly caught Shay's attention. "What kind of baggage?"

It was something John had never spoken of. Not ever. It happened and it was over with, forever to be buried away within his own nightmares and pain. And right now, even though he wanted to tell her all about it, and unload it once and for all, he couldn't. "The baggage," he decided to say, "of being a man who had one long-term commitment in his entire life, a commitment that ended disastrously. That kind of baggage."

She could sense there was more to his "baggage," a lot more, but she didn't question his decision not to go there now. They were like a hot air balloon just getting off the ground. Now was not the time to take on the heavy loads.

"Did you do all you could to make your marriage work?" she decided to ask him. He had invoked his ex-wife as a buffer once. She needed to know if that marriage was as over as the print on their final divorce decree said it was.

But he wouldn't even respond to that simple question. This worried Shay.

"Why aren't you answering?" she asked him.

Because he was ashamed, he wanted to say. "I just.

135

. .," he said stumbling. "No. I didn't do all I could to make that marriage work."

"You cheated on her?"

After she cheated on him, he wanted to say. "Yes," he said instead.

Shay closed her eyes. It was the one thing she always dreaded in a relationship, a cheating man. How in the world could she even think about going down some romantic road with a man who was right now admitting that he was a cheater? She moved to get out of the bed.

And John, shocking himself, began to panic. "Shay," he said, stopping her from moving off of him. "Please don't leave."

"I can't do this," she said, shaking her hand, fighting back the tears. "I can't deal with a cheater, John, I'm telling you I can't."

"I'm not a cheater. I mean, not now."

That was what they all said. Shay moved to get off of him again.

"Shay, what is it?" he asked, refusing to release his hold on her. "Talk to me."

"I told you! I can't do it. I want a man who believes I'm enough for him. Not a man who has to have me and all of these other women. I can't deal with that. I won't deal with that. Every man I've ever been with has cheated on me and I'm not going through that again."

"But I won't be that way, Shay. Not with you. These women I'm sleeping around with are bed warmers.

That's it. They know it and I know it. And as for my ex-wife, she and I were a train wreck, I mean it. We should have never gotten married in the first place. We only did it because of. . ." John's heart began to pound. He couldn't believe he almost went there.

Shay stared at him. "Because of what, John?" she asked.

John felt helpless. He felt as if he had to expose himself fully, warts and all, or lose Shay forever. For some powerful reason he couldn't even verbalize, he couldn't lose Shay. He knew it like he knew his name.

"Because of our son," he said.

Shay didn't expect that answer. "Your son? You have a son?"

A pain so devastating came onto John's handsome face that even Shay could feel the force of his pain. "I *had* a son," he said.

Shay's body froze. She didn't expect this. She did not expect this man to tell her that he had a dead child.

John hadn't expected to tell it, either. Not ever. Or at least, in Shay's case, not this soon. But he knew he had to tell it all. "I was a cop in Baton Rouge at the time, and Blair was my girlfriend. One of my girlfriends," he added. Shay didn't respond. His pain, and the pain she suddenly felt, was too excruciating for her to respond. She just stared at him.

"Blair told me she was pregnant. We fought and then made love, that was pretty much our relationship up

137

to that point, but I married her because I felt it was the right thing to do. And I was committed to the relationship early on. Completely committed. Until, one night, while Blair was away in Virginia attending her sorority sister's wedding, I left work extremely late, was tired on my feet, and drove over to the babysitter's to get our three-month old son. I put the baby in the car seat."

He stopped.

Shay could barely breathe.

John frowned. Even though he was staring at Shay, she knew he was staring through her, at a night long ago. "I put my son in the car seat. But I was so exhausted. I was so drained that I forgot to fasten it." Tears began to appear in John's eyes. "I forgot to fasten him in, Shay. My own son. I forgot to fasten his car seat in. I just sat him in it. I just. . . But I fastened mine. Oh, yeah, I got behind the wheel and fastened my own *got*damn seatbelt like clockwork."

He frowned again. Settled back down. "I apparently dozed off at the wheel because just as I was opening my eyes I blew through a red light. I slammed on brakes but I was T-boned by this other car. And my child, my son, my life, was thrown through the windshield."

Shay's heart dropped.

"The guy driving the other car had on his seat belt, too, so he was fine. I didn't have a scratch on me. The other guy didn't have a scratch on him. But my son. . ." He paused again. Frowned again. "The authorities on

138

the scene said my child was like a flying projectile. They said he was like some unsecured flying missile. Unsecured was how they put it. I didn't secure my son. I failed to protect my own child. And he died as a direct result of my failure."

John steeled himself. The pain was still so raw it felt as if it had happened six days ago, not six years ago.

"What was his name?" Shay asked him.

John closed his eyes. Opened them again. "Malcolm," he said. "We called him Mal. Sometimes I'd call him Malkie."

"Did they charge you?" Shay asked. She had to know it all. She had to know every piece of this devastating puzzle called John Malone.

"They should have. Everybody knew they should have. But I was a cop. You know how it goes. They didn't even file charges against me. It was just an unfortunate accident they said. So, instead of going to prison for murder like I should have, I packed up my wife and we left Baton Rouge. The memories were too thick there anyway. It was as if the air itself reminded us of our loss. And my part in that loss. We couldn't stay even if we willed ourselves to stay. So I accepted a promotion here in Brady. It was so ironic to me, but so typical. My child dies, I don't get a scratch, and I get a promotion on top of that."

That's because God knows, even if you don't, that you're not as hopeless as you think you are, Shay wanted to say. "Your wife came with you to Brady?" she asked instead.

John paused on that, as if she'd just asked a loaded question. "Yes," he said.

"So she doesn't blame you?"

John snorted. "She blames me every day of every hour of every second of her bitter life. And since I couldn't agree more with her assessment, I felt it only proper to bring her along to constantly remind me of what a miserable son-of-a-bitch I truly am."

The sadness of that statement broke Shay's heart. And that compassionate look in Shay's eyes caused tears to trail down John's face. He never dreamed he'd be comfortable enough to share his pain with any one.

"Welcome to my nightmare," he said to her with a smile that was meant to be joyless. Shay wiped his tears away and stared at him. All she ever saw when she saw John Malone was toughness personified. Handsome, great bod, and tough. Now she saw the other side too.

She kissed him.

"I don't think you're a miserable lout, John Malone," she said to him.

John looked at her, as if he was seeking an approval he knew he didn't deserved.

"I think you're a flawed man, a wounded man, and sometimes a very difficult man. But you're a good man too, I think. And that's the part of you we've got to make sure super-cedes all the rest."

John stared at her, his heart recovering. "Does that mean you're not going to leave me?"

Shay almost smiled. It went from her fear that he was about to leave her, to the other way around.

"I don't know what it is about you, kid," Shay said, causing John to smile, "but there's something about you, that's for sure. And I want to stick around to see if I'm right."

John wanted to cry again. He couldn't believe how emotional he'd become.

Shay became dead serious too. "But the first time you decide that I'm not enough for you, the very first time, John Malone, I'm out of here, I declare I am. I can't deal with a cheater. I'm not one of those women who can look the other way and pretend it ain't so. I'm not that woman. I'm not her. So if you can't be faithful, say so now. And we'll shake hands and end this right now."

John didn't know why he wanted to give it a go when everything he'd ever loved always seemed to disintegrate in his hands. His prayer was that with Shay it would be different. That *he* would be different. And somehow he felt a strong urge, a strong need to try. "You won't have to worry about that," he promised her.

Shay smiled and laid her head on his shoulder. He rested his hand on the side of her hair, wrapping her tightly in his arms.

But they both felt slightly more terrified than euphoric.

EIGHT

Ronnie Burk's Toyota Prius turned onto Bluestone Road to conduct what he privately called his morning drive-by. He had to go out of his way to get there, because Shay's home was not on his way to work. But he made the effort anyway. It made him feel good, like he was looking out for her. For over a month now he'd been doing it: drive over to Mickey D's and get his morning coffee, stop by the Piggly Wiggly to get that apple strudel he loved to eat, and then drive by Shay Turner's house on Bluestone Road before getting back on Kincaid to make it to work.

Although he and Shay were both scheduled to begin work at nine a.m., he always arrived much earlier. Usually by seven. Which meant, to do his morning drive-by, he had to leave his home as early as six.

But on this morning, when he drove past Shay's home, he couldn't believe his eyes. A big black and gray truck was parked on her driveway.

"What the *fuck*," he said inwardly as he drove to the end of the street and turned back around. He stopped his vehicle a couple houses down from Shay's house and stared at the truck, his hands now gripping his steering wheel.

For nearly half an hour he just sat there, staring at that truck, at that house, at the window he knew was her bedroom window. And sure enough, just as he

142

suspected, the light came on in that bedroom and then, less than ten minutes later, the front door of Shay's house opened and John Malone came bounding down the steps.

Ronnie could not believe his eyes. He thought it was John's truck all along, but he refused to believe that a sensible girl like Shay would be that stupid. But there it was. John Malone in the flesh. After undoubtedly pounding the flesh off of little Shay. How could she, Ronnie thought, as John got into his big Chevy pickup, cranked up, and drove away.

Ronnie hit his steering wheel.

"How could she!" he screamed.

Shay arrived at the Brady Tribune newsroom with a little extra pep in her step. She had just dropped Aunt Rae off at the Senior Center, enduring her *you're late* routine even though she wasn't late, and was now ready to get to work. Ed Barrington was the first face she encountered.

"Good morning, Ed," she said airily to her boss as she walked past him. He was stooped down talking to an editor at the copy desk.

"What's so good about it?" Ed replied, not bothering to look her way. And then he remembered something. "Oh, Turner, it's you," he said, looking up. "I need to see you in my office," he added.

Shay placed her things on her desk near the back of

the newsroom, and then headed back toward the front.

"Hey, Ronnie, what's up?" she asked as she passed his desk.

Ronnie mumbled something as if he wasn't the least interested, and she kept going.   He was doing all he could to keep his rage from festering. She just betrayed him. She just literally crawled out of bed with another man, and she had the nerve to ask him what was up? Your ass was up, bitch, while John Malone pounded it, Ronnie had wanted to say. But he kept his cool. She needed some tough love, he decided, something to bring her back to reality. And he was just the man to give it to her.

Shay arrived in Ed's office just as Ed did himself. He closed the door and they both sat down.

"Is it about the press conference yesterday?" she asked him.

"Why would you ever think that?"

Shay smiled. "I'd never seen anything like it, Ed. The guy went after me the entire time. I just sat there amazed."

"It was something to see all right. Seeing Malone defend you was something to see, too." Ed said this and looked at her.

Shay hesitated. "Yeah," she finally said. "You think he'll be fired?"

"Who knows?   The mayor suspended McNamara already, pending the outcome of some lame investigation of course, but that doesn't mean Malone is out of the woods yet. He should have known what was going on, even if he claims now he didn't. My bet is that he knew all along and he'll get the ax next."

Shay remained expressionless, although she couldn't disagree with Ed more. "So what's up?"

Ed leaned back. "I'm putting you back on the Queen's Ridge story."

Shay frowned. "But why? Ronnie's handling that story now."

"You both will be handling it. Just as you both will be handling the Dodge story. And Ronnie will be lead on both."

Shay felt as if she'd just been slapped in the face. She stared at Ed. "I break the story. I write the story. I'm the person the source came to. But I'm not good enough to continue reporting on the story? Is that it, Ed?"

"You can report. But you're report to Ronnie and he'll get the byline. It'll be his name on the story."

"Are you saying, are you telling me that we won't even share the byline? It'll just be all Ronnie?"

Ed hesitated. "Yes," he finally said.

"This is really foul, Ed," Shay found the courage to say to her boss. "This is really unfair and this is wrong."

"It's not about all of that, Shay."

Shay was flustered. "Well please tell me what it's about because I don't get it. I keep working my ass off and this is the same shit I keep getting. Over and over.

145

So please tell me what it's about."

"I only do what I'm told, all right? And my boss told me to make Ronnie primary. So I made Ronnie primary. It's politics in this town. McNamara has friends in high places. You should know that."

"But, Ed---"

"No but. Case closed."

Shay stared at Ed. She could see the embarrassment in his eyes, and the regret that he'd been put in such an untenable position, but she felt no sympathy for him. She was tired of this. She was tired of being held back, pushed aside, her rightful stories stolen from her and given to less talented journalists. She stood to her feet. "Is there anything else?" she asked him.

"Look, Turner---"

"Is there anything else, sir?" Shay didn't want to hear it.

Ed let out a harsh exhale. "No, Turner, there's nothing else," he said.

And Shay left his office and headed for her desk. Ronnie looked up as she past his desk, as if he wanted to see her reaction, but her face remained as stoic as she could manage. But when she reached her desk, she balked. The idea of just sitting there as if she accepted this unfair treatment made her turn right back around and head out of the newsroom altogether.

She walked down the hall, opened the door to the stairwell, and hurried through. She stopped in the rarely used, empty stairwell and sat on the top step. She leaned her head against the rail and tried not to feel sorry for herself. But that was a tall order. She had been so hopeful. Her career was finally getting off the ground again and her love life wasn't far behind. But literally overnight, just like that, they'd decided to give a story they knew was rightfully hers to Ronnie Burk. And she wasn't blaming Ronnie, he was taking what was given to him, but that didn't make it any easier.

Her cell phone began to ring and for a moment she didn't even bother to answer it. Until she thought of one particular person, the only bright spot still in her life, and at least looked at the Caller ID. Brady Police Department was emblazed on her screen. She answered the phone.

"This is Shay," she said.

"Well hello there," John said jovially. He was in his office, leaned back in the swivel chair behind his desk, a smile on his face as soon as he heard her sweet, smoky voice.

Just hearing his voice brought all kinds of emotions to the forefront for Shay, too. They had had such a wonderful night together. The best night of sex and conversation she'd had in a long time. And now this. She fought back tears. "Hey," she said.

John immediately detected a difference in her voice. He stopped rocking. "What's the matter, honey?" he asked her.

"Nothing, I was just. . ." The tears began to appear.

147

"Shay, what is it?"

She hated crying to him like some damn baby, but she felt like hell. "They took me off the story," she said.

John frowned. "*You*? Are you kidding me? You're the one who broke the *got*damn story!"

"That's what I said. But they don't care. They're letting Ronnie Burk handle it. He'll get the byline too."

John shook his head. Those assholes! "I'm sorry, babe," he said.

"I'm okay," Shay said, wiping her tears away. "I just found out and it was just a shocker, that's all. But I'll be okay."

"Maybe I'll come over there and have a little talk with Barrington."

"No, John, please, don't. Ed's just doing what the publisher wants. And even if it's his idea, they aren't going to change anything. I'll be okay. I'm used to it."

John closed his eyes. She wasn't even thirty yet and already used to raw deals. If Barrington was in his face right now he'd choke the shit out of him for treating his lady this way. And that was the thing with John now. Shay was officially now his lady. His responsibility. And nobody was mistreating her and expect him to remain silent.

"What about you?" Shay asked him, regaining her composure. "Have they fired you yet?"

John smiled a weak smile. "No, I'm a valuable asset right now. I know where the bodies are buried, so to speak. The conventional wisdom is that I'll be out the door next. The word I'm hearing is that the mayor is contemplating a complete overhaul of the police hierarchy, with me and the rest of the top brass being shown the door. But I haven't heard anything directly from him yet."

"I pray he doesn't let you go. They need you there. You were only doing your job."

"I've been so caught up with running that drug task force that those Dodge murders and the connections we should have drawn a long time ago just never came across my desk. McNamara handled every one of those cases."

"Or didn't handle them, which is the point," Shay said.

"Right," John said. He then motioned for a uniformed officer who was standing outside his door, waiting for him to get off of the phone, to enter. "We'd better both get back to work," he said to Shay.

Shay closed her eyes and nodded her head. "Agreed."

"Sure you're okay?"

"Positive."

"Have dinner tonight?" he asked her.

She smiled. "Sounds good."

"I'll call you."

"Okay, John. Bye." She said this and then killed the call. She remained where she sat for a few minutes longer, her cell still in her hand, her mind bouncing from her budding romance with John to the drag that was becoming her job. All she wanted was a fair shot. Don't screw her over. But she kept getting screwed.

And then, last night, she allowed John to screw her too. Not in the way her job was working her over, but in a more risky, intimate way with far more lasting implications. And she didn't know if she could handle all of this. She came to Brady as a way of starting over after the way she was treated in Birmingham. And already she'd been cheated on and slapped by the man she had once thought was husband material, had been bedded by a cop who had a reputation for bedding females, and now her job had her mired in clay. She felt stuck, fucked, and mucked. And she'd only been in town less than four months.

She left the stairwell and headed back to the newsroom. Her conversation with John did manage to make her feel less besieged, so that was a good thing. And once she got behind her desk she was actually able to concentrate on the work at hand. She was writing a follow up story on the Dodge murders, and although her name would not appear once the story was published, that wasn't going to stop her from doing the best job she could. She still had to eat and pay her bills, byline or no byline, and she wasn't ever going to forget that fact.

Ronnie Burk watched her as she got back to work. He watched her whenever he walked over to the copier, or the fax machine, or whenever he had to show his slug line to the copy editor. And sometimes he'd look back and catch her just sitting there, with those reading glasses on, her big, dreamy eyes staring into space as if she was in some deep thought. She looked like some love-struck teenager to him, and it pained him that it wasn't his love that had struck her.

But for her to prefer a player like John Malone just angered him. *Give me a break*, he thought in his anger. Why all of these women were so nuts about a guy like that was a mighty mystery to Ronnie. And why a sweet, innocent young woman like Shay would feel she had to settle for some old-ass jock like John Malone just didn't sit right with him. She could do way better than that.

He got a chance to tell her exactly that a few hours later, when Shay finally left her computer and went into the break room for coffee.

He followed her.

She was pouring coffee into her cup when he entered. "Want a cup?" she asked him.

"No, I'm good, thanks," he said as he slowly moved toward her. He often wondered why he was so smitten with Shay Turner. She wasn't all that great looking. She looked good, but she wasn't any beauty queen. And her figure was mostly on the small side, something else that never really turned him on.

But she turned him on. Maybe because she wasn't perfect. Maybe because there was an innocence to her

151

that he felt was his duty to protect. And he was going to protect her, he thought to himself, even if it meant drastic measures.

And as she poured her coffee, he stood behind her and couldn't stop staring at that small figure of hers. She was small, but she wasn't boyish. This girl had curves in all the right places. And that ass of hers was so tight, so snugly fit into those blue dress pants she wore, that he was certain a dime could bounce off of it and put somebody's eye out. Then he thought again, about John Malone feeling on that ass, even before he himself had a chance to feast on it, and his rage returned.

"How about that press conference yesterday?" he said as he moved over and stood alongside her.

"It was interesting, that's for sure," Shay said, stirring her brew.

"The way McNamara ripped into you, gosh. He looked like a fool." Shay smiled. "And then for John Malone to try and take credit for your hard work, that was insulting too."

Shay's smile didn't disappear, but it weakened. "What work of mine was he taking credit for?"

"The fact that you wrote about the cover-up."

"Yeah, thanks to Captain Malone giving me the intel to write about it. So I don't get your point. And what was insulting about what he said?"

Ronnie hated the way she was defending that creep, but he fought hard not to show it. "The way he went

152

about it is what I mean," he said. "The way he threw his own boss under the bus. Like, who does that?"

"His boss was lying in his face, and he stood up and called him out on it. I don't call that throwing anybody under any bus. I call that courage."

Ronnie snorted. Inwardly he seethed. "Courage? Give me a break! The only courageous thing John Malone has ever done was when he divorced his good wife, a wife who stood by his side through thick and thin but who he couldn't stop cheating on."

Shay stood erect. "I'd better get back to work," she said as she moved to leave. She wasn't about to stand there and hear him rag on John.

"And the way he still has sex with her," Ronnie threw in, knowing that it would get a rise out of Shay. It did. She turned back around.

"Yeah, isn't it pathetic?" he said when she turned. "He still fucks his ex-wife, pardon my French, but he does. I caught him over there just this morning, yes, I did. I have a friend who lives in the same building where his ex-wife's condo is and he says John goes over there every single morning to sex her before work. And he did it this morning too. Went right over there and screwed her."

Shay's heart was pounding. "I'm sure you nor your friend have any idea what goes on behind her closed doors so, yeah. But anyway---"

"She told him," Ronnie said quickly. Shay looked at

him. "My friend, that is," Ronnie continued. "She told him what goes on when John makes his morning visits. Sex, sex, and more sex, that's the way she put it to my friend."

Shay stared at Ronnie. What kind of game was he playing at, she wondered. "Ed says you're now the lead on the Dodge story," she said.

Ronnie was surprised that she didn't want more details, but he knew how to keep it together too. "Yes. Sorry about that. I was as shocked as you were."

"We need to compare notes, to see where we go from here."

"Right. You bet." Ronnie ran his hand through his spiky blond hair. "I have a couple interviews in a few, but I should be free later today. How's your schedule?"

"I'm flexible. Just say when," Shay said and made her way, quickly, out of his presence.

When she made her way back into the newsroom, however, she stopped in her tracks when she saw John at the front of that room shaking hands with the copy editor. Although he looked so magnificent to her, in his tailored light-brown suit, his boyish brown hair in its usual adorably rumpled mess, she was too amazed that he was in the newsroom at all to be enthralled.

Ronnie came up behind her, wondering if she was standing there because of what he had said to her. When he saw John Malone, he frowned.

"What's he doing here?" he asked her.

Since she had some idea, but wasn't about to share

154

that idea with the likes of Ronnie Burk, she didn't say a word. She watched as the copy editor escorted John into Ed Barrington's office, and then she went back to her desk.

It would be another hour before John left that office. And when he did, both Ronnie, near the front of the city room, and Shay in the back, were staring at him. But he kept it professional. He simply left the newsroom altogether, without so much as glancing at either one of them.

It would be yet another hour after his departure before Ed would do as she had thought he would do earlier, and call her into his office. To undoubtedly cuss her out for allowing John to interject himself in their business to begin with.

As she walked to Ed's office, she determined that she wasn't going to tell him that she had asked John to stay out of it. She wasn't going to throw John under the bus like that. But she wasn't going to just sit there and take Ed's abuse either. So she knew it would be a fine line.

"Sit down," Ed ordered when she walked into his office. He was seated behind his desk, and she could tell he was fuming.

As soon as she closed the door and sat down, Ed let her have it.

"So John Malone's your boyfriend now?" he asked her.

Shay frowned. "Is that what he told you?"

"What the hell else could it be, Turner? I've been the city editor of this newspaper as long as John Malone has been in this town and never once, not ever, has he walked into my office to defend one of my reporters. And, on top of that, he threatened to cut off the entire police department from providing any future intel to the Trib if I didn't treat her right. And that's all he wanted. For me to treat you right. As if I'm treating you like some damn dog around here!"

Shay said nothing. She could have said plenty about her treatment, because John was right about that, but she said nothing. This man was still her boss. She still needed this job.

Ed exhaled, to calm himself back down. "So you're sleeping with him now? Is that it, Shay? You're sleeping with this guy?"

Shay knew what he meant. She turned Ed down, but not John. She knew exactly what he meant. And that was exactly why she held her peace.

"You aren't the only one he's banging, I hope you realize that."

Now he was going too far. "Is there something you wanted, sir?" she asked him.

"Yeah, it's something I want!" *I want to fuck you too*, was what he really wanted to say. But he calmed back down. He wasn't about to tussle with John Malone if it was true and she was now one of his. "You're back on

156

the Dodge story."

Shay didn't expect that. "As lead?" she asked.

"As lead," he said. Her heart soared. "Only continue to work with Ronnie," Ed added. "He makes a good back up."

"Yes, sir," Shay said with a smile, standing to her feet. "I'll gladly work with Ronnie, sir."

"And Turner," Ed said. Shay turned his way. "You're a good kid, I know it even if I don't act like it sometimes. Be careful with Malone. When it comes to breaking a woman's heart, he's the master."

Shay didn't say anything to that. She just left. And once again, her joy was tempered. It was the story of her life. As soon as it seemed as if she was about to soar, her wings always managed to get clipped.

NINE

She didn't see or hear from John again until later that night. Although he had said he would phone to set up a dinner date, he never did. And she wasn't about to phone him. She, instead, went home after work and studied the research notes she had compiled on the Dodge case. If he phoned, great. If he didn't, she wasn't going to worry about it. She wasn't going to let this relationship become the end-all that be-all of her life. She wasn't going to do it.

And it wasn't just because of what Ed and Ronnie had said. She knew John was a ladies' man. She knew that going in. But it was her heart that she had to protect. Because she very well may not be enough for him. Not that it would be her fault if he felt that way, she knew it would be his own damn fault. But that wouldn't ease her pain. John had some great qualities. But he also had some great issues, too. Especially, she thought as she sat on her sofa reading over her notes, if Ronnie's little comment was true and John got out of her bed, and went straight to his ex-wife's.

The doorbell rang just as Shay was thinking about going into the kitchen and finding herself something to eat. She sat her notes on the already crowded coffee table and walked over by her big, living room window. She assumed it would be John. But when she saw, not his big Silverado, but a green Porsche on her driveway, she frowned. She had been certain that it would be John.

She opened the door. When John was standing there, no longer in his tailored suit but now in his jeans and a light brown pullover knit shirt, she was surprised. And she looked past him. "Is that yours?" she asked him.

"Yes," he said, a big smile on his face. "You like?"

"Is it brand new?"

"Not new, no. I purchased it a couple years ago."

"I see. It's certainly sporty," she said as she let him in. That car, for some reason, didn't help lift her mood. It was a player's car straight up.

"What's the matter?" John asked her as he walked in.

"Nothing's the matter," she said as she closed the door. "I hadn't heard from you, so I didn't know if our date was still on."

"Sorry about that," he said. "Every time I thought to phone you I was getting pulled one way or another. But I'm here now. Ready to cook for you. Show me to your kitchen."

She smiled as she showed him to her kitchen. And just like that she felt her mood lightened. John, she was beginning to realize, had a way of doing that for her: easing her load, her burden, her mood. Although, she also knew, they still had the matter of his ex-wife, and specifically his relationship with that ex-wife, to discuss.

As he washed his hands and prepared to cook a

159

pasta dish, she went into the master bath and showered and changed into her own pair of jeans and a UAB jersey. Every time she entered her room now she thought about John stretched out on her bed, completely naked, and the way he kissed her and held her all night. Seeing him again brought it all back.

"Whatever you're cooking," she said as she reentered the kitchen, "it smells great."

"Thank-you my dear," John said and glanced her way. Only he did a second take when he saw how youthful she looked in those jeans and jersey. He'd never bothered with women more than a few years younger than he was, and it was a startling thought to him now. But Shay was a mature young woman, far more advanced than many of the older women he often fooled with, so he felt reasonably comfortable with their age difference.

"I saw you today," she said.

He smiled. "I would have thought you did."

"After you left, Ed put me back as primary on the Dodge murders."

John nodded, tasted his pasta. "Good. He should have."

"You threatened to withhold future intel from him."

"Something like that."

"Why, John?"

John looked at her. "Why do you think? I wasn't going to sit back and let that asshole walk all over you like that. He was wrong and he knew it. Giving your hard work to some damn Ronnie Burk! That wasn't happening. But that's how they do it, Shay. You're a young, black woman in an old white man's game, and they look out for their own. But not this time," he added, and turned back to his pots.

Shay stared at him as he attended to his food. She wasn't accustomed to being taken care of like this. When an injustice at work was done to her in the past, she either had to fight it all alone, often coming across like a bitch, or just forget about it. Mostly she forgot about it, or complained quietly to her boss, except when they left her no choice.

She couldn't take her eyes off of this new man in her life, this big man as he turned around in her small kitchen. He had on a brown pullover knit shirt and well-worn blue jeans, and everything about him screamed power and prowess. In truth, she couldn't stop thinking about his power and prowess, especially in bed. She'd never been with a man quite like him before. Lonnie Resden was good in bed, but his idea of experimentation consisted of spanking her with some new-age belt that left her bruised and battered.

John didn't need any gadgets or aids. His dick was his accessory and man, she thought, did he know how to use it. She never cared to give oral or get oral until John did it to her. She never liked it rough until John gave it to her rough. It was as if he was opening her up to a different world and, with him, it was exhilarating.

And just the thought of his dick inside of her made her vagina tingle. And when he turned her way, as he plated the food, she even looked down, at his package, and couldn't stop thinking about how warmly it made her feel.

John smiled when he saw Shay's gorgeously big eyes trail down to his bundle. He'd had enough satisfied women in his bed to be accustomed to that reaction. But it was different seeing Shay react. He was pleased to know that she was pleased with his performance last night. Because, in truth, he had an encore performance in store for her tonight.

She certainly pleased him, he thought, as he remembered her pliable body, from the sweet smell to the sweet taste to the beautifulness of her entire being. And it was times like these when he hated that he had a bad reputation, and that Shay, by virtue of the fact that she was now hooked to him, would be tarnished with that rep too. To the townspeople she would be just another one of John Malone's ladies. Although nothing, John thought as he took the plated food to the table, could be further from the truth.

"Come on, let's eat," he said as he and Shay sat down at the small table at the small kitchen window.

They ate slowly and small-talked most of the time. An elephant was in the room, clogging up Shay's thoughts, but John seemed oblivious. Until Shay decided to just come out and ask him.

"Are you still sleeping with your ex-wife?" she asked him.

John's fork stalled just after it had picked up a hefty pile of pasta. He sat it back down and looked at her. "What made you ask a question like that?"

"Are you, John?" Shay wasn't backing down. Her fork was playing around with her food, but it was clear where her attention was.

John swallowed hard. "I don't get why you would ask that."

"Did you sleep with her this morning?"

"Hell no!" he said with a frown.

"But after you left me this morning you went over there?"

He hesitated this time, which didn't help Shay at all. "Yes," he finally said.

"Why?"

"What do you mean why?"

"Because that's what I mean. Why, John? Why did you go over there as soon as you left me? Are you still in love with that woman?"

John exhaled and ran his hand through his hair. "I had my cell phone off last night. If I don't turn it off I'll never get any rest. She had left me several messages. I went over there to make sure she was okay."

Shay stared at him. "Why should you care if she's okay?"

KATHERINE CACHITORIE

Again he attempted to smile. Again he failed. "Because she's my ex-wife, that's why. We were married for six years. I loved her once. I can't just pretend that it never happened. She's the mother. . . She was once the mother of my child, Shay, surely you understand that."

Shay didn't understand it at all, if truth be told. When she was done with a relationship, she was done. She truly didn't care if the guy was dead or alive. And she knew it was probably different in a marriage that lasted longer than a minute, but still. John seemed to still have that female in his system big time.

"You do understand," he asked again. "Don't you, Shay?"

"Not really, no," she replied honestly.

"I don't love her. I'm not fucking her. You have nothing to worry about in that department, I assure you. Don't believe anybody who tells you I'm doing anything like that with Blair, because I'm not. I check on her, yes, I do. But that's it. All right?"

Shay looked at him. He looked so concerned that she felt a sense of obligation. And she knew she had to believe him over some gossip Ronnie Burk had heard. She nodded her head. "All right," she said, and John's relaxed look returned.

This was all so new to him. He'd never been in a relationship like this, where he was the one stressing about the future of the affair. He was seriously worried there for a moment that she was going to decide he was

164

too much trouble, and dump him. And if she had made such a decision, he wasn't quite sure how he would have handled it. Or if he could. And that, without question, would be a serious first for him.

He grinned. "You were giving me a heart attack there for a minute," he said.

"I didn't mean to give you any grief. I just don't want any surprises."

John took her hand. "You won't get any, not from me. I'm in this."

Shay stared at him. "All the way?"

He sandwiched her hand between both of his. "All the way," he said.

It was Shay's time to exhale. "Good," she said, and they released hands.

"So," John asked, looking at her almost clean plate of food, "how do you like my crab alfredo? Thumbs up or thumbs down?"

"Up," she said. "With snaps."

John laughed. And then his cell phone began ringing.

"Ah, geez!" he yelled.

Shay smiled. "Turn it off," she said.

He pulled it out, looked at his Caller ID. "It's the station." And was compelled to answer. "Malone," he said into the phone. And then he listened. It was obvious, by the look on his face, that it wasn't good news. "Get those witness statements before they have a chance to compare notes. I'm on my way," he said, and killed the call.

"Oh, I'm disappointed," Shay said.

"You don't know how much I am," he replied. "You go on and finish your dinner. Put mine in the microwave."

The idea that he would be coming back to her tonight warmed her heart. Then she thought about something. "It's not another murder in Dodge, is it?" she asked him.

"No, no, thank God. A drive-by on Stockton. They need a senior officer on the scene."

"You?"

"Me. Dammit." Then he stood up.

"Duty calls," Shay said as she stood up too and walked with him to the front door.

When they arrived at the door, John looked at Shay, at the outline of her breasts within her jersey, and then into her eyes. He pulled her into his arms. "I'll be back," he said. "Are you going to wait for me?"

Shay smiled snidely. "No, John, I'm going to leave my home and go dancing. I never leave my home and go dancing, but I figure I'll do it tonight because you might come back."

He laughed. "You have a smart mouth, you know that?" He gave her behind a swift slap. Then he looked at that mouth. "A gorgeously gorgeous smart mouth," he added.

Shay smiled. And then his lips captured hers.

They moved until her back was   al
front door as he kissed her. She tasted
that he closed his eyes and just relaxe
lips on his. He knew he had to leave, but he couldn't
leave her like this.

He lifted her oversized jersey, revealing those plump
breasts he couldn't wait to taste again. "I thought about
these all day," he said as he squeezed and licked her
mounds.

"What were you thinking about when you thought
about them?" Shay asked as she leaned her head back
and enjoyed the way his mouth made her feel.

"I thought about how big they are," he said,
squeezing them again. "And how tasty," he added,
licking them. And how," he said as he placed her nipple
between his teeth and lifted it, stretching her breasts.
Shay pushed into him when her breast stretched.

"And how what?" she asked.

"And how marked up I left them this morning, and
how marked up I'm about to make them again." He was
on her now, licking and sucking so hard that Shay
wondered if she would come before he even got started
good.

Because she knew he was just getting started. He
removed his gun and holster, putting them on her side
table. Then he unbuckled and unzipped his pants, pulled
them down to his ankles, and then slid her shorts down to
hers. He then removed one of her feet out of the shorts

ogether and lifted her legs, opening them wide, until he nad her legs flapped over his broad shoulders. And that was when the intensity started.

His head moved between her legs and his mouth began kissing her. She closed her eyes as his tongue started licking her folds and then flicking her clit. His hands held her ass in a tight grip as he licked her, and the feeling from front to back rendered her body unable to remain still.

She began to buck against the door as John began to go down hard on her, licking and flicking as if his tongue was going to ram inside of her with the same depth of his dick. She knew she was going to be marked, not just on her breasts, not just on the ass he was squeezing the life out of, but inside of her too. Because he kept going. Because he couldn't stop his tongue from licking her clit and swelling her folds. And she didn't want him to stop. He had her high up, held only by the catch of his huge hands, and her body felt inflamed with desire.

But it couldn't stop there. He needed to feel her mouth on his rod so badly that he knew he had to try it. He was certain she'd never done it this way before, but he had to try it.

He lifted her and turned her body around, to where her bare ass was in his face. She knew immediately what he wanted, and trusted him to be able to hold her. So she leaned her body down in an almost acrobatic move, until her mouth was able to capture his rod. John

168

held onto her as she licked and then went down on him, way down, and moved in and out with the precision he loved about her.

"Ah, yes, Shay, yes," he said as she gave him head. "That's what I'm talking about, baby, that's what I'm talking about!" It was feeling so good to him that he had to turn their bodies around, to where his back was now against the door. His legs were almost buckling as she gave him as good, if not better, he thought, as she got.

His fingers played with her clit as she mouth-fucked him, and then his hand began to rub her ass as his rod became swollen with passion. "Do me, baby!" he yelled as he squeezed her. "Do me, baby, do me!"

And she did him, in a way no other had done him before. He liked it hard and rough and she was giving him hard and rough. Shay felt exhilarated in a sensual daze as he squeezed her ass and she sucked his dick. She had never experienced it like this before. She had never had sex this way before.

"Oh, babe," he said, "We've got to stop."

"Why?" she asked, although she absolutely knew why.

"I'm going to come in your mouth if we don't stop," he said, already throbbing.

And then it became a mad dash for both of them. He lifted Shay back up and then sat her feet on the floor. He turned her around, slamming her back against the door, and then reached down, grabbed his wallet from the pocket of his pants, and pulled out a condom. Shay's body was squirming as he prepared himself. She could hardly wait.

He could hardly wait, too, and that was why, when he entered her, he slid all the way in with one swift drive.

"Oh!" they both yelled, as the feeling of his big rod inside of her, and the feeling of her tight pussy encapsulating him, caused both of them to sigh relief. For they were being relieved.

And then the banging started.

Outside of the very door they were leaned against, Ronnie Burk stood in front of that door just about to ring the bell. He had told Shay that they would meet later to discuss their shared stories, and he had purposely waited until nightfall to come. When he saw that Porsche in the driveway, knowing full well that it belonged to that damn John Malone, he was seething. But he never dreamed he'd catch them in the act.

But he did. They were in the act. As soon as his finger was about to ring that bell, he heard them. First he frowned. What in the world, he said to himself. He was hearing sliding sounds against the door at first. Just odd sliding sounds. But then he started hearing slapping sounds, as if it was flesh on flesh. And he knew exactly what was going on. John was fucking her. And by the sound of it, Ronnie thought, he was fucking her harder than even Ronnie ever dreamed of doing himself. And the flesh pounding felt so hard, so rough, that Ronnie was appalled. How could she allow such savagery to be performed on her small, innocent body?

Instead of ringing any bell, he hurried around to the front window, to see if he could see anything. But he couldn't. He hurried off of the porch and moved swiftly around to the side of the house, where there was a sliding glass door off from the dining room. And that was when he saw them. Both of them. John had her pinned against the front door, his dick wedged deep inside of her, fucking her brains out.

Shay had her eyes closed, but Ronnie was certain she was in pain. The way he was slamming into her, she had to be. And Ronnie was getting a hard-on just looking at her, at the way John had her legs around his back, the way his pants were down around his ankles, the way he was panting as his big, tight ass banged into her. Ronnie quickly unzipped his pants and began jerking off as he watched them. Shay was naked and John was fucking her so hard. Ronnie jerked and jerked. And within a matter of seconds he came. Just like that. John Malone was still banging her, and Ronnie had already come.

He nervously looked around. Fortunately the next door neighbor didn't appear to be at home. Then he grabbed a handkerchief out of his pocket, wiped up his spillage, put his dick back where it belonged, and then headed for the front door, the same front door John and Shay were fucking against. He was angry at her now for making him lose such control.

171

John heard the knocking on the door but couldn't stop pounding Shay. They were in the throes of their climax and no way was he going to allow them to stop. He leaned against Shay, to help moot their elation, but they kept on gyrating in their fast-paced rhythm until both of them constricted into a fantastic release.

And it was only then did they stop.

John was breathing in hard pants, and despite the knocks, they both had to take a second before doing anything else.

But then Ronnie's voice could be heard. "Shay, you in there?" he yelled out.

"Shit," Shay said in a lowered voice. "We're supposed to meet about a couple stories we're working on together."

"Okay," John said, pulling out of her. They both were amazed, but delighted, at how deep down he had been inside of her. It took more than a second for his rod to travel the distance.

"I'll stall him," he whispered to her. "You go get cleaned up."

She moved to do just that, grabbing up her clothes, but John pulled her back. He then kissed her passionately on the lips. "I'll be back for more," he said to her.

Shay didn't believe it possible, but her womanhood tingled again at just the thought of it. "Good," she said smilingly and hurried for the master bath.

"Shay!" Ronnie yelled again.

"Just a minute, Burk!" John yelled back. He then quickly prepared himself, from retrieving his wallet and condom wrapper, removing the condom off of his penis, and then pulling up his clothes. He went into the hall bathroom, to toss the condom and wrapper, and then he headed back up to the front door. After putting back on his gun and holster, he exhaled. By the time he opened the door, Ronnie had managed to calm himself down. Showing his hand to some alpha-male asshole like John Malone would be disastrous. He had to play this right.

He smiled. "Well, hello there, Captain," he said.

"Come on in," John replied, opening the door further.

"Whatever brings you this way?" Ronnie asked as he stepped inside. He expected to smell sex in the air, but he was so inwardly angry he wasn't sure if he did or not. "I hope it's more juicy inside information on our corrupt police department."

"I thought you were off of that case."

"Well, you thought wrong, now didn't you," Ronnie replied in that snippiness of his John knew very well. "Shay and I are both working the case."

"With Shay as lead, though, right?"

Ronnie frowned. "What difference does that make?"

"None whatsoever," John said as his cell phone began to ring again. He looked at the Caller ID. "I've got to run," he said.

"Not on my account surely," Ronnie said.

173

John snorted. "You really flatter yourself, Burk, don't you?"

Ronnie smiled. "No more than you flatter yourself," he replied.

John turned toward the hallway. "Shay, I'm leaving."

"Okay, John," Shay yelled from her bedroom. "I'll be with you in just a moment, Ronnie."

John looked at Ronnie once more, thought he saw something odd about him, but then dismissed it. Ronnie was and always had been an obnoxious twit. He decided to just leave it at that.

"Good night, Burk," he said as he opened the door and headed out.

"Good night, Captain. Don't let the door hit cha where your mammy split cha." Ronnie said this with a laugh. John rolled his eyes at the sometimes gross nature of Ronnie's humor, and kept walking.

As soon as Ronnie closed the door, his smile disappeared. They must take him for a fool, he thought, as he began roaming around the small living room. They must take him for some major league, Kool-Aid drinking, hillbilly fool! Naturally Shay wasn't available to greet him. As soon as he saw Malone's fancy-dancy sports car, he knew she wouldn't be. And the sounds they made! Like two rats making out. He could hardly believe she'd stoop that low.

"Are you decent?" he yelled to her.

Shay laughed, certain he was joking. "I'll be right

174

there, Ronnie," she yelled back from, just as he imagined, the bedroom.

But he didn't wait for her to come to him. He went to her. He moved down the hall toward the sound of her movements like some animal on the prowl. Shay, in her bedroom, could hear his footsteps heading her way too, but was fortunately already dressed and was just combing down her once-wild hair.

"I told you I was coming, Ronnie," she said, heading out of her bedroom. "I had to-"

"Put on your clothes?" Ronnie asked as he stood in the doorway, blocking her path.

Shay looked at him. "Put on my . . ." She smiled. "What are you talking about? And move out of the way."

She attempted to move pass him again. But this time he pushed her back. "What was Malone doing here?"

Shay stared at Ronnie. What was his problem? "That's none of your business," she said.

Ronnie shook his head. "I don't believe you. John Malone? Are you serious? You're fucking *that* player?"

"Okay, now, you're weirding me out here."

But Ronnie couldn't stop shaking his head. He couldn't stop behaving as if he was some scorned man who knew the deal all along. Shay was so baffled that she could barely comprehend the moment. She was so confused that she didn't see the danger.

"You women are all alike," Ronnie said, as if a light

175

bulb had suddenly gone off in his head. "All you want is a big dick. That's all you ladies want. A big fucking dick! Not a good guy. Not a man who treats you with nothing but respect. Not a man who has taken you under his wings and taught you the ropes. Not a man who lays awake every night wondering if you're okay. You want a thug!"

Then he pushed Shay violently, causing her to fall. "Well I got your thug right here!" he yelled as he slammed the bedroom door, unzipped his pants, and began coming toward her.

Shay's confusion was now replaced with anger. She saw the danger clearly now. She wasn't fighting Ronnie anymore, but some man she didn't know at all. Some monster. She scooted on her butt toward the nightstand. She grabbed the lamp so hard that it popped out of its socket, taking the dangling socket cover with it. And she threw it at Ronnie, the entire lamp. But he batted it away as if it was a feather, and it crashed to the floor.

She began throwing everything she could get her hands on, the brush, the telephone, the books she read at night, as she scrambled to get on her feet. But he was upon her too quickly, and he grabbed her by the catch of her jersey, ripping it he grabbed so hard, and slung her to her feet.

"I got your thug right here!" he yelled again as he balled up his fist, lifted his arm as high as it could go, and then crashed that fist against her face with a blow that nearly knocked her unconscious. Her knees buckled by the impact of the blow. And he began hitting her again and again, her blood gushing out all over him, but he wouldn't stop pounding her.

But she was fighting back, throwing punches that never landed, hitting and hitting and screaming as she hit. She was calling John's name. Was John still out there? He could still be in her driveway while Ronnie was nearly killing her! She fought with all she had.

She was fighting against his every move, trying with what little strength she had left to beat him back. She was scratching and clawing but he was so much larger than she was, and so much stronger. She could barely see for the blood, and her heartbeat was beginning to grow faint. She felt barely alive.

And the pain. It was excruciating. She couldn't make sense of any of it. This was Ronnie, wasn't it? Her mentor? Her partner at the Tribune? The one guy she thought was a good guy? Why would one of the good guys, she wondered, be brutalizing her like this?

And as every lick he laid on her drove her closer to unconsciousness, as he was spewing all manner of evil words she could no longer understand, all she could think about was little things.

Sweet things.

Like the hopefulness she felt tonight, when John Malone had her in his arms.

John stooped down at the body in the street, some young drug dealer with dreads, and all he could think about was the senselessness. Another kid gone, and for what? He stood erect.

"They're getting younger," he said to Officer Wayne Peete, who was young himself.

"Yes, sir," Peete replied. "And dumber."

John snorted. "You got that right."

"Can we take him now, Cap?" the medical examiner asked. They had been waiting for John to arrive and view the body.

"Yes," he said. "You can bag him."

"Thank-you," the silver-haired coroner replied. "All right, guys, we're on." He began to instruct his people. John and Peete looked on.

"What did you find on him?" John asked as they watched the medical examiner's team.

"A few dime bags," Peete replied.

"That's it?"

"That's it. He apparently was near the end of his sales for the night."

"Apparently," John replied.

"Sir," another officer said as he approached his captain.

"Yeah, Mike, what is it?"

"Call just came in. An assault over on Bluestone Road. Is it okay if me and Collins head on over there?"

"Bluestone?" John asked.

178

"Yes, sir. They say the lady got worked over pretty badly."

John's heart pounded. "What lady?" he asked and then braced himself. Somehow he knew. But it couldn't be.

"That reporter. Shay Turner. The one that got Chief suspended."

Peete looked at John. He knew Shay too.

John's heart momentarily stopped.

TEN

He jumped into his Porsche and flew through the streets of Brady like a madman. His car wasn't outfitted for sirens, but he didn't care. He ran red lights, blew through stop signs, and made it to Shay's house in a third of the normal time.

The house was cordoned off with police tape by the time he arrived, and police cars were parked along the driveway and the yard. The ambulance was also there as he got out of his car and ran across the front lawn. He hadn't been gone an hour. One measly hour. And now this? His heart was about to pound out of his chest as he slung open the front door, and hurried inside.

The good news, he thought as he entered the home, was that she was the one who had apparently phoned in the incident. Which meant she was still alive. The bad news, he also thought, was that his officer said she had been worked over pretty badly.

"Captain Malone, what are you doing here?" one of those uniformed officers immediately asked when John walked in. It was highly unusual for a man of John's rank to appear at a domestic disturbance scene, unless there was a fatality.

"Where is she?"

"The D.A.?"

"The victim," John asked. He was doing everything

180

he could to maintain his cool.

"Oh," the uniform said, surprised by the wild look in his captain's eyes. "Back there."

John walked toward the back of a house he had just left, and toward a bedroom he was very familiar with.

"What's he doing here?" the same cop asked the evidence tech who was fumbling around in the living room.

"Like how should I know?" the tech responded. "John Malone has been known to bang his share of women. Maybe this reporter's one of them." And they both snickered.

John heard their snickering but didn't care. He had to see Shay for himself.

Paramedics had her already on the gurney, readying her for transport, and Craig Yannick, one of John's detectives, was standing at the foot of the bed. John nervously approached Shay. And when he saw her face, his heart sank. Her eyes, both of them, were swollen shut. Her face was bruised so badly that it looked to be twice its normal size.

"Good Lord," John said when he saw her.

Yannick shook his head. "Whoever did this wasn't playing."

"John?" Shay said, as his voice suddenly registered from within the chaos all around her.

John hurried over to the stretcher to stand beside her. He held her hand, one of the few parts of her body

181

untouched. "Yes, Shay, it's me," he said.

"John?" she asked again.

"Don't try to talk, sweetie, okay? You're going to be all right."

Yannick looked at his boss, surprised that he would use such a term of endearment.

But John was completely focused on Shay. "They're going to take good care of you," he said to her. "We'll get through this."

"Ronnie," she said to him.

John looked around. Was Burk still there? Could Burk tell him who did this? "Is Ronnie Burk still around?" John asked Yannick.

"Burk? The reporter? Not that I know of. I haven't seen Ronnie Burk."

"He's not here, Shay," John said. "Did he leave before this happened?"

"It was Ronnie," Shay managed to say, a tear escaping from a tiny slit within her swollen eye. "It was Ronnie."

Yannick looked at John, stunned. John leaned down to Shay. He could hardly believe it himself. "Are you saying Ronnie Burk did this to you?"

"Yes," Shay managed to say, the pain unbearable, but she had to let them know. She had tried to tell the other cops, but they kept confusing what she was saying. "It was Ronnie. Ronnie did this to me."

"Excuse us, Captain," the paramedics said, "but we

need to transport."

John stood aside as they began hurrying the now gurney-strapped patient out of the bedroom.

"Ronnie Burk?" Yannick said to his boss. "Is she serious?"

John remembered that stupid smirk on Ronnie's face. Remembered his crass joke. "Yes," John said. "She's serious." He began heading out of the bedroom, Yannick hurrying behind him. "And so am I," he added.

The left side door of the duplex was kicked open and John and Yannick entered the smelly apartment. John had wanted to follow the ambulance to the hospital, and Yannick, in the Porsche with John, was surprised when he attempted to. But then John came to himself, realized what little good he could do at the hospital, took a U-turn, and then headed to arrest their suspect.

The suspect was in bed when his door, without warning, was kicked down. He attempted to get out of bed, his heart pounding, but the movement up front was too swift. Before he could even stand, John Malone had hurried in and was already upon him, grabbing him and slinging him to his feet.

"You motherfucker!" John yelled so loud Yannick was afraid the neighbors would hear.

"What did I do?" Ronnie was yelling. "What did I do?"

John slung him against the wall, the impact causing

Ronnie to grimace. "How could you do that to her, you bastard! How could you do something like that to an innocent like her?"

"People are coming outside of their houses now, John," Yannick nervously warned his superior. "Settle down!"

I'll settle down all right, John thought, staring at Ronnie. "Get out and close the door," he ordered Yannick. "Me and Burk here have a little business to attend to."

"Don't you do it," Ronnie yelled at Yannick. "Don't you dare go and leave me with this crazy man! I didn't do anything! I don't know what he's talking about!"

"Get out and close the door," John again ordered Yannick, attempting to cool down.

"But sir---," Yannick started.

"Get the hell out and close the *got*damn door now, Yannick!" John now yelled, his cool gone.

Yannick knew it was wrong, he knew he should refuse the order, but what could he do? McNamara was gone. John was the head honcho right now. He therefore reluctantly did as he was told.

As soon as the door slammed shut, John released his grip on Ronnie. And stepped back. "What's your problem?" he asked him. "You like beating on defenseless women? Is that how you get off? Is that your thing?"

"I didn't beat on her. We were horsing around and it

184

got out of hand, Captain! That's all that happened. That's the truth."

John could not believe it. "Horsing around?" he asked, amazed that he would think him that stupid.

"Yes! You know, we were having a few sex games. Just like she had with you. And everything got out of hand. She wanted it as badly as I did."

John shook his head. What a pathetic piece of shit, he thought. "Well guess what?" he said. "I want it even worse." And then he grabbed Ronnie by the catch of his collar and horsed around with him.

He beat him mercilessly. He kicked him and stomped him and beat him until he was on his knees coughing up blood. He saw Shay's swollen face, her eyes, and he beat the shit out of Ronnie Burk that night. It took all he had not to kill that man.

When it was all over, and Ronnie's face was as swollen as Shay's, John stopped. He just stood there, fighting to catch his breath, as Ronnie moaned like a drowning man on the floor. Then John stepped out of the bedroom, spatters of Ronnie's blood all over his light brown shirt. Yannick, who was nervously standing in the hall, stood erect.

"Cuff him, frisk him, and run his ass downtown," John ordered.

"Yes, sir," Yannick said, staring at his boss, as he hurried into the bedroom.

When he saw the condition of the suspect, he

185

stopped in his tracks.

By the time John arrived at the hospital, Shay had lapsed into unconsciousness. She was hooked up to IVs and heart monitors from her chest to her arms and hands. John's heart dropped just seeing how different she looked from that young woman who was so vibrant and full of life when they were together earlier, laughing and talking and making the kind of love he used to dream about. He just stood there, staring at her, completely oblivious to the fact that two other people were also in her room.

Aunt Rae was seated beside her bed, and Ed Barrington was standing on the opposite side.

"Hello, John," Ed said when it was apparent he hadn't even noticed them, although they were in plain sight. John stood at the foot of the bed staring at Shay.

"Hey," John said, his eyes stayed on her.

"I couldn't believe it when I got the news," Ed said. "Shay, I asked. You've got to be kidding me. Who would want to hurt a sweet kid like her?" Then he looked at John. "Is it true?" he asked him.

There was a hesitation, as it took John longer than normal to realize that a question had actually been directed at him. "Is what true?" he asked.

"I heard Shay identified Ronnie Burk as her attacker. Please tell me it's not true."

"Is that why you're here, Ed?" John finally looked at him. "To cover your ass?"

Ed took umbrage. "That's not fair, John, and you know it. I'm here because Shay is my employee and I care about my employee. That's why I'm here!"

John rubbed his forehead. "Sorry," he said. "I'm just. . ." He stared once again at Shay. Ed stared at the blood spatters still on his shirt.

"Did you talk to the doctor?" he asked Ed. "How is she?"

"How do you think?" Aunt Rae answered. John turned in her direction. "She looks like a truck hit her and then a train sideswiped her and then a plane crashed through her face." Then Rae frowned. "Poor thing."

John looked at Ed. "That's Ramona Baxley," Ed said. "A friend of Shay's."

John looked at the elderly woman with her double chin and her pocketbook hanging from her chunky arm. "You're Aunt Rae," he found himself saying.

Rae looked at him. "That's right."

"You're Shay's closest friend here in Brady."

Aunt Rae stared at him. "That's right. And who are you?"

"That's John Malone, Aunt Rae," Ed said. "He's a policeman."

"I know who John Malone is," Aunt Rae snapped. "I read the papers." She looked John up and down. Saw his thick biceps, his flat stomach, his muscular thighs. "Funny you don't look like John Malone, at least not from how you look on TV, and those pictures of you in the

187

papers. Of course that sorry Tribune is loaded with grainy pictures nobody can actually see, but still. You don't look like my ideal of what John Malone looked like."

"And you don't look like my ideal of what Aunt Rae looked like," John said.

Aunt Rae smiled. "Touché," she said.

But Shay was on John's mind. He walked over to the head of her bed. He began gently rubbing her forehead. He still couldn't hide his rage at what Ronnie did to her. "How's she doing?" he asked again.

Aunt Rae frowned, looked at her too. "Not good. The doctor said she'll be in and out of consciousness for a while still. Poor thing."

"Yeah," John said, his heart breaking at just the thought of what that asshole Burk put her through. "Poor thing."

And as John couldn't stop staring at Shay, and couldn't stop rubbing her small forehead and smoothing down her hair, Ed and Aunt Rae couldn't stop staring at him. For Ed there was that twinge of jealousy. Before this morning he didn't even know John knew Shay Turner like that. For Aunt Rae it was a ray of hopefulness. If Shay could wrangle herself a strong, principled man like she always thought John Malone was, it would be a God-sent. She didn't know John Malone personally, but she saw him on TV defending Shay at that press conference. That should stand for something, she thought. Shay didn't deserve to be alone. Not a good person like her.

188

She only prayed, however, that the affection he seemed to be showing for Shay right now could blossom into something longstanding and real.

Later that night, after Aunt Rae and Ed were long gone, John was seated in a chair beside Shay's bed, his legs crossed, her small hand in his big hand, and his tired blue eyes were closed. He had turned off his always active cell phone and had refused to leave her bedside. And it was this picture, of a still asleep Shay and a sleeping white man with a gun holstered on his hip, that a middle-aged black couple walked into.

John looked up when he heard the door closed. The male appeared to be in his mid-forties, around five-eleven, with a slender frame and a handsome, dark-skinned face. The woman was shorter but not short. John would put her height right around five–six or seven. And her attractive oak-brown face reminded him instantly of an older version of Shay. He stood up.

The mother's hand immediately flew to her mouth as soon as she saw Shay. "Oh, my baby," she said in anguish, and her petite body leaned against her husband.

"She'll be okay," the man said, although his face was also a mask of concern. "You heard what the doctors said. They said it's going to look worse than it is."

"But it looks awful," she said, going to Shay. "It looks just awful."

"Mr. and Mrs. Turner?" John asked them.

The man looked at John. Shay's mother walked over and touched her sleeping daughter.

"Yes?" the man said.

John extended his hand. "Hello, sir. I'm John Malone." They shook hands. John hesitated, just in case Shay had mentioned him to them. But by the puzzled look on the father's face, she hadn't. "I'm a captain with the Brady police force."

"Oh," the man said, less confused now. Although it still didn't explain why this police captain was, when they first entered the room, holding his daughter's hand. Nor the blood stains that were on his white shirt. "I'm Norris Turner, Shay's father, and she's Annabelle, my wife. You know who did this to our daughter?"

"Yes, sir," John replied, and Annabelle looked at him seemingly for the first time. "We have him in custody."

"Thank God," Norris said.

"Who is it?" Annabelle asked. "And why did he do this brutal thing?"

"The who is Ronnie Burk. He was her co-worker. We haven't worked out the why yet. He's claiming it was a sex game gone bad."

"A sex game?" Norris said. "That sadistic son of a bitch! Where is he?"

"In the hospital at the moment."

"This hospital?"

"No, sir. I didn't want him anywhere near Shay."

Norris nodded. "Good man," he said. And then he

190

looked at the blood spatters on John's shirt in a new light.

And they all just stood there, the three of them, and stared down at Shay. It was an awful sight for all three of them, and John could not only feel her parents' pain, but was experiencing his own. But he knew he had to remain strong. For Shay. He therefore went and got coffee for the parents and all three of them eventually settled in chairs around the bed, and silently prayed for Shay's full recovery.

It would be some hours later when a male's voice would penetrate the silence.

"What are you doing here?" he said at the room's entrance and John and Norris turned to the sound. It was Lonnie Resden, looking dapper in his Valentino suit. John immediately remembered him as the ex-boyfriend.

John stood to his feet.

"What are you doing here?" Resden asked again. "What's he doing here?" he then asked Norris Turner.

"You know him?" Norris asked Resden.

"He's the cop that tried to arrest me," Resden said. Then he finally looked at Shay. "Wow, look at Shay." He walked over to her and effectively stood beside Annabelle's chair. "I didn't think it would be this bad."

"He arrested you for what, Lonnie?" Norris asked him.

"He tried to arrest me," Resden said, still staring at Shay.

"Yes, Lon, but what for? Why would he even try?"

191

"I had a little unpleasantness with Shay."

"Unpleasantness?" John snorted. "Oh, is that what they call beating the crap out of a woman now? Unpleasantness?"

"Kiss my ass!" Resden said. "She was the one who beat on me, and you know it!"

"I don't know shit!"

"All right, that's enough," Norris said. And then he exhaled. "May I see you outside, Captain?" he asked John.

John looked at Resden again, and Resden snarled at him, but neither one of them felt compelled to make a scene at a time like this. Especially with Shay in such bad shape, and her mother, who didn't appear to have paid attention to any of their conversation, in such distress.

John looked at Shay again, and his heart pounded against his chest. This was bad enough. He didn't need to add to it.

"No problem," he said, and he and Norris Turner walked out of the room.

"I'm a blunt man, Captain Malone," Norris said as soon as they entered the corridor. "So I won't make small talk or pretend I called you out here for anything other than why I called you out here. What are you to my daughter?" he asked pointblank.

John knew it was still a relationship in its infancy, and they were still working through the cobwebs, but he wasn't going to pretend, either. "She's my girlfriend," he said firmly.

Norris was surprised by his bluntness. He stared at him. "You're a sight older than her."

"That's correct."

"I would guess you're closer to my age than hers."

John felt slightly embarrassed when he put it that way. "That would probably be an accurate guess," he said.

"But you have feelings for her?"

"Yes," John said heartfelt. "Very much so."

Norris continued to stare at him. And John knew the older man was sizing him up. "Funny she never mentioned you."

She never mentioned you, either, John wanted to say. "We're just getting off the ground, to be honest with you. She wouldn't have."

Norris nodded his head. John liked his thoughtfulness. And the fact that he didn't dismiss their relationship out of hand.

"I know she and Lonnie had broken up. I didn't know he had put his hands on her."

"He did," John said. "That's why I don't want him in there with her."

Norris stared at John. Then he walked over to the hospital room, opened the door, and asked Resden to come out. Resden took his pretty time, but he came out.

"What's up, Norris?" he asked Mr. Turner.

"I want you to leave."

"Leave?" Resden said. "Is this bastard telling you---"

"It has nothing to do with Captain Malone. I'm telling you to leave. You put your hands on my daughter. I know her. She wouldn't want you here."

"You're going to listen to this guy?" Resden asked. "All I did was slap Shay. She's the one who beat me up."

"I'm not going to ask you again, Lon. Leave."

"I wouldn't have come. Your wife called me. She wanted me here."

"My wife has illusions of her daughter marrying a successful man, that's all that phone call was about. If she would have known that you'd laid a hand on Shay, that would have been one phone call she would not have made. I assure you of that. Leave."

Resden stared at Norris. "I'll go and tell Annabelle goodbye," Resden started saying.

"No, you won't," John said. "The man said leave. Leave."

Resden couldn't stand the sight of that particular cop, but he wasn't about to tangle with him. He barely escaped a charge the last time. The District Attorney, a friend of Lonnie's, gave him a mighty break. He wasn't pushing his luck twice.

He left.

Norris exhaled. Turned his attention to John again. "My daughter is a very private person," he said.

John nodded. "I know."

"She never, and I mean never discusses her personal affairs with me or her mother. That's why we didn't know there had been an altercation. She phones us once a week and we see her at holidays. That's the way she prefers it, and we're pleased that she's out here living her own life her own way." Norris frowned. "That's not to say that I don't worry about her, because I do. I worry if she'll be okay. But I trust her judgment. I trusted it when she was head over heels in love with Lonnie, although I never liked the young man, but he was an attorney and showed good enough manners and my wife just loved him. So I held my peace. Now you say she's involved with you and also, apparently, with some sadistic co-worker---"

"She's not involved with him. She works with him, nothing more."

"And you know this how?"

"Because I know Shay. She's not involved with Ronnie Burk."

Norris stared at him again. Nodded again. "Okay. But she is involved with you?"

John swallowed hard. "Yes."

"And you both are okay with the age difference?"

"Yes," John replied, "although we never discussed it."

"And the race difference?" Norris asked, more to gauge how John responded, rather than the response itself.

195

"Yes," John replied, "although, again, it wasn't something we sat around discussing. It just is. All of it, my age, my race, her age, her race, just is."

"Quite true," Norris said. "Well. Good. I'll stay out of it then, as I'm sure Shay would want."

And Norris smiled for the first time. John smiled too.

John would eventually leave the hospital, to give the Turners some private time with their daughter. And they stayed by their daughter's bedside for nearly a week. John would come by in the afternoons, just to see Shay for himself, and he and Norris would spend time talking about her progress. The mother, Annabelle Turner, was still a Lonnie Resden fan, so she pretty much ignored John.

Shay was in and out of consciousness the entire time. She'd always recognize her parents and have cogent conversations with them, but she would always fall back asleep. It was the drugs mainly, to help keep the pain at bay, so the parents did not complain. They stayed at their daughter's bedside for nearly a week. John paid to have Shay's home cleaned spotless by a professional cleaning crew, so that the parents could stay at their daughter's home during their visit. They didn't want to leave. But they were both schoolteachers and had classrooms filled with anxious students to return to. They eventually said their goodbyes to Shay, and to John, and left.

196

That next morning, after everybody had gone and John should have been at work himself, he had been sitting at her bedside all night. She had had a rough night. On three different occasions he had to call for the nurse as Shay would toss and turn as if she was in tremendous pain. They would inject her with more morphine just to get her through the next few hours. By then John was too afraid to leave her alone. He, in fact, had contacted Aunt Rae by early morning, and she had said she'd catch a cab and be there to relieve him around nine.

And as that hour approached, Shay began to wake up. She had been in and out all night.

John moved to the edge of his seat and touched her on the hand. "Hello, babe," he said.

"Hey." Her eyes were no longer swollen shut, although her face still showed signs of puffiness. But she was able to get a good look at John.

"You look terrible," she said to him.

He laughed. "Thank-you for your vote of confidence."

Shay smiled, although it was still a weak smile. "I feel awful, if that's any consolation."

"Well, you look marvelous to me because you're still alive."

"Just barely."

"With an excellent prognosis, kid, don't push your luck."

Shay attempted to laugh but ended up coughing. She eventually settled back down. Then she frowned.

"It was Ronnie," she said, forgetting that she had already told him. Countless times.

John nodded. "We know. We got him, sweetie."

"He's behind bars?"

"After a trip to the emergency room, yes, he was placed behind bars."

A puzzled look crossed her distressed face. "I can't believe he would do something like that."

John rubbed her hand.

"It was as if he thought I was in some kind of relationship with him. Like I was betraying him or something. But that's not true. I never came onto him like that."

"He's a very warped individual, Shay, it had nothing to do with you."

"You knew he was like that?"

"No. I doubt if anybody knew he was that sadistic." Then John thought about what he'd been dying to ask since this ordeal began. But Shay kept talking.

"My parents were here."

"I know, sweetheart, I know."

"You spoke to them?"

"Yes. They're wonderful people."

"Yeah. A little overbearing, but they mean well."

"Overbearing?" John asked.

"You know. They want what they want for me. And

198

no matter what I do, they figure I can do better. They want to help me in every way they can."

"But you prefer to go your own way and do your own thing?"

"Right."

"Yes, your father told me."

Shay smiled. "They're both school teachers, they can barely pay their own bills, but Dad's always attempting to help me. I always turn him down. And always will. I won't burden them in any way, shape, or form. Not ever. He's too good a man to be burdened by his grown daughter." Then she paused. "Lonnie was here, too. Wasn't he?"

John nodded his head. "Yes. Your father got rid of him."

"Good." Then she looked at John again. "How did you and Dad hit it off?"

"Very well. I told him you were my girlfriend and he accepted it. Your mother too, I think."

Shay smiled. "She likes Lonnie, but she'll get over him."

John smiled.

"But what about you?" Shay went on. "Have they fired you yet?"

John laughed. "Not yet. I'm still performing a function for the mayor, and he's still searching for the perfect replacement for McNamara."

"So you're certain McNamara's out for good?"

"Oh, yes. In this election year? There's no way the mayor's bringing him back on board."

"Good," Shay said. "And after you go through all the books for them, and give them the info they need, what then?"

"Then I suspect I'll be fired too."

Shay's face took on a worrisome glow.

"It'll be only right, Shay. I was distracted too long and wasn't paying attention to what McNamara and his flunkies were up to. So this isn't about him or me or any top brass anymore. This is about those dead girls and preventing another death."

She agreed. And nodded her head.

"Shay," John decided to ask, "was Ronnie. . . did Ronnie. . . Did Ronnie rape you, Shay?"

Shay shook her head. "No," she said firmly. "But he . . ."

"Beat the crap out of you, I know."

"And he ejaculated on my face after doing it."

John shook his head. "Sick fucker," he said beneath his breath.

"I think he planned to do something like that to me but I think I passed out. When I came to he was gone. And I called 911."

Tears began to drain down her cheeks. "It was so scary, John," she said. "And you know the only thing I could think about while he was brutalizing me?"

"No, sweetie, what?"

Shay hesitated. "You," she said, and John's heart sank. "I wished you were there to help me. Because I knew if you were there, you would beat Ronnie's ass better than I could."

John smiled. "Don't worry," he said. "He got his."

Shay paused. Looked at him. "You beat him?" she asked.

"I beat him, kicked him, stomped him, did everything I was big enough to do to that asshole, yes."

Shay paused again, as if she wasn't sure she could ever condone such violence. Then she nodded her head. "Good," she said.

Over the next several weeks, Shay remained in the hospital with a slow but steady recovery. The Tribune continued to expose McNamara's corruption with front page headlines. Although John Malone was hailed as a hero for exposing the truth, and the media was playing up his hero status for all the town to see, he didn't feel heroic at all, and stayed out of the glare of the media.

He, instead, spent every chance he got in the glare of Shay Turner.

Every morning before he went to work and every evening after he knocked off, he was over to the Brady Medical Center visiting with Shay. Sometimes they'd talk on and on about the community, his latest case, what was going on at the Tribune. They hold hands and talk for hours. And then other times they would just sit there, still holding hands, quietly enjoying each other's company. Often John would be so exhausted that he would fall asleep. And Shay would sit on his lap and hold him.

By the time Shay was cleared for release from the hospital, nearly six weeks after her attack, two monumental events occurred that captivated the entire town. The first one, Chief McNamara's official resignation, she knew about. The second happened on the day of her release, and she knew nothing about it.

The mayor of Brady, in an attempt to quell the growing distrust of the police department by the entire community, but especially the black community in light of the Dodge murder cover up, appointed John Malone as the new chief of police. Shay, at the time the story broke, was signing her release papers. It was already after six that evening, but she didn't care. She was ready to go. More than ready.

She was also a little dismayed. She hadn't heard from John at all that day, which was highly unusual for him, and whenever she called his cell phone it went straight to voice mail. She even called his office once but was told that he was busy, could they take a message. Of course she wasn't about to leave any message, so she said no and hung up. And then hated herself for being so needy. But it seemed to be a fact. She needed John right now.

But she couldn't let that worry her, either. She

therefore showered and changed and waited an hour longer before she was finally escorted out of the hospital in that dreaded, and unnecessary wheelchair. She had phoned a cab, since she had no other way to get home, and she assumed, when the hospital aide came to transport her, that the cab had arrived. But, as if on cue, John slung his Porsche up to the curb just outside of the hospital's revolving doors, right there to pick her up.

"You're going to be riding home in style, Miss Turner," the aide said smilingly as John drove up.

"How could he have possibly known that I was being released at this very moment?" Shay wanted to know.

"Because he called and told them to keep you here until he got here," the aide answered with a smile, as if what she said shouldn't possibly upset Shay. "We could have released you hours ago. But they waited until the time he said he'd be here. They didn't want to disappoint the boss."

Shay found the aide's comment odd, but she let it slide. She, instead, stood up from the wheelchair and walked over to John's car. John moved to assist her, but she waved him off. "I got this," she said with a smile.

John laughed. All of the swelling and bruising were completely gone from her gorgeous face, and but for still walking gingerly, she was none the worse for wear. "All right now," he said as he took her suit case from the aide, "I'm going to be like Aunt Rae: don't get ahead of yourself, young lady." Shay laughed.

203

When he pulled out of the circular driveway of the hospital's patient pickup zone, she looked at him. He was dressed in his usual tailored, double-breasted suit, this one a light tan, but he also sported a pair of dark shades that made him look simply irresistible to her. She was really beginning to like this dude.

"What did she mean?" she asked him.

"What did who mean, love?" John responded. He started calling her that endearment around week two of her hospital stay. And it warmed her heart every time he said it.

"That aide back there. She said they didn't release me for hours because you told them to keep me here until you got here. Is that true?"

John knew Shay wouldn't like that one. "It's true."

But, actually, Shay did like it. She liked it because it showed that he hadn't abandoned her as her irrational mind was beginning to think. "She also said they kept me there because they didn't want to disappoint the boss. What boss? What did she mean by that?"

John smiled. "For a news reporter, you don't keep up with the news."

"What did she mean, John?"

"You know Chief McNamara resigned."

"As so he should, yes."

"Well, our scared to death mayor decided this morning to call a news conference where he announced his decision to appoint me as the new chief of the Brady,

Alabama police department."

Shay stared at him, her heart soaring. "Are you serious?"

John smiled. "I'm the new chief."

"That's great, John!" she said with a grand smile, hitting him on his muscular arm. "Why didn't you call and tell me?"

"Because I wanted to see you when I told you. Because I suspected you would be the happiest person in this town for me. Maybe even this world."

Shay couldn't agree with him more. "You deserve it."

"I wouldn't go that far, but I'm pleased." Then he looked down, from her eyes and luscious lips, to her hefty breasts. "Just as I'm sure you're pleased to be out of that hospital."

"Oh, yes," Shay said as she leaned back against the leather headrest. "Very pleased."

But her joy was cut short when John pulled his Porsche into the driveway of her small rented house on Bluestone Road. The calm and easiness that cloaked her suddenly disappeared. Her face was now a mask of anguish.

"What's the matter?" he asked when he looked over and saw she was no longer that carefree spirit he had picked up from the hospital.

Shay exhaled. "It flooded back," she said.

"The memories?" John asked, and she nodded.

205

John touched her on her hand. "It's okay," he said as tears began to appear in her big eyes. "Shay, it's okay."

"There has to be a lot of blood after what he did."

"There was," John admitted. "I hired a cleaning crew to get in there and take care of it. It's spotless now."

Shay shook her head. The pain of that day was like a tightness in her chest. She looked at John.

John's heart dropped. "It's okay, Shay," he said as he reached over and completely took her hand in his. "It's just that it's still too soon. Why don't you come over to my place?"

Shay stared at him. The vulnerability he saw in her eyes broke his heart. That bastard Ronnie Burk was going to pay dearly for what he'd done to her.

"I'm all right," she said.

"Not here, you won't be. Not yet. Stay with me for a few days, until you're sure."

But Shay still balked. "I have to face it someday."

"But not today you don't."

Shay, however was still unsure. "I promise you, Shay, going over to my place isn't going to be scandalous in any way. I just want you to feel safe right now. Being with me will ensure that."

Shay knew what he spoke was the truth. And the idea of so much as walking through that front door would be too painful to bear right now. She nodded her head. "Okay," she said, and John cranked back up, and backed

206

back out.

ELEVEN

They entered the big, quiet home in Dale's Pointe hopeful but drained. It was a beautifully furnished home and Shay suspected it was probably his ex-wife's taste. But she couldn't afford to worry about that right now. She was still getting her own bearings back. John knew it too, and wanted to immediately make her feel at home.

"I'll show you to your room," he said to her. He had her suitcase in his hand as they walked up the wooden staircase to the second floor landing. The master bedroom was at the end of the hall and John wanted her there, in his room. In his bed. But he knew it had to be her choice.

"Would you like to stay in my room, or the guest room?" he asked her.

Shay knew that John's ex-wife once lived in this home, and undoubtedly once slept in that master bed. She looked at John. "The guest room," she said.

John understood. He walked her to the large guest room and sat her luggage on the bed.

"Nice room," she said.

"Thank-you. So," he said, rubbing his hands together, attempting to relax her and ease her distress, "would you like to get some rest, or maybe I can get fix us something to eat?"

"I would like to soak in a tub, actually, if that's okay?"

"Of course," he said, looking down her body. "You

208

undress and I'll prepare your bath."

It had been over six weeks since he last touched her, and he was aching to do it again. But he wasn't about to pressure her right now. He was just so happy to have her out of the hospital that nothing else mattered. He headed for the adjacent bathroom.

Shay exhaled and began removing her clothes. She still felt uneven, as if her life had suddenly stopped and took a dramatically different course. One day she was going fine, things were actually looking up, and the next moment she was fighting for her life. Thanks to that fool Ronnie Burk! She exhaled again. Nothing she could do about it now, she thought, as she grabbed the oversized bathrobe on the back of the closet door, and put it on.

John was seated on the edge of the tub, his legs crossed, his suit coat off, and his shirt sleeves rolled up. When Shay entered the room she could see his gun and holster on the doubled-sink vanity counter as he ran his hand through her slowly filling bubbled-bath water.

"A bubble bath," she said as she began walking further into the bathroom, "thanks."

John looked at her and smiled when he saw her in his oversized robe. "It fits you beautifully," he joked.

Shay laughed. "It smells just like you."

"Ouch!"

"No, I didn't mean it like that. I love your smell," she admitted. "Nothing to ouch about there."

John loved her smell too. He knew exactly what she

209

meant. Then he stood up and reached out his hand. Shay walked over to him. He untied the robe and slowly removed it, his big blue eyes feasting on her naked body. She didn't have a scratch on her, nor her face anymore, as if that terrible assault never took place. John was pleased that she had no outward signs, he was very grateful. But he knew inwardly she was still reeling.

He held her hand as she stepped into the garden tub. "Thank-you so much, John," she said heartfelt, "for everything."

John smiled. Kissed her on the mouth. "Take your time," he said as she sat down. "I'll see what I can scrounge up for dinner. Call me if you need me."

And he was gone. He was going to give her time to decompress before they launched right back into the sexual side of their love affair, and he knew she appreciated that.

But it wasn't easy. John's dick was throbbing when he removed her robe, and still aching for attention as he made his way into the kitchen. It had been an exhausting six weeks for both of them. And today was no less exhausting. For him it was his first day as chief of police, which was emotionally exhausting in and of itself, and she was just released from the hospital after a month-and-a-half long stint. They both needed to decompress.

John's cell phone rang just as he pulled out a carton of eggs and a bag of spinach. It was Craig Yannick, requesting permission to haul in a young man they believed was responsible for a shooting a few nights ago. Unlike McNamara, John wasn't giving carte blanche to any of his detectives until he had a better handle on what each one was up to. They therefore were ordered today to run every major bust by him first. Especially if it involved drugs or a homicide.

After requesting and getting the details on why they wanted to bring in the young man, John gave the go-ahead. And hung up the phone. He then looked at the food he had taken out, thought better of it, and poured, instead, two glasses of red wine and headed back upstairs. But as soon as he began approaching the guest bathroom, he stopped in his tracks. Shay was in the tub, leaned back, her elbow on the tub's rim with her hand rubbing her forehead, crying.

When John saw her he hesitated. It was all floating back still, he thought. So he cleared his throat, to alert her of his presence, and entered talking.

"I thought this would be a good pick-me up," he said as he entered.

Shay immediately sat erect and wiped her tears away. She even tried to smile but failed. And when she looked up and into John's eyes, his attempt at levity fell flat, too.

He handed her a glass of wine.

"Thanks," she said, gladly accepting it. For her it was just what the doctor ordered.

But John wasn't satisfied at all. She'd been crying,

that much he knew was clear. And he couldn't just toast her, have a drink with her, and leave, that much he knew too. He therefore sat his glass of wine on the vanity counter, and began to undress.

Shay noticed what he was doing as she sipped her wine. She still felt so stressed that she didn't know if his obvious decision to get in the tub with her would be welcomed. She didn't see how anything short of completely erasing what Ronnie had done to her would do her any good. But she didn't dissuade him, either. His hands had a calming effect on her.

And that was what John was banking on as he stripped naked, retrieved his glass of wine, and got in the tub with Shay.

He sat behind her, placing her body in front of his, and for well over fifteen minutes they didn't try to do anything but sip wine and relax. John didn't ask her why was she crying, and Shay didn't ask why did he decide to bring her wine. They just decided that both questions contained obvious answers that weren't worth the effort to ask. They just wanted to relax.

And they did, for over fifteen minutes. Until Shay grabbed the bottle of soap and poured the liquid into her hand. That move alone changed the entire atmosphere of the room because, as soon as she began to bathe herself, awareness crept in. John became hyper-alert to her back against his front, to the upper part of her ass against his penis, to her flat stomach underneath the arm

212

he had around her waist. To her.

And as John began to expand, Shay, too, became hyper-alert to his growing erection, and his arm around her waist, and his rock hard body she was resting against. And when John sat her glass and his on the bathroom floor, and took over the bathing, they both understood where it was leading. His hand caressed rather than bathe her. He moved along her arms and then her stomach and then all across her breasts.

That was when Shay leaned back, when he began massaging her breasts, lathering them, squeezing and rubbing them. By the time he moved down her body, to her womanhood, she was aching for his touch.

And he touched her. He lathered her outside, circling her folds and then slowly, expertly, moving two of his fingers inside of her. Shay's body pressed against John's when one hand continued fondling her breast and the other hand fingered her, as the sensual feelings of both ends of his massages began to give her an adrenalin rush. And when those same fingers began to glide in and out of her, making her so wet inside she could hear his fingers immersed in her saturation, she closed her eyes. And just relaxed to his glide, to his breast squeezes, to his expertise.

John, too, was feeling the adrenalin rush. It had been so long since he was last able to touch her like this that he thought he was going to wear out his hands. He couldn't stop fingering and fondling her. His fingers, in fact, became so saturated with her wetness that he had to lift her body slightly, off of his rock hard penis, before he came right then and there. Neither had planned to go down this road, not this soon, but both knew now that there would be no turning back.

And when his fingering and fondling became too much, and he was almost near the spilling point, he lifted her, wrapped his arm underneath her thighs, and slid his dick deep inside of her wet pussy. They both let out a sigh so loud that it sounded as if they had synchronized their response. But it wasn't something they planned. It was something they had: chemistry. Because they were completely in synch as he fucked her, as his dick moved deeper and deeper into her in slow, arching movements that left both of them full, but craving more.

And it continued. He went up into her harder and harder, longer and longer. The only thing they wanted to feel was dick on pussy. They didn't want talk, they didn't want any other fondling. Just dick on pussy. And that was what they got, for ten, fifteen, twenty minutes of fucking. Straight fucking. Nothing else. John's body was so filled with sensations that his head lobbed back and his stomach muscles stretched to support his gyrations.

And Shay. Words could not express how much she was burning with desire as he fucked her. She reached her hand behind her, and touched the side of his face, thanking him for giving her this moment of pleasure that, for the time being, completely eclipsed all of her painful memories. She felt nothing but his love, his dick, her pussy tightening around every inch of his massive rod. It was all feeling. It was all in the moment. It was exactly what she needed.

And when it was time for her to climax, and time for him to release, they were still in synch. His gyrations increased, as he began to thrash into her with a hard pounding. The intensity had her pushing so hard against his rock hard body that her reaction alone intensified what he thought couldn't possibly get any more intense. But it became more intense.

And they came together. He slammed into her one last time, his dick going up into her so hard and deep that his balls nearly followed. And she tightened around him with such a ferocious grip, and he expanded even wider within her wet, tight pussy, that she found herself screaming in such an extreme delight that it was almost painful. They came. Together. With every inch of their bodies throbbing from the impact.

And they just sat there, still wedged together, their juices flowing out into the tub. John leaned into her, his forehead against the side of her face, both breathing so heavily it sounded unhealthy. And tears appeared in his eyes.

"I love you, Shay Turner," he said to her.

Tears began to well up in Shay's eyes too. "I love you, John Malone. I love you, too."

He closed his eyes tightly. How he could have ever

215

questioned if he would be able to commit to her was a mystery to him now.

After spending the night in each other's arms, John was up bright and early the next morning. He was standing at the center island in his kitchen, drinking coffee, chomping on a Danish, looking over the Brady Tribune newspaper, when Shay walked in. She was wearing one of his shirts, which made him feel warm inside, and although she had just woke up, she looked radiant to him.

"Good morning," he said to her. Just the sight of her brought back the wonderment of last night. And not just the sex part, although that was wonderful in and of itself. But John was remembering how, after dinner, after they had both retired, she left the guest bedroom and came and got into bed with him. And they held onto each other all night.

"You look awfully dapper," she said to him.

He looked down, at his dark green double-breasted suit, and then smiled back at her. "You look gorgeous yourself," he said.

Shay snorted. "Yeah, right," she said as she sat at the center island across from him. He poured her a cup of coffee.

"What's on your agenda for today?" he asked as he poured.

"Good question," she said, grabbing a discarded part

216

of the newspaper to peruse. "I'll probably go by the Trib, see what's up."

"When do you plan to go back to work?"

"Tomorrow for sure. That's why I'm going over there. To see Ed. To see if he'll have me back."

"He'd better have you back," John said. "After what his employee did to you, he'd better."

Shay smiled. "That had nothing to do with Ed and you know it. But yeah, I believe he'll take me back too. It's just that it's been such a long time."

"I know."

"And my workload. I can't even imagine how that's going. Especially since everything seems at a standstill. And nobody's been arrested for those Dodge murders."

John shook his head. "Don't remind me," he said. "We don't even have a suspect yet. But at least the public now knows that there's a serial killer out there, thanks to your reporting. We've just got to nail the bastard. And we will."

Shay looked at her man. At his big, bright, sapphire eyes. "I know you will, John," she said with such sincerity that it warmed John's heart. He felt blessed to have a woman like her in his life. He also felt responsible for that woman, and protective of that woman.

"Shay," he said, a frown enveloping his face. When he didn't immediately continue, she looked away from the paper and at him again.

"Yes?" she asked.

"I don't think it's a good idea for you to go over to your place just yet." He said this and then stared at her.

At first Shay seemed unsure, and then she nodded. "I agree," she said, to his relief.

"Give it a few days," he added. "But under no circumstances do I want you going over there alone. When you're ready, let me know. I'll go with you."

Shay smiled. "What have I ever done to deserve a man like you?"

John smiled. "Deserve me? Are you kidding? You deserve far better than the likes of me. I'm the undeserving party here, and don't you forget that, young lady."

"Yes, Daddy," Shay said, knowing that such an age reference would get a rise out of John. It worked. He balled up a part of the newspaper, and playfully flicked her on her arm. Shay laughed.

"Isn't it beautiful, Faylene?" the waitress asked her boss as she looked at Blair Malone's costume jewelry.

"They're always gorgeous," Faylene said as she walked up to the counter where Blair was seated. She was showing a few of her necklaces to the waitress, a potential client. "Especially those brilliant colors," Faylene added as she picked up a pink pearl necklace.

"That's what I like too," the waitress said. "How much is this one, Blair?" she asked, holding up a turquoise necklace.

"That one is fifteen."

"That's not bad," Faylene said.

"Put it on, try it out," Blair told the waitress. "See how it walks around on you."

"Thank-you, Blair," the waitress said as she put on the necklace.

"Now you can gawk at it and do your work at the same time, "Faylene said with a smile.

"Yes, ma'am," the waitress said and headed back to her station.

"She's going to buy it," Faylene said, "you mark my words."

"I hope so," Blair said. "I used to sell twenty-five of these things a day, which wasn't much, but it was better than nothing. Lately I've been selling nothing."

Although Faylene, a big, bosomy blonde, was known as a looker in her own right, she knew she couldn't hold a candle to Blair Malone. Nobody in Brady could hold a candle to Blair. That was how Blair was able to wrangle that personification of gorgeousness called John Malone in the first place. Now every man in Brady seemed to want the newly divorced prim and pretty Blair. And although Blair fooled around with a few jocks, and had been doing so even before her divorce, Faylene knew that she wasn't really interested in any of them.

"I don't know why you don't get yourself a rich man," Faylene said, "and let him take care of you."

Blair only smiled. People didn't understand. She

219

might be divorced on paper, but she still viewed herself as John's woman. As John's wife. And she always would.

"Anyway," she said to Faylene, "when are you going to buy one of these gorgeous necklaces yourself?"

Faylene laughed. "You're good. I bought one already, remember?" She said this and looked out into the parking lot.

"You bought one so long ago, Faylene, it doesn't even count anymore. Look at this one," Blair said as she picked up a yellow and green flower pendant with a pearl necklace. "It has you written all over it."

John's Porsche drove into Faylene's parking lot and Shay killed the engine and remained behind the wheel. He had insisted that she drive his car. She thought it would be too fast for her, too showy, but she found that she liked it. It reminded her of John: powerful and fast. And it had his sweet cologne scent all over it. This car was all John.

She pulled down the overhead mirror and began putting on lip gloss. She was feeling like herself again for the first time since Ronnie's attack. She was thrilled to be out of the hospital, thrilled to be driving a hot car, thrilled to have herself a hot man. And John was hot, in every sense of the word.

She still couldn't get over how much he stepped up for her. He spent night after night at the hospital with her. Six weeks ago, when he sat at her kitchen table and said he was all in, she wasn't sure if she believed him then. But she believed him now. Because she'd been able to see it with her own two eyes. And even last night, when they made love for the first time in weeks, it felt like more than just sex. She still remembered how his hands felt all over her, bathing her, pampering her, caressing her. Then she smiled again, thinking about just how deftly he caressed her, and got out of his car.

"Hey, Blair," Faylene said, looking out of the big plate glass window of her diner, "isn't that John's car?"

Blair quickly looked at Faylene, and then looked out of the window. "Where?" she asked.

"Right there. Near the drug store alley. That Porsche sure looks like John's car."

Just as Blair saw the Porsche, Shay was stepping out of it. She was dressed comfortably, in a short red summer dress and matching heels, her hair loose down her back, sunglasses on her face, as she made her way toward the front entrance.

"Who in the world is that?" Blair asked, a pang of jealousy immediately cursing through her.

"That's that reporter," Faylene said. "Shay Turner. You know? Ronnie Burk supposedly attacked her, although Ronnie looked worse than she did, so the jury's still out on what really happened."

But Blair didn't know anything about that. "Never heard of her," she said, as she stared at Shay.

Shay, oblivious to the stares, walked into Faylene's

221

like she had many times in the past, lifted her shades on top of her head, and made her way to an empty booth.

"But one thing about it," Faylene continued as they both watched Shay, "she's driving John's car."

"Yeah," Blair said, her anger growing. "How disrespectful can you get?" She left her jewelry on the countertop, surprising Faylene by her sudden lack of concern for her bread and butter, and headed toward Shay's booth.

Shay didn't see her coming until she had placed her drink order, the waitress had walked away, and she was now opening the menu. When Blair took a seat at her booth, however, Shay looked passed the menu. And then closed it.

"May I help you?" she asked the older woman.

"Why are you driving my husband's car?" Blair asked her pointblank

Shay's heart began to pound. This must be the ex-wife. The very beautiful ex-wife, Shay inwardly noted. "And you are?" she asked.

"I'm Blair Malone, his wife. Why are you driving my husband's car?"

This threw Shay. She took a moment to take it in. "Don't you mean your ex-husband?" she asked her.

"Why are you driving my husband's car?" Blair asked again.

"Not that it's any of your business, but he gave me permission to drive it."

222

"Like hell."

Shay hesitated. "Okay, now, this is getting kind of unnecessary. I think you need to take up any issue you have about that car with him."

"I'm taking it up with you, bitch!" Blair said so forcefully that it astounded Shay, and caused others at nearby tables to look their way. Including two uniformed officers in a side booth. "And I want to know why is some cheap, trash-barrel whore like you driving around town in my husband's car? Don't you know better than to be bothering with another woman's man?"

Shay was stunned by her aggressiveness. "You're divorced," she said.

"And you believed that?" Blair said with an oddly chilling smile on her face. "Honestly? Are you *that* naïve?"

Shay knew better than to let the ranting of some bitter woman throw her confidence in John, so she didn't respond. She knew a confrontation wasn't worth it. Especially not with so many eyes anxious for gossip and possibly even a knock-down drag-out.

"How old are you anyway?" Blair asked her.

Shay said nothing.

"He doesn't like young girls," Blair continued. "Never have. And you look to be barely twenty-one."

Shay started to tell her that she wasn't as young as that, but she didn't even go there. Telling this woman that she was twenty-six, not twenty-one, wouldn't change her impressions of her one iota. She therefore remained silent.

"I don't get it," Blair said, a puzzled look on her face. "Why in the world would he give you, of all people, the keys to his car? He never even liked for me to drive his precious car, but he lets you drive it? His whore? Seriously?"

Now Shay was getting tired of this fast. "Look, lady--"

"Mrs. Malone is my name."

"Good. Because I have one too. And it's not bitch or whore or any other derogatory name. And you will not sit up here and call me those names."

Blair laughed one of those joyless laughs mixed with anxiety and jealousy. And Shay had had it. She came to grab a quick breakfast and then head over to the Trib. But when it became obvious that this woman wasn't about to leave her table, and was begging for a fight, she wasn't about to sit there and argue with her. Or fight her. Not over some man. Not over a man who was this woman's husband for six long years. She therefore decided to find another place to eat her breakfast altogether, and just leave.

But Blair wasn't about to just let her leave. Not when she saw how much younger Shay was. Not when she saw up close Shay's smooth black skin. Not when she looked into Shay's big, golden-brown eyes. She couldn't just let it go. It would be like being robbed and raped in broad daylight, and then ignoring it.

When Shay stood up to leave, Blair stood up, too, and slung Shay back around. "I'm not through with you, bitch!" she said so forcefully that one of the officers stopped eating.

Shay looked at Blair's hand on her arm and then into Blair's pretty face. "Take your hand off of me," she warned her.

"Make me, bitch," Blair warned her back.

Shay angrily flicked Blair's hand off of her but Blair quickly retaliated, spitting into Shay's face, the saliva cruising down toward Shay's mouth.

And Shay's retaliation was swift too. She slapped Blair so hard that Blair stumbled back, lost her balance, and then fell over a chair, crushing it to the floor. The officers quickly hurried to the ladies and grabbed Shay. Shay was stunned when they slung her to the ground and began handcuffing her.

"She spit on me!" she yelled repeatedly, but the officers didn't seem to be listening. They knew Blair Malone was Captain Malone's ex-wife. They figured they could get brownie points on this one. They therefore grabbed Shay, took her to their patrol car, and tossed her inside.

By contrast, Blair was assisted to her feet, and asked if she needed an ambulance.

TWELVE

John was leaned back behind his desk talking with Craig Yannick, the detective he was seriously considering promoting to become his second-in-command, when his door flew open and Wayne Peete, without knocking, hurried inside.

"Excuse me, Cap. I mean, Chief. I mean . . . I didn't know somebody was in here."

Yannick frowned. "And because you didn't know somebody was in here that gave you license to just barge on in?"

"No, sir, but---"

"But what, Peete?" John asked. "What is it?"

"Those idiots just arrested Shay Turner, sir."

John heard it, but it didn't register at first. When it did, he jumped to his feet. "Arrested her?" he asked angrily. "What the fuck for?"

"For slapping Mrs. Malone."

"Mrs. Malone? Who the hell is. . . You mean *Blair*?"

"Yes, sir."

"Geez," John said as he grabbed the suit coat off of the back of his chair and hurried for the exit. "Where is she?"

"They have her downstairs, in a holding cell," Peete said, hurrying behind him.

But he couldn't keep pace with the boss, not this

time. Because John took the stairs, hurrying down them so swiftly that he barely remembered touching one. And he burst into the holding section of the jail.

When he saw Shay sitting in one of the cells, his heart dropped. "Open it," he ordered the jailer.

"Sir?" the jailer asked, stunned to see the chief on site.

"Open it," John said again, this time a little harsher. When the jailer started moving, but not swift enough, John almost lost it. "Open it now, dammit!" he yelled.

The jailer jumped fast to the sound of John's roar and quickly fumbled with the keys and unlocked Shay's cell. As soon as he did, John pulled her out of that filthy place, and hugged her. "Oh, babe," he said, to the jailer's shock.

But John didn't give a damn. There would be hell to pay, he thought as he held her, when he found out who was responsible for this.

He spent the balance of that day with her. He took her to breakfast, this time at the high end Carriage House restaurant, and then to the mall where they walked and talked and shopped like kids. John fielded many phone calls from his staff, and endured even more stares from the townspeople, but he didn't care. He wanted everybody to know that she was his. That he and Blair were yesterday news and would always be yesterday news. Shay Turner, he wanted to get the word out, was his woman now.

He also ordered Craig Yannick to suspend the two arresting officers pending an investigation into Shay's arrest. If they saw the whole thing, as Shay said they did, then they had to have known that Blair was the instigator; that she spit on Shay first. In Brady spitting in someone's face was an assault by any definition, and as officers they knew it. And they also knew that it was Blair's ass that they should have hauled in.

Just thinking about it angered John, so he stopped thinking about it. He just wanted to spend the day with Shay. And he did. They spent all day together. And that night, after walking seemingly all around Brady and having a picnic at the beach, they were happily exhausted. They showered together, with John putting his dick inside of her as they bathe, and then they curled against each other in John's bed and slept like babies.

Shay woke up early the next morning. This was to be her first day back to work and she was anxious to get started. She looked over at John. He still had his arm around her in the bed. She smiled at him and at his sometimes over-protectiveness. Then she lifted his arm enough to slide out of bed. He moved too, onto his back, but remained asleep.

Shay got into the shower and John continued to sleep when the front door of the home was unlocked and then opened. Blair Malone entered the home that was once her residence for almost six years, and made her

228

way up the stairs. Early this morning a former, busybody neighbor had phoned and told her that John had himself a black woman at his home. Blair knew immediately that it had to be that Shay Turner, the chick who had been driving his car. The chick who had slapped her and knocked her down. She couldn't believe John would betray her like that. She hung up the phone, dressed quickly, and hurried over.

Once she made her way up those stairs, she walked along the second floor corridor and down to the master bedroom effortlessly. Before the divorce, this was her home. Her home and John's home. And she knew this place like the back of her hand.

She knew John was sleeping around. Hell, he was sleeping around during almost the entirety of their marriage. So the mere fact that his big dick, horny ass had some woman was nothing new to Blair.

But she never received any report about him bringing any of his women to their home. Not ever. And to think that he would choose Shay Turner of all people, that violent black bitch, to be the only woman he ever invited to lounge around in their home, was incredible to Blair. Shay Turner of all people? After what she did to Blair? Just thinking about it caused her anger to rise with every step along that corridor she took.

By the time she arrived at the closed door of the master bedroom, she was seething with anger. But she knew she had to keep her wits about her. She wanted to check this bitch right. She didn't want to give up any of the element of surprise. So she opened the door to the master bedroom gingerly, with great anticipation in her hate-filled heart. She was ready to pounce, but she knew she had to take it easy.

As soon as she opened the door, she could hear the water running in the shower. And she could also see John, stark naked, lying alone on the bed. She looked down the length of his ripped body, at his pecker just lying there so peacefully, and her heart swelled with anger, hatred, and love. Her emotions were just that confusing. She walked over to him slowly. Why did he have to look so damn handsome all the time? And tears began to fill her eyes.

She sat on the edge of the bed. Then leaned down, took that wonderful dick she knew so well, and put it in her mouth.

Shay pressed off the water in the shower and stepped out of the stall. She dried off quickly, wrapped the towel around her small body, and brushed her hair up into a band-held ponytail. This was her first day back to work and she wanted to look serious and strong.

She looked at herself in the mirror. John often said she had a strong but also a vulnerable look about her, and he always seemed fascinated by her face. When she looked at herself in the mirror she saw cute, yes, but nothing like what John apparently saw. But that was the beauty of their relationship. It was more than just skin deep. Their relationship was layers deep, with each seeing in the other what they couldn't see in themselves. It was wonderful actually. Especially after these last six weeks when she relied so heavily on his love and his strength. She hated relying on it, but loved knowing that she could. That was why she felt that their relationship was so special. Because she could rely on him, and he could rely on her. She made a funny face at herself in the mirror, smiled at her silliness, and then grabbed up the front of her oversized towel, turned off the bathroom light, and made her way back into the bedroom.

She didn't realize a third person was in the room until she had already walked over to her side of the bed. She saw to her amazement, on the opposite side, Blair Malone knelt down at John's side. She also saw how Blair had John's penis in her mouth, licking it like a lollipop. When she looked up and saw that Shay was looking at her, she didn't even have the pride to stop. She, instead, took his rod all the way down to the back of her throat.

"John!" Shay blared, astounded by what she was seeing.

"Yes, what," John said as he jumped awake, causing Blair to fall back on her butt. When he realized she was there, he was as astounded as Shay was. "What the fuck are you doing in here?" he demanded to know, jumping out of his bed.

Blair quickly backed up and stood up. Only her eyes

231

were on Shay. "You can't have him," she said, moving toward the foot of the bed, her eyes trained on Shay. "Nope. Made up my mind. You can't have him."

"Get out of here, Blair, what the fuck's wrong with you!" John yelled as he reached for a pair of pants thrown over a chair on his side of the bed. "And get out now!"

But Blair only had eyes for Shay. "You can't be with him," she was saying. "He's my husband."

Shay's heart was hammering. She'd already seen how foolish this woman could be. "He's your *ex*-husband," she said, "and you need to get out of here."

"Me? Get out of my own home? Bitch, who do you think you are?"

"Bitch, who do you think you are?" Shay asked. "Your ass the one running up in here starting something." Shay was getting angrier by the second. This was the same chick who had spit in her face. Now this? But she was ready for her this time.

But as quickly as she thought she was ready, she realized she wasn't ready for this crazy woman at all. Because it changed on a dime. John was still demanding that Blair get the hell out of his home. He was even beginning to move toward her to forcibly remove her. Shay was still arguing with her, word for word, making it clear that she wasn't going to stand for her foolishness this time around. And then Blair pulled out the gun.

Everything stopped when she pulled out that gun.

"See bitch," Blair said, "I got your foolishness right here!" And she pointed it at Shay, and fired.

"*Nooo!*" John screamed as soon as she pointed the gun. Before she fired he was leaping across the bed. As she fired he was throwing his body into Shay's small body and knocking her to the ground. The bullet whizzed past his ear and lodged into the back wall. And Blair fired again. And again.

The second and third shots missed too, as John had completely covered Shay. But he knew he had to do it. He slung around, grabbed his sidearm off of the nightstand, then flipped onto his back, pointing his gun at Blair.

"Don't make me do this, Blair! Don't fucking make me do this!"

But Blair wasn't listening. John's movement left Shay exposed, and she aimed to kill her. She saw red. She saw Shay, and she saw red. But before she could fire her final shot, as she was just about to do, John fired his first and only shot.

One shot was all it took.

Blair buckled, looked at her husband as if amazed that he would have even thought about harming her, and then fell over.

"Shay!" John yelled, his gun still pointed at his ex-wife, his heart in his shoe. "Tell me you're okay!"

"I'm all right," Shay yelled back, sitting up from the fetal position John had thrown her into, looking up with

233

what he recognized as pure terror in her eyes.

John went over to Blair, and checked her pulse.

He then sat back, on his haunches, and dropped his still smoking gun.

"Is she going to be all right?" Shay asked, standing to her feet. "Is she all right?"

John looked at Shay with what she knew to be pure terror too, and then he went to her. He pulled her into his arms. "No, baby," he said, his brows knitted. "No."

And although he held Shay, although she felt his protective arms around her, she felt as barren, as alone, as unprotected as a fruitless tree in the middle of a desert.

Police now swarmed the chief's home and John and Shay now sat quietly on the edge of the living room sofa. Shay had put on a pair of shorts and a t-shirt and John was in his trousers and a sweat shirt. Neither had on shoes. Both looked as if they'd seen the gates of hell and were still horrified by the view.

"Sit back, babe," John urged Shay as he put his arm around her and they both sat back on the sofa. There was no way there were going to find lemonade in these lemons. It was just that bad.

It only got worse when Ted Fletchette, the town's mayor and John's boss, arrived at what was now considered the crime scene. He stepped in slowly, looking from right to left as if he had to make sure the coast was clear. When he saw John and Shay, he walked in their direction.

Ted didn't speak. That wasn't his style. He just took a seat in the chair flanking the sofa and looked at his chief of police. It seemed to him that the scene itself, of cops everywhere, of a dead ex-wife in the ambulance outside, of neighbors who also happened to be voters standing out on their lawns wondering what in the world was happening here, spoke for itself.

Then he exhaled. "You put me in shitsville, John," the mayor eventually said. Shay looked at him. "There's no cute way to put this," the mayor continued. "I'm screwed. I mean, think about the irony here. My first chief of police was as crooked as a curve and now my second chief of police just killed his wife! They're gonna run me out of this town on a rail!"

Shay couldn't believe how the mayor was turning this awful tragedy into an indictment against his political future. She almost said something, but John squeezed her. So she held her peace.

"All we can do now," the mayor went on, "is mitigate the damage. I'm suspending you immediately, pending the outcome of an investigation. Craig Yannick will be in charge for now."

Shay could not believe it. "You're suspending him?" she asked. "What did he do?"

"What do you think he did, Miss Turner? He killed his wife!"

235

"He killed his *ex*-wife because she was trying to kill me! He didn't just kill her. He was saving my life!"

"Yeah, well, I don't know that, now do I? And I wasn't talking to your ass, anyway."

"That's enough, Ted!" John said. "I'll accept your suspension, but I won't accept you speaking to Shay that way."

The mayor threw his hands in the air. "Sorry," he said. And then his voice began to rise. "I guess I don't know how to be politically correct when my entire career has just been fucked!" Some of the police officers in the room looked his way. Then the mayor stood up angrily. And walked back out.

The days that followed were a blur to Shay. Everywhere she went the townspeople gave her funny looks and made annoying comments as if she and she alone were solely responsible for what happened that night. John was indeed suspended pending an official investigation and was ordered, by the mayor himself, to stay away from Shay until they could get to the bottom of what really happened. Shay, too, wasn't allowed back to work at the Tribune pending the investigation's outcome, and was strongly advised, by the newspaper's attorney, to have no contact with John Malone.

But they didn't know what they were asking of them. John and Shay had become the other's best friend, soul mate, partner. They broke the no-contact orders almost immediately. First by phone. Every day and night they spoke by phone. But as the investigation dragged on, from one week into two, John couldn't bear it anymore. He had to see for himself just how Shay was holding up.

He phoned her by week two and told her to get in her Beetle and drive, two towns over, to the backside of the Big Wal-Mart parking lot.

Shay arrived first, sitting quietly in her VW, and then he arrived, in his Silverado, and she got out and got into the truck with him.

At first they just sat there, staring at the few cars traveling in and out of the grocery store, and then John looked at Shay. She was still, like him, badly shaken.

"You okay?" he asked her, concerned.

She looked at him, to make certain he wasn't kidding. "No," she said as if it was obvious.

"It's not your fault, Shay. You did nothing wrong."

"That's what you're saying. That's not what everybody else is saying."

"Then everybody else are damn fools! I caused this. Me. Not you. Not. . ."

Shay looked at him. "Not Blair? Is that what you were going to say? That it wasn't Blair's fault, either?"

John frowned. She could see how torn he was. "It was her fault, of course it was her fault. But---"

"But what, John?"

John ran his hand through his already rumpled hair. "What do you want me to say? That I bear no blame

237

here? My bad decisions caused the life of my son, and now I had to take the life of his mother. They both died at my own hands, Shay. And when you have to face a truth like that, a truth that stark, you don't give a damn about the circumstances or the context. You just don't. If it wasn't for my actions they would both be alive today! And then to drag you into this." John could barely contain his grief. "That's the worse part of it all. You had to get tainted with my craziness. Now they're calling you a slut and a whore and a home wrecker. *You*! All because of my decisions. We can dress this up however we want, but it's all because of me."

Shay understood his anguish. She was anguished too. Every time she thought about that bloody scene in that bedroom it made her so disoriented that she didn't know if she was going or coming. It was bad. And they both knew it.

A few days after they met in the Wal-Mart parking lot John was exonerated of all wrongdoing, and he was fully reinstated on his job. Although he was ready to get back into action, it wasn't the same. Because Shay was still traumatized. Because it kind of felt like too little too late. And on the day he showed up at Shay's home, to tell her the so-called good news about his reinstatement, she had already made up her mind.

They sat at her small kitchen table. The silence in the room made even their least movement sound loud.

238

"Are you sure about this, Shay?" John asked her, his blue eyes so troubled they were troubling Shay.

"I'm positive," she said. "My parents have been asking me to come ever since that night. They've been begging me to come. But I kept telling them no. I kept telling them that I was fine. But I'm not fine, John. I still feel as terrified as I did the night it happened. I need some time away."

He reached for her hand and placed it in his. Only his hand was shaking. "When will I see you again?"

"We can still see each other," she said with great hope. "I'm only moving to Philadelphia, not out of the country. Of course we'll still see each other."

"But are you sure you can't just go for a few days and come back?" John asked her.

"Yes, John," she said. "I'm certain. I'll be back, I promise you, I'll come back. But right now it's all still too raw, it's still too painful. Remember when your son died and you had to get out of Baton Rouge? How you said you could feel the pain in the air itself? That's how I feel. I've got to leave. At least until the rawness of it wears off."

If it ever wears off, John thought sadly. Then he looked into Shay's big, bright eyes. Tears began to well up in his. "I'm going to miss you so much," he said, and Shay quickly jumped from her seat and hurried to his. He pulled her onto his lap and wrapped her into his strong, muscular arms. He squeezed his eyes shut as he held

239

her.

They sat there, hating the position life had put them in, but understanding there was no other way. She had to leave, to regroup now, while she still could. John understood that. Then he garnered the strength to lean back and look her in her eyes again.

"Do you want me to go with you?" he asked her.

Shay smiled and placed her small hand on the side of his face. "Yeah, I can see you staying at my parents' home with me like some teenager. No, babe," she said. "That'll only make it worse. The people of this town need you on the job. And you need your job. And I need to know that you'll be okay."

"But I can't bear knowing that you'll be alone in some strange city---"

"It's not a strange city. It's my parents' home. And I won't be alone. I'll be fine, John. I just need time to exhale, that's all. And soon the sting won't sting anymore, for both of us, and I'll come back."

John smiled too, revealing, Shay thought sadly, every second of his thirty-seven years. He reached over and kissed her long and sweet and desperately on her lips. Then, when their lips parted, he nodded his head. "Yes," he said. "You'll go to Philly, spend some time with your parents, and then you'll come back to me."

It sounded like a definite plan, a good plan, but it wasn't a plan at all. Just hollow words. Just words to make it through the moment. And somehow, in that deep recess of their hearts that they weren't able to even acknowledge right now, they both knew it.

They kissed again, and held each other again, as if they were still determined, despite the odds, despite those hollow words, to keep their love alive.

THIRTEEN

Two Years Later

"Sure you don't want cheese in those grits?" Faylene asked John Malone as she poured fresh coffee in his coffee cup and marveled at the man who ate his breakfast, same time every morning, same spot at the counter, inside her popular diner. It was a scorching day already in Brady and his suit coat was in his car. But even in his long-sleeved, pristine-pressed white dress shirt Faylene could still see the stark definition of his ripped abs and those mighty biceps she always dreamed of squeezing. And even after he turned down her offer of cheese, and continued to eat his breakfast, she lingered behind the counter anyway. Before Blair died she used to envy that woman so much. She had herself a real man and didn't seem to appreciate it. Now that Blair was long gone Faylene was determined to take her spot. But she knew, with John Malone, she had to tread lightly.

"I heard y'all found another girl last night over on Hash Street," she said, her light blue eyes staring into his dark blue ones. "Please tell me it ain't true."

John chomped down the last of his bacon and sipped from his freshly brewed coffee, inwardly warmed by the smooth, clean taste. He could always count on Faylene to give him great coffee and good conversation every time he stepped foot into her establishment. He could also count on her to flirt with him.

"You know I don't discuss my cases," he said, glancing down at her breasts, her implants like massive mounds bunched together and jutting from the top tip of her white blouse, threatening to break free. Faylene was a beauty, a woman considered a blonde bombshell around these parts, but her appearance, with the big hair and the big breasts and the overt flirtatiousness, was a tad too much for John's taste. He thought about screwing her many times in the past, certain that she would be a more than willing bedmate, but he always decided against it.

"But it's true, isn't it?" she asked. "Y'all did find another one last night?"

John sat his coffee on the saucer. "Yes," he admitted. "But it's not the same m.o. The thirteen women Willie Glazer's soon to go on trial for killing were duct taped, strangled, raped. And they were all prostitutes from Dodge. That wasn't the case with the girl we found last night."

"She wasn't found in Dodge, but over on Hash Street, right?"

"That's right."

"Was she strangled too?"

"No. She was stabbed, but don't you go blabbing that around, Fay."

"But some in this town already declaring Glazer's

243

innocent, and the fact that there's been another girl killed only proves that Glazer didn't do those other thirteen killings. They gonna lump that new dead girl in with the ones he's about to go on trial for killing."

"You just stay out of it," John said, pointing his fork. "I don't want you talking it up with your customers all day long, Faylene, now I mean it. The last thing I need is for these folks around here to start believing we arrested the wrong man."

"Some blacks already believe it. From what I hear they're planning some kind of protest march all the way to the courthouse when the trial begins."

John didn't want to be reminded of that headache. The last thing this powder keg of a town needed right now was some protest march, and he'd already made that clear to the town's black leadership. "Don't believe everything you hear," he said. "You have too little information to be gossiping about any of this right now."

Faylene placed her hand on her considerable hip and smiled. "Do I look like a gossiper to you?"

John quickly nodded his head. "Yes," he said with a smile of his own.

Faylene laughed that booming laugh of hers and winked at John just as one of the younger waitresses walked up beside her.

"Faylene," the waitress said, "what I'm supposed to do with this?" She was holding up a newspaper coupon.

"Don't you see me and the chief talking?"

"Yes, ma'am, but she won't take no for an answer."

Faylene frowned. "Who won't take no for an answer?"

"That lady over there in the big hat. I told her we ain't running this special no more but she says it was in today's paper and it didn't have no expiration date and she expects us to honor it."

Faylene sighed. "I'm not the boss, John," she said as she reluctantly took the coupon from the waitress's hand. "They don't work for me. I work for them."

John snorted, drank more of his coffee. The waitress, some brown-eyed young redhead with freckles out of this world and stacked high breasts to rival Faylene's, gave him one of those *yes, I'm available* smiles he knew so well. She was barely eighteen, young enough to be his daughter, but was flirty as hell. That was the problem in Brady. Far too many unattached women, far too few unattached men. And an unattached man like John Malone was considered the top of the heap.

"I told Ray over at the Tribune not to run this anymore," Faylene said. "But that douche bag does it anyway."

"Can we honor it?" the waitress asked.

"We have no choice," Faylene said, handing the coupon back to her. "I'll call the Trib later and give them a good cussing out."

"Yes, ma'am," the waitress said with a smile and left.

Everybody knew what kind of potty mouth Faylene could have.

John's cell phone began to buzz just as the waitress left. He pulled it out, checked the Caller ID.

"But really, John," Faylene said, "we're talking another dead girl here, even with Willie Glazer in jail. Don't you think it's time for people to start panicking?"

"No, I do not," John said. "This is Malone," he said into his phone.

"There's been a car wreck over on Bainerd, sir," the voice on the other end said.

John frowned. "Who the hell is this?"

"Oh, I'm sorry, sir. I'm Officer Malvaney, sir."

Malvaney? John thought. *Who the hell is Malvaney?*

"I'm new," Malvaney answered his unasked question.

"And what is it again?" John asked him.

"There's been an accident over on Bainerd. I was told you'd want to know."

"How many casualties?"

"Casualties, sir? Oh, no, sir. No casualties. It wasn't that kind of accident. One car was pretty badly banged up, but it's basically a fender bender."

John could hardly believe it. His men knew better than to disturb him at breakfast unless it was vital. "Why would I want to know about some fender bender, Malvaney?"

"Captain Yannick told me to phone you."

"Is Craig there?"

"No, sir. I called the station and he told me to phone you."

"You still haven't answered my question. Why are you interrupting my breakfast over some *got*damn fender bender?"

Faylene smiled. John was a lot of things, but patient wasn't one of them.

The officer, however, didn't skip a beat. "Because Shay Turner is involved, sir," he said.

John's heart rammed against his chest. He knew he had to have heard him wrong. "Shay Turner?" he said with a frown. And just the mention of that name caused Faylene to stop fluffing her hair, and stare at John.

Her shock, however, was dwarfed by his.

"That's why I called you, sir," Malvaney continued. "Miss Turner is involved. When I phoned the station to run her license, that's when Captain Yannick told me that y'all, that you and Miss Turner, that is, used to be sort of like. . . Sort of. . . that y'all were friends."

John knew exactly what the young man was insinuating. Ever since that night when he had to shoot and kill Blair, he and Shay had been intrinsically linked. She'd been gone for two years, but that still didn't stop the gossip. The very nasty, untrue gossip.

"Cap told me to phone you before I let her go," the officer continued.

But this still didn't make sense to John. What was

Shay doing back in Alabama when she all but told him she was never coming back here? They tried to keep their love alive after she left, with John traveling to Philly every single weekend, but the anguish of that night was still too fresh for both of them. Then she got a job in Philly and decided she was going to stay even longer than they had planned. John was crushed by her decision, and she was anguished by it, even though they both declared it wouldn't change their relationship one iota.

But their relationship had already changed. Because it never really got off of the ground. Because there was always too much drama swirling around them. Because they cared for each other so much that they couldn't bear to see the other in pain. So John accepted her decision, although he didn't like it. And they settled on a long-distance love affair.

But soon the daily grind of running a police department began to get in the way. First there was yet another tri-county drug sting operation with the Feds that consumed all of John's weekends. And then, a year after Shay had left, the major arrest of Willie Glazer, the Dodge serial killer, that managed to split the town in two. Willie Glazer was a drifter, a man who was born in Brady and hailed from a good family, but who got on drugs at an early age and never got straight. He would spend many months in town and then hitch-hike his way across the country again, and then come back for a few more months.

It was during those visits back, John and his men believed, that Glazer killed those women. Many disagreed, including Glazer's family. They believed he was being railroaded because he was a drug addict who drifted in and out of town. It was easy, they felt, to pin those crimes on him. They had no DNA, no eye witnesses, nothing. And when Glazer confessed to the murders and then claimed he was forced into confessing, his family blamed John.

There were charges and countercharges. John, who used to be a hero in the black community, was now being portrayed as a villain. He met daily with older black church leaders, who were on his side and weren't about to defend some drug addicted drifter like Glazer, and younger civil rights activists who were more than willing to stand up for Glazer. It was an all-consuming period of time and became darn near impossible for John to get away.

But he and Shay kept trying. They spoke every night on the telephone, although it would sometimes be after midnight before John could phone her, and Shay once came back to town herself to see him at the new home he had purchased.

But it wasn't the same. The pain was still too raw. She returned to Philly the next day, tried to find some normalcy there, and they both decided to give their relationship a little cooling off period. That was two months shy of two years ago. They had both, technically, moved on. Although emotionally was another story.

But why, John wondered, was she back? Had she decided that she had cooled off enough and was now back for good? Was she ready to start their relationship again, or only ready to live her own life without him as a part of that life? It was confusing and scaring the hell out of John.

"Was she . . . was anybody hurt in the accident?" he asked his officer.

"No, sir. Like I said it was just a fender bender. But when Captain Yannick recognized the name, he said that I should phone you."

"The accident happened where on Bainerd?" John asked.

"Two blocks west of Moose Kernan, sir."

"I'm on my way."

"Should I take her to the station?" the officer asked.

"Didn't I tell you I was on my way?" John snapped. "You don't take her anywhere."

After killing the call, John held his cell phone a moment longer, a frown enveloping his face. He still was unable to reconcile the fact that Shay was back in town; that the woman who still haunted his dreams was within reach of him again.

"Did you know she was back?" Faylene asked, her eyes riveted on him.

"No," John said pointblank as he sipped the last of

250

his coffee and stood to his feet.

"Funny she'd come back and not even tell you about it."

It was hardly funny to John. "How about that," he said absently, tossed a twenty on the counter, and headed for the exit. The red-headed waitress returned to Faylene's side just as the chief was walking out.

"Did I hear that right?" she asked as she handed the coupon and ticket order to Faylene. "Is Shay Turner back in town?"

Faylene sighed. "That's what the man said."

The redhead shook her head. "The nerve of her to come back here."

"Who's Shay Turner?" another waitress, a new one, asked as she walked up.

Faylene balled up the coupon, a sadness coming into her bright blue eyes. "A thorn in John Malone's ass if you ask me," she said with bitterness in her voice.

Shay stood patiently against the driver side door of her aging Volkswagen Beetle and asked the officer again what was taking him so long. The way he was on the phone, and then writing, and then on the phone again made it seem as if he'd just captured an escaped convict. The other driver had been given his paperwork and was well on his way. But the officer, for some reason, still had her detained.

Her return to Brady could not have gone any worse.

251

Her goal was to keep a low profile. Go see her old boss at the Tribune this afternoon, pray he takes her back, and then attempt to start all over again. Quietly. But now she was standing on the side of one of the busiest roads in Brady, her Beetle banged up to where it wouldn't even start, and her savings account was just enough money for her to survive a good month. Now she had what could turn out to be a costly car repair bill to contend with. This was not the return she had envisioned.

And Barney Fife here, she thought annoyingly, seemed determined to keep her detained far longer than it could possibly be necessary. He was seated in his police cruiser behind her car and appeared to her to be on the phone again. Although she was waiting on the tow truck and couldn't exactly go anywhere until it came, she still didn't understand why the officer hadn't given her an unsafe driving ticket or whatever he was going to give to her, and set her free.

She quickly realized the reason, however, when she saw that familiar Chevy Silverado drive past her, pull over to the side of the road, and then back up to the front end of her car. She steeled herself as John Malone stepped out of the truck in his always pristine-pressed dress shirt, his big gun holstered on his hip, his muscular, athletic body walking toward her with that same sensual swagger that caused her to dream about him the first time she met him.

It had been almost two years since she'd seen him,

two long years, but that didn't mean her feelings for him had diminished. Not by the way her heart was pounding as he approached her. She'd had many other men to take a shine to her since she left Brady, men who would be classified as darn good catches by even her standards, but her heart was still with John. Her heart kept roaming back to Brady, and to a certain gruff police chief who always seemed to relax her. But who, she knew, she no longer had any claims to.

John walked slowly toward her. He knew the toll those rumors and gossip had taken on her. That was why his heart always ached for Shay Turner. They had tried to blame her for everything, including his divorce, which occurred before he even met her. But that didn't stop them from labeling her with vicious home-wrecker whore labels that were nowhere near the truth. Those labels were, in fact, the polar opposite of the kind of young lady Shay really was.

And that was why, when John was forced to do the unthinkable to his ex-wife, the firestorm that followed and built against Shay was directly because of her relationship with him, and the fact that he had insisted she spend a few days at his house rather than her own. And he felt guilty about it. Even as he walked toward her now, his heart hammering against his chest at just seeing her again, he still felt guilty about it.

When he reached her side, with his blue eyes blazing against the bright morning sun, his heart swelled

253

with emotion. He still could not believe it. Shay was back. After all of this time she was back. After night after night of worrying about her, wondering if she was okay, getting a hard-on just thinking about her, she was back within his grasp.

With the sun reflecting off of her soft brown skin, giving it a golden glow, she looked like a tall drink of chocolate loveliness standing before him. It looked as if time had not only stood still for her, but had granted her more of that unpretentious but regal elegance he'd always found endearing about her. She wore a pair of white hip-hugging pants, a sleeveless silk purple blouse low-cut enough to reveal a tasteful but nonetheless enticing amount of cleavage, yellow, white, and purple stiletto slipper shoes, and a bright yellow scarf tied in a slant around her neck. Her long hair was draped down her back in a curled underthrow, and her soft brown eyes were covered by rose-colored, tinted glasses. She was inside and out, for John Malone, the very definition of what it meant to be beautiful.

"Hi," she said when he made it to her side. She wanted to remove her glasses, to get an unobstructed view of the man who put all others to shame, but she didn't trust her eyes. Just seeing him again was already making her feel heady, and too emotional, when she couldn't afford to shed any more tears.

John was feeling those emotions too. As he glanced down at her cleavage and then back into her wonderful face, not only his heart but his penis was throbbing at just the sight of her. This wasn't good. How in the world was he going to be able to hold out a second longer, when, in truth, he wanted to pull her into his arms right where they stood? That was why he said good morning to her, but then immediately looked from her to the considerable damage to her car's front bumper and dented hood.

"What happened here?"

The question, for some reason, threw Shay. She was expecting something far more personal. Like how are you? Or, what in the world are you doing back here? But he had decided to keep it professional. So could she.

"I didn't stop in time," she said.

John's eyes looked back at her. Oh, how he wanted to feel her in his arms. "Were you hurt at all?" he asked her.

"No, thank God. Neither was the guy in the other car. He said he barely felt the bump."

"Hello, chief," the young officer on the scene said as he scrambled out of his cruiser and hurried toward his boss. He had been on his cell phone, running his mouth with his girlfriend, and hadn't realized John had arrived.

"Malvaney, is it?" John asked the officer without looking at him. He, instead, looked once again at the damage.

The officer smiled. "That's right, sir."

"This is quite a bit more damage than you had led me to believe," John noted.

The officer's smile disappeared, and anguish replaced it. "I didn't mean to mislead you, sir."

Shay could have told John that the damage looked worse than it was, and would have probably not even been reported at all but for his young officer being nearby when it happened and, by blaring his sirens and rushing over, removed the choice.

She watched John as he walked around to the opposite side of the bumper. She'd known attractive men in her day, very attractive men, but John Malone, in her mind, always stood head and shoulders above them all. He had a face that was more wide-jaw than angular, a smooth rather than sharp nose, full lips for a white guy, and narrow blue eyes that glistened against his tanned skin and gave him a deceptively gorgeous look. At first glance you didn't see it. You only saw a fairly nice looking man, but nothing spectacular. But you looked again and wow, you saw it as if you could hardly believe just how beautiful he really was. For Shay, and for most women, John Malone had that kind of wow factor in spades.

He also had a ripped, athletic body, all thighs and biceps, that could still rival a twenty-year-old's any day of the week. And that look of unyielding control he always had on his face exuded a kind of strength and power that Shay used to find intimidating, but eventually found downright sexy.

"This is a little more than a fender bender, officer,"

256

John pointed out to Malvaney and then looked at him, a look of slight irritation on his face.

Malvaney swallowed hard. He knew how rough on rookies Chief Malone could be. "Yes, sir, I agree, sir, but what I meant to tell you was that nobody was hurt or in any serious peril is what I meant. And the other car barely had a scratch."

"That's because it was some bubble Chevy from the eighties," Shay said. "It was built like a Mack truck. The guy didn't even want my insurance information. He said the little scratch his car sustained fit right in with the other dents and scratches, so it was no big deal. But your officer wrote it up anyway."

"He did his job," John said firmly. He didn't allow anyone, not even Shay, to question the judgment of his officers unless that judgment was a blatant violation. He therefore moved his attention away from the car's damage and back to Shay. He began walking back toward her. His heart was hammering as he approached her. He was surprised at how just seeing her again was affecting him so strongly. And he wondered what in the world was it going to take to ever get her out of his system. A two-year absence didn't work. By the way his heart was hammering, by the way his emotions were all over the place, it only seemed to make his feelings for her even more intense.

His eyes began to trail down the length of her body as he approached her, pleased to see that she had gained a little weight. She was always small, and would probably always be petite, but the last time he saw her she was so wrapped up in the trauma of what they had gone through that she had lost weight.

Shay noticed his perusal of her body as he approached her. She never quite knew what to do whenever his eyes would assess her that way, and they used to assess her often that way. Not that she would complain; she used to love whenever he showed that level of interest. Now, however, given her unfair reputation before she left town, given her need to get it right this time and avoid as much controversy as she possibly could, she wasn't at all sure if she could handle that level of interest right now.

He looked back into her eyes, placed one hand in his pant pocket, the pocket on the same side as his holstered weapon, and exhaled. "Have you tried to crank it?"

"I tried, yes. But it won't crank."

"Ah," John said in that sympathetic way she used to adore.

"Yeah, it was like the last thing I needed. I meet with Ed this afternoon and now I don't even have wheels. Geez. Some welcome home."

John stared at her. He could already see the anguish in her eyes. "Have you called a tow truck yet?" he asked her.

She nodded, was about to say yes, but Malvaney

interrupted her.

"She told them to tow it to her house," he said with a grin. "I told her what good's that gonna do? Why not have it towed to a repair shop so it can get repaired?"

Because I can't afford a repair bill right now, Shay had wanted to say to the eager officer when he first came up with the bright idea, and she still wanted to set him straight. But she wasn't about to expose just what kind of dire straits she really was in to him or John Malone or anybody else.

John could sense her hesitation. He decided to briefly change the subject. "So were you just passing through?" he asked.

"No, actually," she replied. "I plan to stay."

John was amazed. He stared at her. "You plan to stay?"

"That's right."

And when was this plan hatched, he wanted to ask. "Where are you staying?" he asked instead. "Malvaney mentioned your house? What house?" When she left town two years ago, she left for good the small house she was renting.

"It's a house Aunt Rae left me."

John frowned. "Aunt Rae? She died?"

"Yeah." That was perhaps the biggest regret of Shay's decision to leave Brady. She also had to leave Aunt Rae behind. But they did stay in touch, talking on the phone every week. Aunt Rae even broke down and started allowing the Senior Center's transport van to pick her up every morning. She soon started complaining about that too, although she never missed a day riding it.

"She didn't want a funeral, you know she was kind of eccentric. She wanted her body cremated with no ceremony, she was firm on that. The attorney handling her estate didn't even tell me about the death until after the cremation. He only called me then because she left everything she owned in this world to me. Which was only her house. She died a year ago."

Shay swallowed hard. John could understand easily how that old woman could take so completely to Shay even though she didn't know her that long. He understood it perfectly.

"She passed last year," he asked, "and you're just now taking possession of the house?"

Shay nodded, a bewildered look on her face. "That's right."

John stared at Shay. He understood. When she left Brady she was in a bad state. She'd been through too much. He had been doubtful that she would ever come back this way.

John's cell phone began to buzz. He pulled it out and looked at the Caller ID. It was the station. "Malone," he said. He looked at Shay as he listened on the phone. She seemed flustered to him as she stood there, her small arms folded in a carefree pose, but her face revealing a sense of dread. Coming here was a major

LOVING HER SOUL MATE

move for her. And that house she inherited was hardly
the catalyst. He wondered, however, what was.

"Okay," he said into the phone. "I'll be there."

He killed the call. And made up his mind. No way
was he going to continue to pretend that he didn't have
strong feelings for this woman.   These gossiping
townspeople be damned. "Get your things," he said to
her.

Shay, however, didn't understand. "My things?"

"Your suit case, or whatever else you have in the
trunk. I'll take you where you need to go."

"Thanks, Chief, but I know you're a busy man. I can
wait for the tow truck."

"No, you can't," John said so firmly it surprised Shay.
"What tow company are you using? Rick's?"

Shay hesitated, her big eyes attempting to follow
where John was going with this. "That's right."

"Malvaney?"

"Yes, sir?" Malvaney replied as he stepped up
toward the twosome.

"Wait here for Rick. Have him tow Miss Turner's car
over to Ace Garage."

Shay began to panic. She couldn't pay for any
repairs right now. Not until she was certain Ed was going
to give her her job back. Because if she didn't get the
job, she'd need money to survive until she found a new
one. "John, look, I appreciate what you're trying to do,
but I would prefer to have the car towed to the house until

261

I can---"

"Tell them to get in touch with me if they have any questions," John continued to tell Malvaney. "And to send the bill to me."

"Yes, sir," Malvaney replied and glanced at Shay Turner. He still didn't get it. He still couldn't see just what it was about her that had the chief treating her as if she was somebody so special. To him she was just another black woman. Cute, yes, she was cute all right, but hardly fantastic looking. Faylene, whom everybody knew had the hots for the chief, looked way better than her. He just didn't get it.

Shay didn't exactly get it either. Not when so many women around town were always clamoring to be in John Malone's bed. And not when John had to know that those same rumors of their torrid love affair would start flying yet again.

"May I speak with you privately, Chief?" she asked him.

But his cell phone began buzzing again. When he saw the Caller ID he held up a finger to Shay. "Malone?" he said into the phone, and after a brief moment he frowned. "What do you mean you can't find it? Didn't I tell you to tear that place upside down last night? Without that evidence we're screwed!" He began moving away from Shay and toward his truck, his voice rising with every step.

And Shay gave up. She needed transportation, no

doubt about that. And if Ed hired her on the spot, as she was praying he would, she'd need wheels right away. Although she would pay her own repair bill, she wasn't going to turn down his assistance with a ride. Not when her interview with Ed was mere hours away.

But as she got her luggage out of the trunk, with Malvaney helping her, her brows knitted in frustration anyway. Because it was all so disheartening. She came back to Brady hoping to be this independent island, a woman who would avoid all controversy and just do her job. But she hadn't been in town a full hour and already needed John Malone's rescue.

Her return home could not have possibly started off any bleaker.

His truck pulled into the circular driveway of his ranch style home in Pace Harbor. It was a sprawling brick home of well-maintained shrubbery and an elegantly-maintained dark green lawn. A statue of Apollo was in the middle of the circle as a fountain overflowing with rich spring water, and a double-car garage at the end of the curve gave the home an almost too-traditional-for-John-Malone suburban feel. Pace Harbor was one of the most exclusive neighborhoods in Brady, home to many of the town's movers and shakers. Shay, however, had only been to his new home once, when he first purchased it and she returned to Brady for that weekend.

But the fact that it was new didn't help. The fact that

it was new caused the memories of his old home, and what happened in that old home, to flood back that weekend like a tidal wave. Shay left Brady early that next day.

He unbuckled his seat belt and got out of the car. She fully expected him to run inside to get whatever he needed to get and then drive her to her own new residence. But he, instead, walked around to the passenger side of the car, and opened the door.

Shay looked at him warily when he opened the door. The reason she hated being beholden to people was because she felt beholden to them, and would come off as ungrateful if she didn't comply with their every whim. But John knew her. She had turned him down once. . .

John knew her all right, and he could see the hesitation, or maybe even the fear, in her creamy-soft brown eyes. But it was now or never. Sink or swim. Yes or no.

He crotched down to her. They were now eyeball to eyeball. He took her hand and held it between both of his.

"I want to welcome you home properly," he said to her with all honesty. "And I can't do so out here."

Shay's heart pounded when he made such a blunt utterance. It was as if he had decided that he wasn't dancing their mating dance any longer. It was as if he was making it clear that he still wanted her, but she had to decide, here and now, if she wanted him.

Shay stared at him with a look so filled with anguish that it broke John's heart. But he couldn't run around that mulberry bush with her all over again. His feelings were still too strong, even after a two-year absence, and he had to know where she stood. She either wanted to be with him, or she didn't.

Shay understood clearly what he was implying. Because she knew it too. All that time away, all of those lonely nights, had increased her feelings for him, not decreased them. And she didn't have the energy anymore to keep dancing either.

That was why Shay managed to release her fear and smile. She wanted to be with him. She knew it all along, but especially during those dark nights after she left Brady. Her decision, now, was as firm as his.

When Shay smiled through her fear, it warmed John's heart. He felt a swell of emotion so strong he thought he was going to cry. But he held it together and continued to hold her hand, to squeeze her hand, as she got out of his truck.

FOURTEEN

They didn't waste time. As soon as the door of his home closed shut, he was in front of Shay, placing his hands on her beautifully toned bare arms, moving closer to her beautifully lithe body. His brows were knit now, as pure emotion was beginning to overtake him.   It was uncharacteristic of John Malone, and nobody had ever seen this side of him. Except Shay.

"I miss you so much," he said to her, still rubbing her arms. "There wasn't a day that went by that I didn't want to pick up that phone and call you or just get in my car and go to you. But you made it clear you needed your space, you needed time away, and I accepted that. Because I knew you did." He paused to avoid becoming almost too emotional. "I thought you had left me, Shay. I didn't think you would ever come back. And I was trying to keep going, to go on with my life. But I could never get you out of my system."

Shay placed her hand on the side of his gorgeous face. It was only nine am and already he had a five o clock shadow. She smiled. "I know," she said. "I haven't been able to get over you, either. And you wouldn't believe how I tried." They both smiled.

He pulled her into his big arms, something he had wanted to do since he first saw her standing on the side of that road. "I hope that trying didn't include a man," he said against her perfumed hair.

"And what if it did?"

"I'd understand it, but I wouldn't like it."

Shay smiled. "No, there hasn't been another man. I've kept myself for you."

John's heart swelled when she said those words. He closed his eyes.

"What about you?" Shay asked, pretty certain his answer would be the exact opposite of hers. "Have you kept yourself for me?"

John hesitated. Shay inhaled, to steel herself for what she knew would be a no. Then he spoke. "Yes," he said, and she let out a relieved, and delightfully surprised, exhaled.

"The truth is, I haven't been with a woman since the first time I made love to you," John continued. "You were brand new to town then," he said, his lips brushing her smooth, brown cheeks. "You were such a newbie and you didn't know what the hell you were doing," he said with a smile. She smiled too. "But I think I loved you even then, Shay." He found her lips and kissed her so passionately that she could feel his body pressing closer into hers, and she pressed closer too. She threw her arms around his neck and squeezed him as tightly as she could.

"You don't know how much I've wanted you," John said as he kept kissing her, his breathing almost tortured. "Every night I wanted to see your face, to hold you, to

267

fuck you, Shay. I wanted to be so deeply inside of you. I wanted you so badly I couldn't sleep. I wanted you to want me."

"I want you, John," Shay said as they kept kissing. "I've always wanted you."

John lifted her into his arms. She wrapped her legs around his thighs and her arms around his neck. "Oh, John," she said as their kissing became even more passionate, "what are you doing to me?"

"I can't stop, Shay."

"I know."

"I've got to have you. I've got to feel my dick inside of you."

"Oh, John," Shay cried as he began carrying her to his bedroom. "I want to feel it too."

"You want it?" he asked her as he hurried.

"Yes. I want it." She didn't think she could ever want anything more.

And he wanted it even more than that.

"What time is your meeting with Ed Barrington?" he asked her.

"It's at one," she said. "What about you? Don't you have to be at the police station?"

"Says who?" John asked as he began carrying her through his living room, down his long hall, and into his master bedroom. "I'm the boss. And I'll be there when I get there."

Shay leaned back with a smile and allowed him to

kiss her cleavage as he carried her.

But as soon as they entered that bedroom, and he sat her down on the bed, her heart began to pound. This was the moment they both had wanted for so long, and the pressure of being here with John Malone, a man who could take her to school and back in the lovemaking department, began to overwhelm her.

John could see the apprehension in her big, expressive eyes. And he forced himself to slow down, and to knell down in front of her. "I'm rushing you into this," he began.

"No," she said, shaking her head. "It's not that. I want it too."

"Then what's the matter, sweetheart?"

But Shay couldn't say. She just suddenly looked so bewildered.

John stayed knelt in front of her and pulled her into his arms. It's all right, babe," he said, moving closer to her. "It's all right."

Shay wrapped her arms around him. They'd had such a complicated relationship when she lived in Brady. He was fast becoming her advisor, her best friend, her father, mother and brother all wrapped into one. But for the last year and eight months he hadn't been her lover. Now he was about to take that mantle in her life once again too. And maybe that was her apprehension. When she lived in Brady he quickly became the most dominant person in her life, supplanting all others. When she was happy, she called him. When she was sad, she called him. When she was lonely, she'd have to see his gorgeous face just to feel relevant again. He already had her heart. Now he was about to have her body once again. And that realization, that there would no longer be any part of her life that was not closed to him, had her trembling.

He could feel her tremble as he held her. And it devastated him. It made him feel like a louse, like some sex-starved teenager wanting it no matter how the female felt about it. But this was Shay, and her feelings meant more to him than her body ever would.

He removed his holster and placed it, with his gun, on the nightstand. Then he lifted her and got onto his bed with her in his arms. They laid side by side, and he pulled her closer. "It's all right," he said to her again as he held her. "It's going to be all right. I'll never hurt you, Shay. I'll never hurt you."

Shay had tears in her eyes as he held her. He rubbed her hair and kissed her cheek and comforted her in her distress. This was the John Malone she had always loved so much. This was the wonderful man who treated her with such kindness from the first day they met. Nothing in her life was going right. Ever since she was let go from her dream job in Birmingham, nothing had gone right for her. And her parents were so overbearing in Philly, so determined to control her life. She felt even more suffocated there. As soon as she got a job, at a decent newspaper in Philly, she immediately got her own place and took care of herself. Her parents didn't like it, but they eventually accepted it. Because they had to know that the idea of being taken care of by her parents, at her age, was unbearable to her.

Yet, as she lay in John Malone's bed and allowed him to hold her, to comfort her, he was doing exactly that. Taking care of her. Being there for her. Loving her. But somehow, with John, she welcomed his care.

The Brady Police Department was abuzz with news of Shay Turner's return. Everybody who was there two years ago remembered the toll it had taken on their chief and the pound of flesh the town had extracted out of Shay's reputation. Not because she had done anything wrong. They knew the chief's marriage was in shambles long before he even met Shay. But the fact that her reporting was responsible for Chief McNamara's dismissal, and the fact that she was in that house the night John had to kill his own ex-wife, affected every one of them.

And that was why she would get no sympathy from John's men. John Malone stood by her, even when it was hurting him with the mayor, who could rescind his appointment as chief at any time. But he stood by her. Even to this day, his loyalty to an ambitious reporter like Shay Turner was inexplicable to them.

"You should have seen how arrogant she was,"

271

Malvaney said to the officers standing around Captain Yannick's desk. Yannick was there too, his burly arms folded, as his disdain for Shay Turner grew with Malvaney's every word. "You would have thought she was Michelle Obama or somebody the way she was demanding that I let her go as if I was detaining her for no reason. She even had on shades and was shaking her leg and she just turned my stomach. But when the chief got there he set her straight."

"John stood up for you?" Craig Yannick asked.

"Yes, sir, he did. She tried to act like I had no call stopping her but Chief Malone told her to back up right there, that I was doing my job. You should have seen her face when he disputed her that way."

"Good," Yannick said with satisfaction. "Maybe her aura has finally worn off on him."

"I never understood it myself," Detective Kincaid, a tall, tough-as-nails black woman, said. "Shay Turner's nothing to write home about. I mean she's a nice looking woman, but the way Chief seemed to be so smitten with her."

"Well, you know what they say."

"What they say, Cap?" Kincaid asked with a smile on her face. Everybody in the Brady Police Department just loved Captain Yannick's witticisms.

"The sweeter the berry, the blacker the juice," Yannick said and they all laughed. Malvaney, however, frowned.

"I think it's the other way around, sir," he said.

"He knows, son," Kincaid said. "He knows."

"And from what I heard," Yannick continued, "John Malone tapped that black juice so hard and so often that it went from sweet to prune." They laughed even harder. "From wet to dry." Even more laughter.

"What the hell's so funny?" John Malone asked when he came up front from the interrogation room. All of his officers, except for Yannick and Kincaid, nervously and hastily dispersed.

"You know me," Yannick said. "Just joking around. How did it go?"

John exhaled, and leaned against a desk near Yannick's. "Terrible. We've been back there nearly nine hours with that fool and he still won't confess."

Kincaid smiled. "Maybe he's not such a fool after all."

John looked at Kincaid with a searing look. Kincaid cleared her throat and wiped that smile off of her face.

"But you're certain the boyfriend killed that girl?" Yannick asked.

"I'm as certain as I can get. Every piece of evidence we have points to him."

"You know what those young activists are saying," Kincaid said. "They're saying that the fact that another girl was murdered while Glazer's been in jail only confirms his innocence; that he's no more the Dodge serial killer than they are."

273

John shook his head. "Nobody's spewing that nonsense but those so-called leaders who love to get their names in papers but don't give a damn about their community. They know this girl died on Hash Street, not in Dodge. They also know Glazer's guilty as sin for every one of those Dodge killings. And he's going down for what he did."

"How's Pamela reading all of this?" Kincaid asked. "She's certain our case against Glazer is strong?"

"Hell yeah," John replied. "She's a good DA. She agrees with me."

Yannick smiled. He knew how the chief and Pamela Ansley had a pretty close friendship.

John continued. "Glazer killed every one of those women he's on trial for killing, and boyfriend back there killed that woman we found last night on Hash Street. We've just got to make sure he confesses."

"Want me to have a go at him, Chief?" Kincaid asked with a grin.

"No," John said pointblank. He knew what kind of "go" Kincaid meant. "I want you to get him out of the interrogation room and put him back in his cell. I don't want any black eyes or accidental fallings or any of your bullshit, either, Kincaid, understand? The eyes of this town are on us right now and you'd better not fuck up."

Kincaid smiled. "Come on, John. Do I ever fuck up?"

"Yes!" both John and Yannick replied in unison.

274

"I'll have another go at him in the morning," John continued, "but right now I'm going home. I'm dead on my feet. See you people tomorrow," he said and headed for the exit.

Kincaid shook her head. "He nearly killed Ronnie Burk after Ronnie attacked Shay, and he's pointing a finger at me? Why is he always so hard on me?" she asked her captain.

"Because he knows your ass," Yannick said, and they both laughed.

Then Yannick thought about it. He saw something distracting about John Malone today, something unsettling, as if seeing Shay again had affected him far more than Malvaney could even begin to understand. Yannick didn't understand it either, but he thought he saw that same kind of wariness, that same kind of intense concern, that only Shay Turner's presence seemed able to elicit from his boss.

Shay was in Aunt Rae's kitchen wiping down the cabinets and countertops when she saw a flash of light swerve onto the driveway. She left the tiny kitchen, walked through the adjacent tiny living room, and looked out of the bay window. And there was John's big Chevy Silverado parked behind his Porsche. He had given her the keys after he had held her in his arms, in his bed, for nearly two hours. He said for her to drive it to her meeting with Ed Barrington, and that he'd get with her later tonight.

She remembered how apprehensive she felt. The townspeople would know, she knew, that she was driving around in John Malone's Porsche again. She had gotten into an altercation with Blair Malone the last time that had happened. And the talk would crank right back up. But John didn't give a damn. He said people will talk even if there was nothing to talk about. And they, he had told Shay, were just giving them something to talk about. Shay laughed at the time, and said his logic left a lot to be desired. And they kissed, long and passionately, as she accepted the keys.

Before she returned to Brady, she would have never dreamed that their relationship would have moved back to such an intense level this quickly, but she was glad he didn't hesitate. She wanted him. She wanted his kindness and his friendship and, yes, his love. She wanted to be his lover. And although she wasn't sure if she could fully deal with the backlash such a relationship could produce, she wasn't about to give him up because of that. After the way she was lied on and treated even when she and John were playing it as safe as safe could get, she wasn't allowing the people of this town, or anybody else, to dictate who she choose to love.

John was still seated in his truck, on the phone with someone. But just knowing he was coming to see her lifted her heart. Her meeting at the Tribune with Ed Barrington had been an unqualified disaster, with her former boss, a man she used to respect so highly, all but calling her an unethical bitch who had no business anywhere near journalism. The idea of such a person working for a prestigious newspaper like the Tribune, he continued, was out of the question. She knew she needed a friend after that. And not just any friend. She needed John.

He got out of his truck and looked at the little white house before him. There wasn't much to it, really. It was small and rundown, in serious need of a paint job, a yard job, and even a roof from what he could see of it this time of night. It was a far cry from that cute house she used to rent on Bluestone Road. But this one fit right in with the neighborhood. To the right of her new home was a hangout house, rundown too, with a group of shirtless young men shooting dice and listening to loud rap music. Across the street was an apartment complex that was always the center of police raids and drug busts from way back. And down the street, not a hundred yards from Shay's new home, was where they found two of the Dodge murder victims. If her goal, in coming back and settling here, was to have him so worried about her he could barely stomach it, she'd already succeeded beyond her wildest imagination of success.

He walked up to her front porch, all eyes in the vicinity, he knew, on him.

Shay opened the screened door as soon as he stepped onto the porch. "Hey," she said with a smile.

277

"Hey," he said as he opened the door wider and stepped in beside her, kissing her on the lips as soon as he walked in.

When she let him in, and he crossed the threshold, his eyes immediately trailed down, to her short, thin t-shirt, to her light blue Puma shorts, to her blemish-free, shapely legs enticingly familiar to him. But his eyes trailed back up and found themselves resting on her chest, on her well-endowed, braless chest.

When Shay realized why he was staring in that area, she immediately began to move toward the sofa.

"I didn't expect to see you tonight," she said as she walked.

"And why's that?" he asked, following her. He could kick himself for being so obvious. "You're back in town. I told you I'd be over. Why wouldn't you expect to see me?"

She glanced back at him. He was awfully defensive. "It's kind of late is what I meant."

He lifted his head slightly, in acknowledgment of what she meant, and watched as she sat on the sofa, placing her feet underneath her butt. She looked so young to him, so vulnerable sitting there, with her hair now swept back in a thick, French braid that revealed the beauty of her small, round face. He wanted to sit next to her, so he did.

He crossed his legs and turned toward her. He now had on his suit coat so his gun wasn't visible, and she could tell he was taking pains to keep it concealed as kept his suit coat flapped well over his waist area.

"So this is the house," he said, looking past her. The inside was in remarkably better shape than the outside, but still, in his view, not good enough for Shay.

"This is it," she said. "Poor thing did her best to keep it up, but I think as her health suffered, so did this place."

John looked at her. "You're serious about living here permanently?"

"Yes, John, I'm serious. It just needs some TLC, that's all."

"I understand that. But the neighborhood, Shay---"

"Is bad. I know. But there's a lot of good people here too. And the good outweighs the bad by a long shot, trust me." She said this as she reached behind her shoulder and grabbed a small box. John's eyes stared at the nipples jutting out from underneath her t-shirt as she reached. And just like that he was getting a hard-on.

"Look," she said, handing him the box.

"What is it?"

"Open it."

He did. A small pair of pink, knitted gloves were inside.

"The neighbor next door gave them to me."

"Next door? Where all of those hooligans are hanging out?"

"That's her grandson and his friends. They're harmless."

t her. "And you know this how?"

y when I used to come over and visit

:ool. He really liked Aunt Rae and she

nly person uptight around here is you."

John snorted. She may have a point there.

He looked at her. And began to rub her hair. "You're a wonderful sight after a horrible day, you know that?"

Shay smiled. "You aren't so bad yourself."

John couldn't even manage a weak smile. Not because he wasn't pleased that she thought so, but because his mind was still on her. And her beauty. And her sweetness. And the fact that the outline of her gorgeous nipples were poking against her thin shirt and driving him insane. He moved closer to her, and kissed her on the lips.

Shay returned his kiss. Gladly. It had been a long day for her too, a horrible day just as his had been. And she needed a release. She needed it badly.

"Oh, you taste so sweet," John said as he kissed her. He pulled her into his arms and deepened his kiss.

Shay moaned too as he moved down, from her face to her neck, and down further, which, she had suspected, was his intention all along. Because he lifted her blouse and attacked her breasts. Kissing and sucking her nipples, running his tongue along her mounds, drinking up every ounce of her chocolate sweetness.

"Oh, Shay," he said as he pulled her onto his lap,

tossing her shirt completely off, and lapping on her breasts, unable to stop sucking them. Shay leaned back and let him suck. It had been so long. Now it felt so good. She lifted her breasts higher, so that his mouth could enjoy them in full. And he did. He couldn't get enough of her.

He lifted her and carried her to the bedroom. She had to direct him, when he'd come up for air long enough to pay attention. He wanted her so badly he could hardly think straight. He just had to get inside of her. That was the only thing on his mind. Find relief inside of her.

It was a small bedroom, less than a third of his own massive master, but Shay had already cleaned it and made it her own. He laid her on the bed and undressed himself quickly, placing his gun and holster on the nightstand, his eyes never leaving hers. And when he removed his pants and briefs, revealing a penis so thick and stiff, her womanhood began to tingle.

He leaned over and removed her shorts, rendering her naked too. When her womanhood jutted out of her panties like a welcoming delicacy, she could see that lustful look drape his sweet blue eyes.

"Oh, baby," he said as if he hurt, as he moved halfway on top of her and grabbed her nipple with his mouth. His hand began massaging the second breast, causing her to squirm with delight and move her body closer to him. She felt that warm sensation pierce through her as his tongue continued to caress her

281

nipples, moving around the outer edges and then licking the inner hub.

But he didn't stop there. His mouth moved up, to her mouth, and began kissing her so passionately that he moved her body further onto the bed. He crawled his naked body completely on top of hers, his tongue intermingling with her tongue in a long, passionate kiss that had her hand slicing through every inch of his silky brown hair. He wrapped his arms completely around her as he kissed her. She felt his stiff penis against her womanhood, as he rubbed it against her, as he kissed her in a way that she had never experienced. If she had any idea a night with John Malone would be this deliciously intense, she jokingly thought, she would have been back long ago.

After his kiss finally eased enough for her to catch air again, he moved over, to her ear, to the side of her neck, and moved, once again, down to those ripe nipples of hers. He seemed to be a major league breast man, as he seemed unable to get enough of her breasts. He sucked them and licked them and fondled them. He moved back up to her mouth, kissing her there, because he loved her taste too, but he always returned to her breasts.

And then he started moving down, to her stomach, to her outer thighs, and then to her womanhood. He loved the look of her sensually smooth brown skin as he kissed her, as he moved from her thigh to the outer folds of her vagina. And then, to her eternal delight, his tongue moved in.

Shay thought she was not going to be able to bear it when she felt him glide over her clit with tongue lashes that made her want to scream. He knew what he was doing. Of all the men she'd had in her entire life, none of them could compare to the way John Malone made her feel.

John felt the same way about Shay. He'd sexed more women than he ever cared to admit, but Shay was doing something to him. She was making him feel passion again. Not the kind born out of boredom or a need to feel he was not alone, but the kind born out of love and the need to know that he could actually love. Because he loved Shay. He probably knew it years ago, when he first laid eyes on her. And all he could think about, as she explained why she beat up her boyfriend, was why in the world was this sweet, young girl making his heart hammer? He loved her. And the way she made him feel as he made love to her only confirmed that love.

He continued to kiss and suck her clit in such an intense way that Shay's body was lifting off of the bed in tremors of delight. He couldn't stop sucking and licking her. He squeezed her ass as he tongue-fucked her. And all of her grunts and groans didn't make him ease up, as he knew he should, but it made him lick and suck and fuck her harder. So hard that even he couldn't bear it anymore.

283

He moved up her slender, naked body, and shoved his dick in her with an urgency that bordered on panic.

He closed his eyes as his penis felt her pussy for the first time in nearly two years. And as he began to move inside of her, deepening his penetration, he wrapped her in his arms again. Shay closed her eyes too, enraptured by the feeling. She knew it would be intense and passionate and downright sensual. But she had no idea it would be this incredible.

His massive tool felt so full inside of her. It felt as if he was massaging every inch of her vagina. And all she wanted to do was move to the rhythm of his gyrations. And they moved. In unison they moved. A slow motion dance so sensual, so intense, that John kept holding her tighter and tighter as he fucked her. He couldn't let her go.

Shay loved the way he held her. She loved the way he knew how to slide in at just the right angles, with just the right gyrations that hit her on the spot every time he slung that rod. It was as if he couldn't miss. Her folds caved in around his thickness, creating such a resistance that his every movement felt so sharp and tight inside of her. She was, in fact, amazed at how he kept expanding. Just when she thought he could not possible engorge any larger, he did. The further he pushed inside of her, the larger he became.

And when he released, when they came, it felt like a drenching to Shay. John even screamed out a scream so primal and loud that she wondered if the neighbors could hear him. And his gyrations began to increase. She screamed too, when he increased, as the intensity became too much.

"I can't take it, John!" she yelled.

"Yes, you can, baby," he said as he pounded her. "Yes, you can, babe!"

And she did take it. He didn't stop, not for a moment, he didn't slow down, either. He couldn't even if he tried. Because it felt so good. And it felt so right. This was the woman he wanted. And he thrashed her with his love.

When the feelings pulsated their last gasp and ebbed, they both felt as if they had just run a marathon. They felt exhausted. They felt drained. But they felt so triumphant that it thrilled and enthralled them.

Afterwards, as they lay arm in arm, both so drained that they could hardly move, John began to feel a tension began to settle in Shay's naked body. He looked at her. When he lifted her chin to his face, he saw a troubled look in her eyes.

"What's wrong?" he asked her.

But she didn't say anything.

"What is it, Shay? Don't tell me you're regretting what we just did?"

"No, no. Not at all. I'm glad we're back together."

"Then what is it?" When she still wouldn't say, and

that troubled look only heightened, he guessed. "Is it this house, this neighborhood?"

"No, John, it's nothing like that. I like it here. There's a nice spirit in this place."

"Then what?" He thought about it. "Is it that meeting you had with Barrington?"

And as soon as he said it, the look in her eyes confirmed it. "Yes," she admitted.

John's heart began to race. "What happened?" Nothing from Shay. "He took you back, didn't he?" Surely, John figured, even an idiot like Ed would gladly rehire his best reporter.

But Shay moved over onto her back, her face now looking up at her high ceiling. "No," she said. "He wouldn't take me back."

John frowned. "Why the hell not? What happened?"

"It was awful," she said, closing her eyes and then opening them again. "Ed treated me like I was a piece of trash. You should have heard him, John. It was as if all of those lies about me breaking up your marriage and causing your ex-wife to do what she did were true in his eyes. He even began to suggest that what Ronnie did to me, and the fact that he was now in prison, was all my fault too. As if I somehow came onto Ronnie and led him on or something. It was like he. . . It was as if he---"

John placed his hand around the front of her body and began massaging her. "It's okay," he said.

Shay stared into nothingness. It was still raw, still

painful to her. She actually thought Ed was an ally. She just knew she'd always have a home at the Brady Tribune.

"He even had the nerve to say that I wasn't worthy to work for his newspaper," Shay went on. "He said that. He said I wasn't worthy to work there."

She paused, still battling the pain and disappointment. And the tears. "When I tried to tell him that he had it all wrong, that I wasn't guilty of what I was being accused of, he didn't want to hear it. He said even if I didn't break up your marriage I should have never been involved with you anyway. You were a divorced man, why couldn't I be involved with you? It made no sense, and I think he knew it, but it was as if he didn't want to have anything more to do with me."

John placed his fingers on her mouth as her tears began to form. "To hell with what he said. You hear me, Shay?" She looked at him, her tears slowly sliding down. "Ed Barrington is an asshole and we don't give a damn what he has to say. We know the truth. That's all that matters. To hell with him."

Shay's bright brown eyes stared into his bright blue eyes and then she laid, once again, against him. But she wasn't telling him the whole story yet. Not just yet. Because as soon as Ed treated her like dirt and turned her down, she pounded the pavement looking for work. She would flip burgers if she had to. But nobody, not even a burger joint, would hire her. And that was a shame.

But she was a journalist. So she decided, instead of contemplating leaving town again, to go to the lesser known newspapers in town. The first, the Marchman, turned her down cold. They didn't need another reporter, not even one of her caliber. The second newspaper, the Brady Beast, accepted her on the spot. The Beast, as it was called, was the town's smallest newspaper and was popular primarily in the African-American community. It was known almost exclusively for its dogged reporting and its criticisms of the Brady power structure. A power structure that had John Malone at its center.

That was why she held her peace. John would not approve of her working for the Beast, not by the way he was always complaining about their coverage of his police department, and she knew getting him to accept her new position would be a tough sell.

But it wasn't as if she had options. She was a journalist first and last, and she had decided to return to the only town she had ever felt was home, a town that used to treat her warmly until her hard hitting reporting became a threat. The Brady Beast was a major step down for a reporter of her caliber. She knew that. But it would have to do for now, whether John approved or not. She wasn't allowing him or anyone else to be in control of her decisions. And since the Tribune said no, and the Marchman said no, and even Mickey D's said no, she had to go where at least she could pay her bills. And she'd just have to work for the lesser competitor and work hard until it became the Tribune's equal. It was a challenge to Shay. And, given how John felt about the Beast, a risky one.

"Shay?" he said, when her mind seemed to be miles away. She looked at him. He had been dying to ask this question ever since Malvaney phoned him with word of her return.

"Yes?"

"Knowing what you were up against, why did you come back to Brady?"

Shay smiled. It was as complicated as it was simple. "Because as bad as it was here, it was worse in Philadelphia."

John looked at her. "Worse?"

"Yep. There was a lot of loneliness. And drift. And the fact that they treated me as if I was just this hick reporter from Alabama who didn't know squat. I mean, that's the way it is in the newspaper business. It's a small club and they guard their little turf like mama hens. And because I was new and young, I could forget about that. The biggest story I ever got there was a report on a missing manhole cover." John smiled. "I kid you not. In the year-and-nine months that I worked for the Philadelphia Chronicle, that manhole story was the highlight of my career."

She sighed just thinking about it. There was even a glint of concern in her eyes. "And so I thought about the house Aunt Rae had left me, and I thought about the good days I had here before the bad days came, and I, of course, thought about you, and so I gave Ed a call. I told him I was thinking about relocating back to Brady and wanted my old job back. He wasn't jumping up and down, but he never does anyway, so I thought the fact that he said he'd meet with me was just a formality."

Another pause. "So it all started lining up perfectly for me, and all signs were pointing to Brady. Besides, the Chronicle was already whispering about laying off a ton of reporters and I knew I would most certainly be in that group if it happened, given the fact that I contributed nothing worth a damn my entire time there. So the writing was on the wall really and I decided to go back home. It had been like a nightmare just before I left here, yes, I can't even front. It was awful. But I missed this place. And I missed working here." She paused. "And I miss you."

John pulled her tighter into his arms when she said those last words. And he knew, as he held her, that he was all-in once again. He would have to take care of her, not just financially, which would be the easy part, but emotionally, which would be the test. And as she lay in his arms, and as she trusted him to be her man again, his heart was hammering against his chest. There had never been a woman who made him feel so alive and so inadequate at the same time. And for a jackass like Ed Barrington to call this woman, this virtuous woman, unethical and unworthy had him so angry he was practically enraged.

But he kept his feelings in check. For Shay. For this young lady who was nothing short of gold in his arms.

FIFTEEN

Nearly an hour later Shay was fast asleep. John lifted her and laid her between the sheets. And just looking at her nakedness caused his maleness to react and want her again. He wanted to squeeze those breasts and taste her again. But his humanity, and that decency Shay once told him was what she liked the most about him, wouldn't let him do it. He knew she had to be emotionally spent after a day like this day, and needed her rest. He therefore pulled the covers up on his sleeping beauty, stared at her for a long, long time, kissed her on her forehead, and left.

But he didn't go home. Even though he was so exhausted he could barely keep his eyes open. He, instead, drove across town, to a home in the Brady Hills subdivision, after getting the address from his resourceful dispatcher at police headquarters.

The doorbell chimed through the stained-glass door and was eventually opened by Ed Barrington, City Editor of the Brady Tribune newspaper.

"John?" Ed said with surprise in his voice as he tied his brown bathrobe around his body. "What are you doing here? Come in."

"No. I'd rather stay out here."

Although Ed found it odd that he would turn down an invite to come inside, he nonetheless stepped outside, onto his wraparound porch, and closed his front door.

"Forgive me," he said as he exited his home, his small eyes puzzled, "but I'm rather surprised to see our chief of police on my doorstep this time of night. Is it about the arrest?"

John frowned. They hadn't made that arrest public yet. "What arrest?"

"The arrest of the boyfriend of that victim from Hash Street. My sources tell me that Pamela's getting ready to charge him with murder. Is that why you're here?"

"You had a meeting with Shay Turner today," John said, not about to discuss that arrest with him.

Ed suddenly seemed less sure-footed. "That's right."

"You called her unethical. You accused her of being responsible for what happened that night with my ex-wife. You said she wasn't worthy to work at your sorry excuse for a newspaper."

Ed just stood there.

"What's the matter?" John asked, walking closer to him. "You got nothing to say now? You had a lot to say when it was Shay."

"Now look here, John, I don't know what she told you but it wasn't the way she's making it out to be."

"So you're calling her a liar now?" John asked, moving even closer, completely obliterating Ed's personal space.

"I'm not calling her anything, all right? I just---" He

293

tried to back up but found that his back was against his storm door. John backed up. "I just don't think she's the right fit for our newspaper right now, that's why I didn't give her the job."

"And that would have been fine. You could have told her that. But to insinuate that the reason you don't want to rehire the best reporter you've ever had is because of her lack of ethics is what I can't believe."

"That wasn't what I was saying. I was saying that I didn't want to take my readers through that again."

"Through what again? What the fuck does any of what happened between me and my ex-wife have to do with your readers?"

"Nothing, but---"

"That's all you talked about. How Shay supposedly broke up my happy marriage when we both know my marriage to that crazy-ass ex-wife of mine was in shambles the moment after we said 'I Do!'"

"Okay," Ed said, "you're right. It wasn't about that. I just didn't want to rehash what happened all over again."

"So you throw Shay under the bus? Is that it? What has she ever done to you, Ed, but give you her all?"

The emotion in John's voice stunned Ed Barrington. He knew John had the hots for Shay, but he always assumed it was only just a sexual thing. Even Ed, on occasion, had the hots for Shay Turner. He attempted to smile. "Damn, John," he said playfully, "that pussy still that good after all this time?"

John grabbed Ed by the catch of his robe so hard that he feared he could crush him. "You listen to me you sawed-off sonafabitch! If you ever even think about disrespecting Shay Turner again, I will personally kick your ass. Do I make myself clear, Barrington?" When he didn't immediately respond, John slammed him against the back of the storm door. "Do I make myself clear, Barrington?" he asked again.

"Yes," Ed said quickly. He knew making an enemy of the chief of police would be a nightmare for his newspaper. When he gave Shay the boot, he had no idea they would still be this tight. If he had known, he realized, he would have hired Shay on the spot. "Look, I'm sorry, John. I didn't mean to---"

"Don't tell me you're sorry. You tell it to Shay. Understood?"

Ed hesitated.

John slammed him again. " Understood?"

"Yes! I understand, dammit! I'll, I'll take care of it tomorrow. Now if you like."

"Not now, it's late. She's asleep. Tomorrow."

"Okay," Ed nodded, wondering lustfully if John had just left the sleeping Shay. And if John had just put a pounding on her that caused her to have fallen asleep. The idea of a dick inside of Shay Turner, a woman he'd always wanted to get his dick inside of, was giving him a hard-on. "I'll take care of it," he said.

John exhaled, and released Ed.

Then John hesitated. "For the record," he finally said, "she had nothing to do with what happened in my marriage. Nothing. And if you ever say to anybody that she did, you'll have to answer to me. Understood?"

Ed nodded his head, amazed that a hard-hearted man like John Malone could actually care for somebody. "I understand," he said. But this time he seemed to mean it.

John was a little embarrassed by his strong arm tactics, he already had a reputation for being too brutal with people, but those tears in Shay's eyes broke his heart. And he was serving notice that she was not going to be their whipping girl this time around.

He left. And this time he did take himself home.

The next morning and Shay was on the road early. It was her first day of her new job and she was already antsy. The mechanic had already said that her Beetle wouldn't be ready for another few days, so she ended up with John's Porsche again. Not that she mind driving it. She loved driving it. It was just that she wasn't all that crazy about the attention driving it would automatically bring on her.

But she wasn't trying to live her life for other people now. She had too much to lose now. She therefore drove it proudly and drove it into the first free parking space she could find outside of the Brady Beast newspaper building. Her cell phone started ringing just

296

as she did.

She answered before she stepped out. When she heard Ed Barrington's voice, she frowned.

"Good morning, Shay," he said so casually that it stunned her.

"May I help you?" she asked, still wondering what nerve he had calling her at all.

"I know you're wondering why I'm phoning."

"It has crossed my mind, you'd be right about that. Now what is it?" Her patience, and respect for him, flew out the window during that so-called meeting yesterday.

"I was calling to see if you were still interested in the job."

Now she was really baffled. "Excuse me? What job?"

"The job here, at the Tribune. I'm offering it to you."

Shay frowned. "You're offering me . . . wait a minute. Yesterday I wasn't worthy to step foot in your precious building, but today I not only can step foot up in there, but I can work there too? Is that what you're telling me?"

"That's what I'm saying, yes, Shay, I'm offering you your old job back."

This man must be out of his mind. What was wrong with people? Did they think she was made of stone and their insults didn't hurt her to her core? "I don't get your point," she said. "Why would you be offering me a job you told me you wouldn't allow me to have if I was the last journalist on earth, Ed? What are you talking about?"

"I didn't say that."

"You did say that."

"Now look, I'm not going to argue with you. I'm offering you the job, okay? Now you can take it or leave it."

"Fine," Shay said, amazed that it wasn't already obvious. "I leave it," she said, and slammed shut her phone. And then she turned the whole thing off.

She just sat there, to compose herself. What the hell, she wondered. How could he think that she'd want anything to do with him or his newspaper ever again?

Then she thought about John. She cried on his shoulders once again and he held her just like he used to do. Put her to bed too. And knowing John, knowing how enraged he could sometimes become, she could just see him driving right over to Ed's house and threatening him with bodily harm if he didn't what? Give her the job? That made no sense. Surely he didn't think she would work for Ed Barrington after the way he treated her.

Unless, she thought again, he didn't think she had any other prospects. It wasn't like Brady was this big town loaded with newspapers. There were only three. And maybe he didn't think she'd lower herself to work for the other two. He never knew that she not only interviewed at both of those "lower" newspapers, but the lady who interviewed her for the Brady Beast hired her on the spot.

Only she didn't mention that bit of news to John.

Especially since she knew he would flip his lid when he did find out.

And although she was grateful for his help, she had to remind him that she could fight her own battles. Although, she thought as she got out of his Porsche, you wouldn't know it by the way she went crying to daddy last night. As if she was some kid. You also wouldn't know it by the way she just stepped out of daddy's car. She smiled and shook her head. This homecoming was about as low-key, about as unassuming as a lion in the streets.

She continued to smile as she grabbed her briefcase off of the backseat, her shoulder bag off of the front seat, and hurried for the entrance of the large, rustic building.

Although the Brady Beast newspaper was located on the building's top floor, the fourth floor, the dilapidated-looking elevator was out of order and she therefore had to walk up stairs. Or run, because she was running late. Running late for her first day of work, at a newspaper that was her absolute last choice, in a return to Brady that could only be described as unsettling.

Two years ago, or even two months ago, working at a place like this would have been unthinkable. But that maddening meeting with Ed Barrington put an end to any illusions she had of returning to the way things used to be. She left the Tribune after that meeting, sat in her car in tears for nearly thirty straight minutes, this close to calling John even then and telling him how badly Ed had treated her.

But she didn't stay in that weakened state very long. Because Shay Turner was practical if she was anything. She knew she had to eat, and had bills to pay, so she therefore picked up her little wounded pride and drove herself to some burger joints and restaurants around town, and then to the next newspaper in town. And finally ended up at the Beast.

By contrast, the Brady Beast was so thrilled to have a reporter of her caliber, so eager to have that tough-as-nails reporter once known as No-nonsense Shay, that they hired her on the spot. And she was grateful. Very grateful. But to pretend to be overjoyed would be a lie. For a reporter with Shay's background and experience to accept a job at a small in every way daily like the Brady Beast was akin to the president of a major university becoming its janitor. It was a job, yes, it was an honest day's work, but there was really no comparison.

But now, as she sat in the small newsroom where paint peeled and water spots dotted the ceiling, as she waited for the editor to come and meet her in person for the first time, she wondered if she had made the right decision. Was it nothing more than foolish pride that caused her to thumb her nose at Ed's change of heart and turn down his offer? Would that same pride cause her to want to work doubly hard to prove some point to them? She leaned her head back and closed her eyes. Her prayer was that it wasn't so; that she didn't come all this way, take this decidedly humbled position, just to prove a point.

When she opened her eyes, however, she didn't feel rejuvenated, or even at peace with her decision. She was startled. For standing before her was a tall, muscular white woman who was staring unabashedly at her. She had thick, red hair and a round, kind face. She smiled a perfectly straight, perfectly white, toothpaste-commercial smile.

"Hello there," she said, extending her hand. "I'm Paige Kent."

Shay immediately knew the name. She was the Brady Beast's senior editor and the woman who her interviewer said would be her supervisor. She stood quickly, and shook her hand. "Miss Kent. Please to meet you."

Paige smiled. "No you didn't call me ma'am. How old are you?"

"Twenty-eight."

"Well, I'm thirty-one. Which is, unless my math fails me, a distinction without a difference. The name's Paige. No more ma'am from you."

Shay nodded. "Yes, ma'am." Then, when she looked sidelong at her, Shay smiled: "Just kidding."

Paige smiled, too, and looked down at Shay's small but curvy body, up at her long hair made sleek in a straight, layered style, and into her pretty, oak-brown face. Her remarkably gorgeous face, she noted. Then she pointed at her. "I knew I was going to like you. Now come," she added, walking away from her. "Let's talk."

Shay quickly grabbed her briefcase and shoulder bag and followed her rather masculine-walking supervisor across the newsroom. Other reporters glared at her as she walked with Paige, as if her presence there meant instant competition. When she got into the small, but neat office, Paige seemed to have picked up on that, too.

She leaned against the edge of her desk, legs stretched out and crossed at the ankles, and pulled up the sleeves of her sweat shirt. "They won't make it easy for you," she said. "Not because of anything you've done, but because they know your history."

"My history?" Shay asked nervously. Was she talking about John's ex-wife and that craziness that night?

Paige quickly clarified. "They know that you once worked for the Tribune, which every one of them has tried to do at some point in their careers and didn't make it. And they know about your relationship with Chief Malone. At least the relationship you used to have with him."

"Why would my relationship with anyone be of concern to them?"

"Because they're human beings, Shay. And because they thought such an affair was inappropriate for a professional journalist."

Shay found that rather judgmental, but she let it slide.

"They won't make it easy for you," Paige continued. "But I think you're tough enough to take it."

"Sure thing," Shay said, attempting to sound tough, although she didn't feel so tough.

Paige smiled, as if she understood it, too. "Before I forget," she said, reaching behind her and grabbing a press badge from off of the desk. "Here are your credentials."

Shay took the badge, which bore her name and, underneath, the newspaper's name, and she smiled. "That was fast."

"Oh, we're thrilled to have you, make no mistake about that. You're our lottery pick. Our prized catch yet. We have a lot of high hopes riding on you."

Shay didn't know what to say to that. She didn't know if she should be flattered to be so highly thought of, or to be suspicious that this newspaper was even more small potatoes than she had thought.

"Thanks," was all she could manage to say.

"Anyway," Paige said, rising and causing Shay to rise, too, "your desk has your name plate on it, so you can't miss it. Why don't you drop some of your gear and get on over to the police station."

"The police station?"

"Yeah. I want you to interview Willie Glazer. I don't know if John Malone told you about the case?"

Shay hesitated. She didn't like the way she put that. "I've heard about the case, yes," was all she'd say.

"Good. His trial begins in three months."

"That trial is still three months away?"

"Yep. Thanks to our slow-as-molasses criminal justice system. And all of the continuances the defense has filed."

"But why would you want me to interview him? I thought he confessed."

"He did. But he now says it was a coerced confession. And I mean he denounced that confession the very next day after he supposedly made it. Our readers don't believe it was a true confession at all. They aren't buying it."

"But I still don't get your angle. What can I bring to the table that's not already there?"

"Since you just got back in town you aren't tainted yet by all of the back and forth. You can take a look at the case with fresh eyes. It'll be like coming full circle for you. You are, after all, the person who blew the lid off of those Dodge killings cover up to begin with. And again," she added, "our readers don't agree that the cops have the right man. They think Glazer's innocent. It's a case that has torn this community apart, right down racial lines."

Shay nodded. John had told her about it.

"Yeah, Glazer's a kind of drifter who drifts in and out of town," Paige continued, "but he comes from a good family. Some blacks aren't buying him as the Dodge serial killer. They think Malone's just covering his ass.

They figure it's because it's been such a long time that he had to pin it on somebody."

That sounded nonsensical to Shay, but she let that slide too. "How are things looking for Glazer?"

"Awful. It doesn't look good for him at all. I've got a reporter covering the trial, so don't worry about that angle. I want you covering Glazer. Work some of that magic you used to work when you were with the Tribune. Get access to him. No other reporter's been able to, but I have confidence in you. Get a good story for us like you did for the Trib. Which, reminds me, I do have a question. Why aren't you back working with the Tribune?"

Shay didn't hesitate. "They didn't want me back," she said.

Paige nodded. "I appreciate your honesty," she said. Okay. Good." She said this and began walking behind her desk. "Close the door behind you, will you?" She immediately picked up his phone and began pressing buttons.

She didn't waste words, Shay mused, as she stepped out of the office and began a search for her desk. She found it, near the front of the newsroom, by the file cabinets. Well kid, she thought with a smile, remembering how her desk was in the back of the newsroom at the Tribune, you're moving on up. Then she shook her head, and took a seat.

305

John Malone stood at the wall-sized window in his third floor office and looked out at the town around him. From the slow-moving traffic, to the unhurried steps of the pedestrians, to the clean, and quiet, and sanity, it was a far cry from his days back in Baton Rouge. When he first arrived here the slow pace, the easiness, drove him crazy. Now he welcomed the ease. And understood it. And became increasingly agitated whenever his peace was disturbed.

Which was why he had been trying to get Shay on the phone all morning. He had a realtor friend of his who was willing to work with her, but first he had to convince her that she needed to move. The idea of his woman living in such a crime infested area was disconcerting to him on every level and he wanted her out of there as fast as she would agree to leave. He also knew that getting her to agree would be a tall order. But he had to try.

And that was why he tried her cell phone once again. And it went straight to voice mail once again.

"May I help you, Miss?" the white-haired policeman asked as Shay walked up to the visitor's desk outside the jail section of the Brady Police Department.

She smiled. "Yes, you may help me. I'm here to see one of your prisoners: Willie Glazer."

"Willie Glazer?" the officer asked incredulously. "And you are?"

"Shay Turner," Shay said, displaying her newly

306

minted press pass. "With the Brady Beast."

The officer chuckled. "What, you couldn't get on at a real newspaper, dearie? Had to bring up the rear? The Brady Beast. Give me a break! Look lady, ain't no reporter gettin' in to see our most celebrated prisoner, and especially not one from that sorry excuse for a newspaper like yours. Every time something goes wrong in this town it's the cops fault. Always blamin' us. Always whippin' up the masses into a frenzy over a bunch of nonsense. Brady Beast. Don't mention that name in my presence."

Shay tried not to show her displeasure with the officer's disrespect. He was, after all, just venting some beef, real or imagined, he had with a newspaper she could not account for because she'd only been in its employ all of one day. She was also surprised that he didn't know who she was. But then again, she thought, two years was a long time ago. Most cops probably didn't remember her name. They undoubtedly remembered the circumstances surrounding her name, but probably not her name. So she held back. Until he kept on talking.

"So why don't you run along," he said, "and write the kind of stories the Beast is famous for. Those stories that have everything to do with making a cop look bad. Or, since you're so young and pretty, you can be their current events reporter. Yeah, that's more to your liking, ain't it, dearie? You can write stories about the prom, or the apple blossom parade, or I know, the watermelon festival."

Another cop, seated down from him, chuckled too.

By now Shay was inwardly fuming, especially when the officer laughed again, full of himself and what he considered his clever joke. She exhaled. Hated to do it, hated it passionately, but that darn pride again. "I wish to see John, please," she said purposely vague, and the officer, as she had expected, looked at her strangely. He knew who John was, but he seemed surprised that she would know John.

"John?" he said. Even he wasn't allowed to call the chief by his first name.

"That's right. Chief John Malone. A friend of mine. Please tell him I'm here and wish to see him."

The officer was still smiling, as if he didn't quite believe her, but Shay could see the cracks in his confidence. "You know the chief?"

"I do. Call him, please."

His smile was now gone, as he stared at Shay. After a moment he picked up the phone, albeit reluctantly, and dialed an extension.

"This is Madge."

"Hey Madge, this Cliff. Chief in?"

"And who wants to know?"

"Some female. Claims to be a friend of his. Can you check it out for me?"

"And get my head knocked off because she's full of

crap? You can check it out for yourself. I'll put you through."

Cliff took a deep breath as Madge clicked off and, within seconds, the chief's always impatient-sounding voice clicked on. "Yes?" Malone said and Cliff, out of habit, sat erect.

"Yes, sir, this is Cliff downstairs. Have a woman here wanting to get in to see Willie Glazer, sir."

"So? You know we aren't letting anybody in to see him now, unless it's his attorney or a family member. Is it either one of them?"

"No, sir."

"Then get rid of her officer, and stop bothering me."

"She says she knows you, sir."

"She knows me? Well who is it?"

"A Shay Turner. Says she works for---"

"I'll be right down," Malone said quickly and hung up. Cliff, astounded, hesitated then hung up, too. He looked at Shay. Cleared his throat.

"He'll be right down, ma'am," he said, and the other officer looked at him. "You can have a seat right over there. Would you like some coffee, or maybe some tea?"

Shay wanted to smile, but she didn't. "No," she said. "Thank-you." Then she walked over to a group of metal chairs against the wall and sat down. She should have felt some sense of vindication, given the officer's nasty little remarks, but she didn't. Why did she let that idiot cause her to pull out her John card and plunge him, once again, into her problems when that was the last thing she wanted to do? And she did it just because some desk cop disrespected her? She didn't even know the joker, how could she allow him to have such power over her? Was her pride that sensitive now?

"Chief Malone," she heard Cliff's voice say and she looked up just as John was walking toward her, ignoring the officer. He looked grim like he usually looked and wouldn't take his beautiful blue eyes away from her. He was in shirt sleeves today, which highlighted his thick, muscular arms, and, as usual, Shay's heart beat quickened at just the sight of him.

"Hello, John," she said when he made his way up to her.

He sat down beside her. "I've been trying to reach you all morning," he said. "Where have you been?"

"Really?" she said. She reached into her shoulder bag and pulled out her cell phone. It was only then did she realize that, after talking with Ed, she had angrily turned it off. "My cell phone is off."

"That much I've already gathered. Why is it off is the question? And what is this about you wanting to see Glazer?"

Shay swallowed hard. She hadn't planned on telling him right here and right now, but here was as good a place as any. "Today was my first day at work," she said. "I didn't want any distractions."

John didn't say anything to that. He stared at her.

310

"Your first day at work?"

"That's right. And I didn't want any distractions."

Shay could tell that he was confused. But before she could tell him anything, he placed his hand on the press badge around her neck and turned it over. *Brady Beast* was written in bold, semicircle letterings. John looked at those words and then looked into her eyes.

"They hired me on the spot," she said.

"I'm sure they did," replied John.

"Upset?"

"Hell no," he said, standing to his feet. She stood too. "At least you'll be doing what you love. It beats crawling back to that asshole Ed Barrington."

"So you weren't the one who told Ed to call and offer me my job back? You didn't talk to him?"

"I talked to him, yes. But I didn't tell him to offer you any job. I told him to apologize to you."

Shay's heart swelled with love for this man. "Thanks."

"So he offered you the job?"

"Yes."

"I hope you told him to go fuck himself."

Shay smiled. "Something like that, yes."

"Good," he said. John then stared at her. His feelings for her had always been strong and intense, but now that she was back within his grasp, his feelings seemed stronger and even more intense. It was as if he was suddenly realizing just what her two-year absence

311

really meant to him. He was seeing what he almost lost in a new light, and it was a disturbing realization.

"So why were you trying to reach me all morning?" she asked, hoping he would say something sweet, like he was calling to say he loved her.

"I wanted you to meet with a realtor friend of mine."

Shay looked at John. "A realtor? Why would I need to meet with a realtor?"

"She can help you find a new home."

"I have a home."

"In Dodge, Shay."

"I like my house. It's paid for. I'm not about to sell Aunt Rae's house just so I can stay in some supposedly better neighborhood. Crime is everywhere, John. There are no safe havens."

"I know that. But---"

"No but. I have a home that's paid for, and I intend to keep my home. Case closed. For real."

John stared at Shay. Those two years away had toughened her too, although, he'd be the first to admit, she was already pretty tough. He exhaled. "I just want you safe, babe."

"I understand that. But I feel like I'm safe. My neighbors are nice people. They're poor, yes, some of them are very poor, but they're good people. I like where I'm living."

John nodded. "Okay," he said, especially since he knew, right now, he didn't really have a vote. "So you want to see Glazer?" he asked her.

"That would be great. My supervisor, Paige Kent, I don't know if you know her?"

"I know her."

Shay wondered why he said it as if Paige was a bitter taste in his mouth. "She wants me to hear what he has to say."

"I can tell you what he has to say. 'I'm innocent, I didn't do it,' that's all he always says."

Shay smiled. "Understood. But I sort of have to hear it directly from the prisoner before I can put it in a story."

John snorted. And then walked, with Shay following him, back over to the desk cop. Cliff stood to his feet.

"Take us to the visitor's room, Cliff, and then call up Glazer."

"Yes, sir, Chief," Cliff said and immediately pressed the button that opened a steel side door. He then hurried through the door. John and Shay, with John placing his hand in the small of her back, followed Cliff.

Cliff unlocked a tiny visitor's room where Shay could sit down and talk to the prisoner by way of phone and a bullet-proof window. Shay was surprised, however, when John walked into the room with her. She had expected a private conversation with Glazer.

John knew she had wanted some privacy, but no way was he leaving his woman back here with this killer. Even though it was virtually impossible that he could get

313

out, John still wasn't taking any chances.

Shay didn't like it, but she didn't say a word. He was already breaking protocol by allowing her back there to begin with. She wasn't about to play the diva and push it.

She took a seat in the chair while John, standing beside her in his gorgeously-appointed Armani suit, pulled out his handkerchief and wiped down the phone that she would be using to communicate with Glazer. When he finished he leaned toward her and they kissed on the lips.

"I'm sorry it didn't work out for you at the Trib," he said as he kissed her again.

She smiled faintly. "Me too. But I plan to do my best for the Brady Beast."

John placed his hand on the side of her face, a look of consternation on his face. "You deserve better than the Beast. If it was up to me you'd own that *got*damn Tribune and fire Ed's ass."

Shay knew what he meant. "Thanks," she said. "Thanks for the vote of confidence."

"What are you thanking me for? You're my woman. I'll do anything for you."

John's words hung in the air like an alien object. He was stunned that a man like him, who was rarely emotional, would have said such emotional words. And Shay was stunned too. Because something between them changed at that very instant. And it was an earth-shifting change they couldn't even begin to verbalize.

314

They stared into each other's eyes.

Although John Malone was still the most attractive man Shay had ever known, those burdens he bore were beginning to show in his face. His youthfulness was fast becoming a thing of the past, and he was beginning to look every inch of his thirty-nine years. Although, Shay also noticed, he was still the best looking, sexiest, most desirable thirty-nine year old she'd ever seen.

John, however, saw Shay in just the opposite light. To him she didn't look anywhere near her twenty-eight years. It was as if time had stood still for her, in a wonderfully youthful, vibrant way, and time was accelerating for him. And he, too, knew it was the burdens he bore. Of losing his son, of being forced to kill his ex-wife, of being responsible for a police department that had him in crisis mode almost every day of every week. But his heart was relieved to see that those two years away had helped Shay. They had devastated him, but they had helped Shay. It made their separation worth it when he saw just how much she'd been helped.

Willie Glazer, a short, light-skinned black male with curly red hair, entered the prisoner's room still in shackles. He walked up to the chair in front of Shay's window and plopped down. Although both hands were chained, he was able to retrieve the telephone without effort, as if he was well familiar with maneuvering in chains.

"Who are you?" he asked her as soon as the phone

315

hit his ear.

"I'm Shay Turner, a reporter with the Brady Beast," Shay said, pulling a pad and pen from her shoulder bag. "And I take it you're William Glazer."

"Willie," Glazer said, and then looked over at John. John was now leaned against the wall behind Shay, his big arms folded like a prison guard. Glazer frowned. "Why he got to be here?" he wanted to know. "I don't want that bastard sitting in on my conversations."

"Tough," John said. "Now get on with it."

Shay waited until she had Glazer's attention before she began her questioning. But it was a fruitless interview. Because John was right. Every answer he gave was the same: I'm innocent, I didn't do it. Over and over. He would never deter from his rock hard profession of innocence.

Shay was accustomed to that. She'd been a reporter long enough to have interviewed many prisoners. All of them were always innocent. But, by the end of her interview with Glazer, she was kind of confused. He admitted many things unfavorable to him. He admitted being a drug addict. He admitted being strung out on drugs during that entire year when thirteen prostitutes were killed. He even admitted hanging out with hookers. But he kept insisting that he never killed anyone.

As she and John walked down the corridor toward the exit door, his hand once again in the small of her back, she was concerned. "That was strange," she said.

316

"What was strange about it?" he asked.

"The way he admitted so much. It's been my experience that liars never cop to anything. They claim to be as innocent as the driven snow on everything."

"Or," John said, "they're more sadistic than your average liar and know how to finesse it."

Shay didn't say anything to that. She knew she wouldn't have a willing audience with John. He arrested Glazer and as far as he was concerned they had the right guy. Pointblank. She'd run her feelings by Paige.

John held her by the arms when they reached the exit door, before he pressed the request to exit button. Shay looked into his eyes.

"I don't want you to get caught up in any drama that newspaper loves to whip up, Shay," he said to her. "Don't get caught up in it. I want you to remain the level-headed journalist I know you are."

Shay smiled. "I will. You know I will."

"That's my girl," John said, as lines of age appeared on the side of his eyes. And once again that feeling of inadequacy, of not being good enough for her, began to overtake him. He squeezed her arms. "Take care of yourself out there," he said, kissed her hard on the mouth, and then pressed the button.

SIXTEEN

Over the next three months Shay did take care of herself, working stories for the Brady Beast that quickly moved her to the top of the heap of Beast reporters. Not that it was much competition. Most of the reporters who worked there weren't very good to begin with, and those who did have it in them were already burned out shells of what they used to be.

But Shay was soaring. Almost every story she wrote ended up with the choice byline at the head of the page. Paige began to rely on her more and more, giving her only the best stories to cover to begin with, which only added to her meteoric rise to the top. John was pleased with her success, but he also continued to caution her about the Beast. It had a way, he once said, of eating its own. Don't get caught up in the drama. One false move and they'd kick her to the curb faster than she could blink.

Shay smiled when he said that, and kept working hard.

And she was also constantly working the Glazer story, attempting to find a new angle, a new wrinkle, something new. She interviewed his parents, his respectable friends, his drug addicted friends. But everywhere she looked, every lead she followed, turned out to be a dead end. And his trial date was fast approaching.

318

Her relationship with John was also a major part of her existence. They both were working their brains out, sometimes fourteen hour days for each of them. But they always made time to have dinner together at least a few times every week. No matter what. Either at Shay's home or John's, or sometimes at a fancy restaurant. They'd always enjoy a meal and talk about anything, everything, except their work. They didn't want to bring the work into it. And it was a wonderful idea. Until, two days before the Glazer trial was set to begin, Shay received two phone calls that instantly changed their calculations.

She was working at her desk in the newsroom of the Brady Beast. It was a story about a septic tank leak over on the south side that had many residents smelling the stink for days on end. Shay was dramatizing their plight. Her story, which she was already told would be the lead for tomorrow's paper, had to have a lot of human drama enfolded into it. So she was working feverishly on that end of the story, when her desk phone rang. She quickly answered, her eyes still on her computer screen.

"Turner," she said quickly.

"It's me, babe, hi," John replied.

She smiled, and leaned back. "Well, hello there, stranger." They hadn't been able to see each other for nearly a week. She understood: the Glazer trial was coming up in two days and he and his men had been working overtime to prepare for any community unrest that might occur. "What's up?"

"A dinner party, at Mayor Fletchette's, tonight."

"Okay," Shay said slowly. Surely this bit of news had nothing to do with her.

"I've been told, by none other than the mayor himself, that my attendance is mandatory."

"Really? That's kind of high school."

"And if that phrase doesn't fit our beloved mayor," John said, "I don't know what does."

Shay laughed.

"Anyway, I want you with me."

Shay's heart dropped. It would be the first time they would be stepping out on the Brady social scene. And to let their first time occur at such a high-profile event. "You sure, John?" she asked him.

"I'm positive. I want you with me." He exhaled. "I know you wanted to keep a low profile, babe, I know. But I don't want to hide the best thing about me under the radar. I want you with me. Out in public. On my arm."

Shay smiled. He was certain. "Then I shall be with you."

She could tell that he smiled too. "That's my girl," he said the way he always said it, they talked a little small talk, and then hung up.

Shay hadn't hung up the phone five minutes when it rang again. And once again it was a police chief. But it wasn't John.

"Chief Cobber, did you say?" she asked as the man

on the other end of the phone had a deep-southern voice.

"Cobbler," he said, "with an L."

"And you're the police chief in Hurley, Mississippi?"

"Yes, ma'am."

Shay had never heard of Hurley, Mississippi. Why in the world would its' chief of police be calling her? "How may I help you?"

"It's about that fellow you have in your jail there, that Willie Glazer fellow."

Shay hesitated. "What about him?"

"Well, it's kind of embarrassing really. But here goes anyway. I'm calling because I had him in my jail for two whole weeks."

"And?"

"And then I let him go. He wasn't the car thief we were looking for."

Car thief? Now Shay was confused. "I don't understand."

"What I'm saying is that he couldn't have killed three of those thirteen girls y'all saying he killed. He was in my custody when three of those girls were killed."

Shay's heart began to pound. "He was in your jail---"

"For two straight weeks, that's right, the same two weeks y'all saying three of those girls were killed. There's no way he could have killed them. At least not them three."

Shay could hardly believe it. "And you have proof of all of this?"

321

"I'm looking at my records right now."

Shay's heart began to pound with excitement. But then she remembered John's words of caution. Don't get caught up in the drama, he'd told her. So she exhaled, and slowed this train down.

"Now wait a minute," she said. "We've had Glazer incarcerated for nearly a year now. There's been article after article, news story after news story about him and his alleged crimes. Yet you wait two days before his trial to come forward with this rather startling information?"

"I know. That's why I'm embarrassed. I never put two and two together. We don't follow the story closely here in Mississippi, mind, like y'all following it in Alabama. But we do follow it. And I was following it. But I never put two and two together until I saw this channel 9 broadcast here that said his full name. It was the first time I learned his full name. And that's when I remembered. I didn't remember his face, but I remembered that name. I remembered how strung out on drugs he was. He was like a drifter and was hitch-hiking around with some other druggies, but apparently the others had moved on. He was too high to keep going and that's when I found him, high as a kite on the street. I thought he was the guy who had stolen a car from this car lot earlier that night. That's why I arrested him. When I caught the real thief, I let him go. I never thought about that guy again, until I heard his full name on Channel 9. And I checked it out."

The man had said a mouthful. Shay didn't even

know where to begin. She didn't even know Glazer's full name. "I'm a little confused, sir."

"Okay, let me make myself clearer. Glazer's full name is William Cletis Glazer. It's the Cletis that I remembered."

"Why would you remember Cletis?"

"Because that's my name, too," the chief said and Shay's heart began to pound again. Because it made perfect sense. Although his name, Cletis Cobbler, didn't.

"So you heard his middle name, remembered you had a guy locked up once with that middle name, and you checked your records?"

"That's right. That's when I saw it. It was William Cletis Glazer. I remembered talking to him about his middle name. He was too strung out on drugs to talk to me, though. But it's not that common a name, not even here in Mississippi. And it was spelled the same way mine was spelled."

It sounded too good to be true. But if it was, Shay couldn't help but thinking, she could win a Pulitzer for something this big.

"Why didn't you go to the Brady police, sir, if you have this evidence?"

"Because I'm a cop myself, miss. Yeah, Hurley is small, I'll grant you that. We're a predominately black town with only three hundred residents. We're small as small can get. But I'm a cop and I know how cops can be. I don't want my evidence disappearing before you

323

have a chance to see it. And I know it sounds far-fetched, but believe me, I'm a cop. It happens."

Shay nodded. She believed him. "Can I drive over now, sir, and see your records for myself?"

"You can drive over, but not now. I'm closing shop for today. But drive over tomorrow morning. I'll be here."

Shay got the address from the chief, hung up the phone, and then contacted Glazer's attorney to get some info on one sticking point. Then she hurried to Paige's office. When she laid out what she had, Paige sat down.

"Do you believe him?" she asked Shay.

"I don't know. Glazer did confess to those killings."

"A confession," Paige reminded Shay, "he now says he was forced into making."

"I know. I plan to check the story out, at any rate. But I have my doubts."

"So do I," Paige said, "which is a good thing. And there's still the question of why Glazer didn't mention this arrest if it occurred when this chief says it occurred."

"Glazer did mention it," Shay said. "That's the intriguing part. I just got off of the phone with his attorney, because I had that same question in my mind too. But according to the attorney, Glazer did tell him about being arrested. Only Glazer believed he was locked up in a jail in Georgia at the time of some of those killings. He didn't remember the town or anything else, just that he believed it was Georgia. And he was so high and then so sick from being forced to detox back then that he didn't remember much of any of it. But his attorney tried to get info anyway. He contacted every Georgia jail they could find. And he found out that Glazer had been in a Georgia jail all right, but he had been there over five years ago. Long before any of those girls were killed. So that was that."

"And his lawyer never thought to check Mississippi?" Paige asked.

"Never crossed his mind. But why would it? They'd already proven that Glazer had his dates off by at least a few years. They figured there was nothing more to check out."

"Glazer is a mess of a human being," Paige said. "He spent years drunk or high or both almost every single day. He once said he couldn't remember being sober for ten minutes in the last ten years. But he still deserves justice."

Shay nodded. "Right."

Paige smiled. "Do you realize what this means if that police chief is telling the truth, Shay? The prosecution says that every one of those thirteen crimes were identical. Identical was the word they used in their press conference. Which means---"

"If Glazer was locked up in a Mississippi jail at the same time that three of those murders had been committed," Shay interjected, "then how could he have committed those three particular murders?"

"Right."

"And," Shay went on, "it will call into question whether or not he committed any of those murders."

Paige nodded. "But wait a minute. What if Pamela Ansley and her prosecution team claim copycat?"

"They can't," Shay quickly pointed out. "I read all of those old news reports. At that same press conference Pamela Ansley said that the copycat theory was out of the question because the killer used certain methods that she and the police never made public."

Paige leaned back. Satisfied. "Go see this police chief tomorrow," she ordered. "In fact, I'll go with you."

Shay smiled. She knew she was on to something now.

"And Shay," Paige said when Shay was about to leave, "I know you and Malone are close, but you cannot, under any circumstances, give him a heads up on this story. If you do, and his cops get to that police chief, his evidence might suddenly disappear. You heard what the man said? He was calling you because he knew you were searching for the truth. He's a cop himself. If he believes his evidence is safer in your hands, you had better believe him. He knows you want the truth. He also knows what Malone and those cops of his want."

"And what's that?" Shay asked.

"They want a way to disprove the truth," Paige replied.

And although Shay loved John, she also knew he was one of those cops who believed what he believed

326

and would stick to his belief even, perhaps, in the face of new information. Eventually he would see the light. But he was a cop through and through. It would take an awful lot to get him to that light.

She therefore agreed with Paige, to a point. She would keep it under wraps for now. At least until she had a chance to eyeball and photocopy the evidence for herself. Then, she decided, she would have to tell John something. At least before he reads it in the paper for himself.

John arrived at Shay's house driving his Porsche and wearing his seldom worn pinstripe suit. He parked behind Shay's completely repaired VW Beetle and just sat there, behind the steering wheel. He dreaded going to some dinner party tonight, especially when they were still working out the logistics for the upcoming Glazer trial and he didn't have this kind of time. But the mayor was his boss, and he had made it an order. He had no choice.

He got out of his car and lumbered toward the front porch. The usual crowd of young people were next door, playing their loud music and drinking their bottles of beer. One of them, shirtless and skinny, yelled, "Yo, Chief!" and John glanced his way.

"Don't hit that thang too hard now!" the young man said to laughter from his friends.

"Why don't I toss you in a cell so they can hit yours,"

327

John yelled back, and the young man's buddies fell out laughing again.

John walked up the steps, across the porch, and rang Shay's bell. When she opened the door, in her sleek white cocktail dress with red heels and earrings, her hair to one side in a sweep down the front of her dress, her big eyes like a glow of light, John lost it.

"Ah, geez," he said as he made his way into the house, slammed the front door, and grabbed Shay by the hand.

"John, what are you doing?" Shay asked smilingly as he all but dragged her down the hall and into her bedroom. By now she knew what he was doing as he laid her on her back with her legs over the side of the bed.

"Oh, baby," he said as he slung off her panties, opened her legs as wide as they could go, dropped to his knees and began tasting her.

Shay began to move around on the bed as he tasted her. It no longer mattered that she'd just put on that dress. It no longer mattered that she'd spent hours in front of the mirror beautifying her hair. She preferred John. She preferred his mouth devouring her pussy as if it was water on a deserted island. And he had to have it. He licked and kissed and sucked so long that her pink pussy turned red.

And then he stood up, unbuckled and unzipped his tailored pants, dropped them to his ankles, and got on top of her.

"I need it bad, babe," he said as he slid his rod into her. "I need you!"

Shay pushed her body against his as she felt his entrance. She needed him, too. She wrapped her arms around him as he pumped on her in hard thrusts up her vagina. He was grunting as he thrust into her, and she was sighing as the feeling became a kind of lingering tingle. And her pussy started throbbing.

John didn't know what had come over him when he saw Shay at that front door. He didn't know if it was the fact that she looked so damn attractive in that white dress. Or the fact that her hair was pushed so adorably to one side. Or the fact that her eyes seemed to just glow. Or even the fact that that kid next door had jokingly told him not to hit it too hard when all he could think about was hitting it as hard as he could sling it.

Or, as he was beginning to believe as he fucked her long and harder than that kid next door could have ever imagined, he loved her. And he had to show his love.

He laid his body down on top of her gorgeous body and pumped on her in a way that made him feel lightheaded. He loved this woman. He loved every inch of this woman. This was the woman he wanted to spend the rest of his life with, there was no doubt in his mind about that.

"Oh, Shay," he said as he rubbed the side of his face against the side of her soft, sweet, velvety brown face. "I love you," he said, unable to shield himself any longer. "I love you so much!"

Tears were in his eyes as he said those words and Shay closed her eyes. They'd been through so much together. Could they make it? Could they actually make it this time?

"I love you too, John Malone," she said as his dick lashed deeper into her pussy as if her words alone spurred it on. And he held her tighter. And she held him tighter. And nothing as minor as their clothes, her hair, the fact that they were already running late, was even on their radar screen.

They fucked long and hard. He thrashed into her over and over and over again. He couldn't stop pounding her. She couldn't stop lifting her body higher to facilitate his pounding. They wanted to demonstrate their love. They wanted to shout it out. They were in love. They were secure in each other's arms. They were now in this together.

And nothing, not even the rain, wind, or any other storm that decided to break, was ever going to matter to them more than they mattered to each other.

The dinner party was held at the mayor's lakefront estate and John and Shay were among the last arriving guests. They had showered together after their long, sweaty romp on the bed, and had made their way to the mayor's estate as quickly as John's Porsche, breaking all kinds of speeding records, could get them there.

And when they stepped out of that Porsche and the valet gladly took the keys, and John looked over at Shay, he felt like a man who'd won the grand prize. He knew he was looking at her through rose-colored glasses now that he was finally acknowledging his love for her, but he couldn't help it. She was hot. And it wasn't any physical heat he was talking about. His love for Shay went far deeper than the physical. His love for her was transcendental. It was on a level that made him feel as if he'd finally found his soul mate. It made him feel as if he'd finally found that one woman who made him want to be a better man.

Although it was already common knowledge among the town's elite that their police chief had hooked up again with that Shay Turner, they had rarely seen the two of them in public together. This would be their opportunity to do a little gawking, both John and Shay knew it was so, and they also knew this joint appearance would only stoke the flames of that night two years ago.

But they didn't care. The people of this town could believe what they wanted to believe, but they refused to care. And sure enough, Shay wasn't in the mayor's home two minutes before she would past by a group of ladies and hear the little rumblings.

"Oh, is *she* the one?" one lady called herself whispering as Shay walked by.

"He left Blair for *that*?" was another common refrain.

331

But Shay wasn't trying to let those old biddies ruin her night. She had John in her heart. All they had was gossip.

John, too, wasn't thinking about the talk. He spent most of the evening laughing and talking and admiring how freely Shay laughed and talked. It was as if she was in her element now. Yes, they were gossiping about them. Yes, he wouldn't trust any of them as far as he could throw them. But that didn't stop Shay from enjoying herself. And that made him proud of his woman. Her spirit, her smile, her vivaciousness outshined every female in the room. Especially the gossipers. Especially those who thought it not robbery to rob Shay's good name.

But then the mayor made his appearance and walked down his winding staircase to applause from his guests. At first he did his usual meet and greet and was thrilled with the way his dinner party was turning out. Until he saw Shay. Until he saw John with Shay. He immediately whispered in his aide's ear and made his way to the library. Shay saw him leave, but never dreamed it had anything to do with her.

It had everything to do with her.

The aide told John that the mayor requested his presence, along with Miss Turner's, in the family library. John's jaw clenched, because he knew it was going to be some bullshit, but he took Shay's hand and made his way into the library.

"What is it, now?" she asked John as they walked.

"The mayor wants to see us."

Shay leaned into John. "Should I be worried?"

John snorted. "If he even thinks about offending you, he should be worried."

Shay smiled and allowed John to lead her into the lion's den.

The drive back to Shay's house was a quiet one. Shay was looking out of the side window, and John was seated behind the wheel staring straight ahead. And although they were holding hands, they both were mired in their own deep thought. But both of them were thinking about the same thing.

What John had said to Mayor Fletchette.

They had been in his library for only a few minutes. The mayor was going on and on about how he won reelection by the slimmest of margins and needed to be above reproach. He didn't want the townspeople dredging up any of that "old stuff," he declared, and Shay Turner was a part of that "old stuff."

"Is there anything else?" John asked his boss.

"You don't seem to understand the position you two are putting me in, John," the mayor insisted. "I barely survived that last election! I don't want them rehashing that old drama. And every time they see you with that woman they'll be rehashing it!"

Then John blurted out a response even he didn't see

coming. "Well they had better get used to it," he yelled, "because this woman is going to be my wife!"

Shay was stunned. The mayor was stunned. And John was darn near flabbergasted. Did he just say that? Did he really? And he didn't take it back.

Now they were heading back, to Shay's place, and neither one of them could find the words to say. They had never so much as mentioned the idea of marriage. Yes, they'd known each other a long time now. Yes, they'd been in a deeply committed relationship ever since her return to Brady. But marriage? That was a different ball of wax. No matter what anybody said to her, she knew being the wife of a man and being his girlfriend were two entirely different things. Were they truly ready for that?

For Shay it was a question of priorities. She was just getting her career jumpstarted yet again. The idea of throwing a husband in the mix would be unsettling on every level. And especially a husband like John. He was no meek and mild, passive man who would let her do whatever she wanted to do. That would have been great, but that wasn't John. Not that he would try to run her life, he wouldn't, but he would certainly have a major say in her life. And he would seek to correct her and protect her if he thought she was headed down the wrong road. He would wear the pants, without a doubt.

She would still have her freedom, she believed, but she also knew she would have to answer to John. That was just the way it would be, and she knew it. And sometimes she loved the idea of having somebody who was looking out for her. But other times she wasn't sure if she could get used to giving somebody else a say-so in her life. John, she knew, if she went down that road with him, would have the deciding vote.

John ran his hand through his hair as he drove and stared into the night. He still couldn't believe he had blurted out those words to the mayor. And he said it with such conviction, as if it was no news to him. Or to Shay. And Shay, poor thing, he thought as he glanced over at her. She was mortified when he blurted it out. She couldn't believe it, either. *Now, hold on there, buster*, he had expected her to say. *Who said anything about marriage*?

He looked down, at the way her hands were folded in her lap; at the way she was staring out the side window as if she was staring at a future with him. And it was scaring the life out of her.

John's heart squeezed in agony as he looked back out of the window in front of him. He felt like a man trapped in his own skin, and the only way he could break free was to turn himself inside out. Because that was what it would take to be a husband to a woman like Shay. He couldn't go to her with bullshit. He couldn't go to her half-stepping. He had to go to her bearing his soul.

His car stopped on her driveway and he got out and opened the door for her. They were still silent as they slowly walked up to her porch and then her front door. The boys next door were no longer outside, and the once raucous neighborhood was now eerily quiet. Shay pulled out her door key. John took the key from her and unlocked the door. He'd done it many times before. He, in fact, always took the key from her and unlocked the door. But this time, for Shay, it seemed to portend what she could expect in a John and Shay union: John would lead the way.

"Coming in?" she asked him as she moved to enter her home. He always came in.

But this time he balked. "No," he said, "I'd better get home and try to get some sleep."

She nodded. And although she understood, she also felt a stab of pain.

"Goodnight, Shay," John said to her, and leaned into her. They both closed their eyes as he kissed her on the lip. And when they parted, Shay could see the anguish in his eyes. He seemed more spooked by his blurt-out to the mayor than even she was.

"Go inside and lock the door before I leave," he said. And although he said the same thing every time he bought her home at night, it sounded like an order this night.

But she went inside, and locked the door.

John went back to his Porsche, cranked back up the loud, revved engine, and made his way down the quiet street that would lead him home, on the other side of town. Marriage, he kept thinking. Where did that come from? Marriage? Seriously?

Then he got onto Belcher Road and stopped at a red light. And he remembered tonight and how he felt when other men were checking out his woman. At first he was flattered. He knew what they meant. But then, if he'd ever admit it, he became a little fearful. What if she found one of those men more suitable than he was? What if one of those men didn't carry the baggage he carried and wasn't so gruff and tough the way he was? What if she fell in love and married one of them?

His heart sank.

And although the light turned green, giving him permission to go forward, he turned around, giving himself permission to go back.

Shay, in her bathrobe, had just taken off her clothes and was pouring herself a bath when she heard the banging on her front door. She froze at first, because she knew. Somehow she knew it would be him. But then she got in a hurry, because she wanted it to be him. Desperately.

After looking out of the peephole, she slung open the door. John, as was his way, barged inside.

"It won't work, Shay," he said to her. And her heart plummeted.

"What won't work?" she nervously asked him. "If we got married?"

337

"If we don't get married it won't work. No matter how much I pretend, it won't work. I can't live without you."

As soon as he said those words Shay flew into his arms.

"I can't live without you, darling," John said, tears in both their eyes. He lifted her up as he held her. And then he sat her back down, and leaned slightly back from her.

"Is marrying me, Shay, too much to ask of you?"

Shay smiled. And touched the side of his handsome face. "No, John. It's a wonderful thing to ask."

John stared at her. His heart preparing to soar. "Will you marry me?" he asked her.

Shay's heart pounded. "Yes," she said. "I will marry you."

And John smiled, and grinned, and lifted her in the air again. Only this time he felt lifted too.

SEVENTEEN

Paige and Shay drove to Hurley, Mississippi early that next morning, and met with the police chief. The chief, a big, burly black man, had his jail records ready for their perusal and his story was the same one he had told to Shay. He didn't connect the dots. The name Willie Glazer didn't ring a bell with him at all. Except when that anchor on the Channel 9 broadcast mentioned Glazer's middle name. *Cletis*. The chief's first name. It was only then did he remember that he had a prisoner there, some years ago, who had that same name. He checked, and was amazed when he saw the name William Cletis Glazer, and that Glazer was actually strung out on drugs and in his jail cell when three of those thirteen women were killed.

Shay and Paige had already confirmed that Glazer's middle name was indeed Cletis. With this evidence, and the chief's willingness to go on record, they felt they had their story. They drove back to Brady, a five-hour drive, and prepared their blockbuster of a front page story while they drove. It would premiere in tomorrow morning's paper. And although Paige told her not to give John a beforehand notice, Shay wasn't about to let a story this big blindside him completely.

She tried to reach him as soon as she left the Brady

339

, but he was still in meetings and
ed. Instead of going home, she drove
herself in with the key he had given to
up lying across his bed.

ne woke up, around two that morning, she
was naked, between the sheets, and his dick was
between her legs. He was kissing her ear.

"I knew you would wake up," he said with a smile.

Shay smiled too. "What if I didn't wake up?"

"I think I could have managed without you," John
said to laughter from her. Then he turned serious. "You'll
never know how pleased I was to see you in my bed. It
was such a long, draining day. Thank-you for being here
for me."

Shay knew there was an additional reason why she
was there, but he didn't give her a chance to express it.
Or at least she didn't want to express it just yet. Not
while he was kissing the back of her neck, and fondling
the front of her breasts, and rubbing her clit with his
massive tool. Not while she squirmed when he poked his
finger into her pussy and began to slide it in and out, over
and over, and then added another finger.

She leaned back against him, as his rock hard front
jutted against her soft back. He was naked too, the gold
chain around his neck was pouncing, as he grabbed his
dick, slipped it into her folds, and began to thrash her.
She cried out from his pounding, because it felt so good.
And he grunted out from the intense way she always

340

made him feel. Only this time he wasn't fucking his girlfriend. He was fucking the woman who was going to be his wife. And it was an exhilarating feeling.

He thrashed into her for nearly twenty straight minutes. What he had assumed would be a quickie turned out to be so laced with passion that it was anything but quick. But when he whipped her pussy one time too many, causing her to squeeze in climax, causing him to clench in release, his juice poured into her with a few more thrashes that left them both pulsating and pleased.

It would be just before dawn, around five am, hours after they both had fallen asleep, before they both would wake up, and she would tell him. She knew it wouldn't matter if she had told him when he first came home, or at five am now. But she still wanted him to know before he saw it in the paper.

At first there was no response.

She turned around, to face him. "Did you hear me?" she asked.

He was on his back, and his eyes were closed again. She shook him. "John!"

"It's what?" he asked her, startled, opening his eyes again and lifting his head slightly. Then he laid his head back down and pinched the bridge of his nose. "I'm sorry, babe. What did you say?"

"I know you're tired, but I need to let you know."

"Let me know what?"

"We have proof that Glazer couldn't have killed three of those thirteen women."

At first he just laid there. Then he looked at her. "You have *what*?"

"We, the Brady Beast, have proof that Willie Glazer didn't kill three of those women. I'm not supposed to tell you, but I didn't want you to be completely blindsided when the morning paper hits the stand." *And the shit hits the fan*, Shay wanted to add, but didn't.

John just stared at her. "What kind of proof do you have?"

"The police chief of a small town in Mississippi showed us proof that Glazer was in his jail for two solid weeks at the same time, over that two-week period, when three of those prostitutes were killed. There's no way Glazer could have killed those three women, no way, John. Which calls into question whether or not he killed any of those women. Especially since our District Attorney Pamela Ansley has made clear that one perp killed all thirteen."

John frowned. "And you believe this police chief?"

"I, why yes, why wouldn't I believe him?"

"A guy sits on information like this for a whole year after Glazer's arrested and then, just before the trial of the century is set to begin, he busts out with the big news? And you don't see why his so-called news would be at least a little suspicious? You can't possibly be that bad a reporter, Shanay."

Shay knew he was angry. He only called her by her full name when he was angry as hell with her. Then he lifted his naked body over her and got out of bed.

"What did Pamela say?" he asked her as he began putting on his pants.

Shay sat up in bed, the covers around her waist, her bare breasts revealed. "The DA?"

"Yes, the DA! What's wrong with you? Who else do you think I'm talking about? Since you didn't bother to get any comments from me, surely you got some from Pam."

Shay knew he'd be upset, but she never dreamed he'd be this upset. "I was going to call and get comments, but Paige decided against it."

"Oh, I'm sure Paige did. If it'll fuck with the police she's all for it."

"That's not fair, John."

"Like hell it's not! You decided to wait until that shit of a newspaper hits the stands to tell me that our entire case against Glazer is fucked, and you're calling *me* unfair?"

"I couldn't give you any heads up on my story before we went to print, and you know that! What if you tell one of your men, and they tell our competitor, then our competitor trumps us on a story we busted our asses on? I can't do that to my employer. You know I can't."

"But you can do it to me?"

"It hasn't anything to do with you!" Shay yelled. "I'm

343

a journalist!"

"You're my woman!" John thundered back. "First and last! You hear me, Shanay? First and last! I'm your man first and last! If you're going to be my wife, you had better understand that."

"Oh, so, I have to answer to you about my job, too, is that what you're saying? There will be nothing about my life that I'll have control over? You'll control it all?"

John took a moment to calm himself back down. "I don't want to control any of it. I just don't like the way you handled this. And if I don't like the way you handle something I'm going to tell your ass I don't like it. You could have phoned me, Shay."

"I tried to phone you! I tried, John. But you were in meetings and they couldn't disturb you. I even left messages for you."

"When did you first find out about this so-called chief and his new information?"

"The police chief phoned me the day of Mayor Fletchette's dinner party."

"What?" John asked, astounded. "You knew about it then and didn't tell me anything?"

"I hadn't seen the evidence for myself. Paige and I went to Mississippi yesterday morning and saw the info."

John could not believe that either. "Mississippi?" he said. "You went to Mississippi yesterday?"

"Yeah, to follow the story."

"And there I was, thinking you were safely at work,

doing your job, when you were in *Mississippi*? And you didn't think I needed to be aware of that fact?"

It didn't sound unreasonable at the time, Shay thought. But now, the way John pointed it out, she realized her problem. She couldn't jump up and do whatever she wanted when she wanted and how she wanted without at least letting him know. That was the deal now. She had a man now. A real man who wasn't going to take a backseat in her life.

"I didn't think about it," she admitted.

John ran his hand through his hair. He stared at her. There was a lot she didn't think about. "Go on," he said.

Shay reluctantly continued. "After we got back into town and the story was in the queue, I tried to reach you. That's why I came over here. And I knew if I told you last night or if I told you this morning it wasn't going to make much difference, I know that. Especially since the story was already locked and loaded and ready for this morning's distribution. But I still wanted to give you a heads up."

He just stood there, his shirt in his hand. His pants on but unzipped. "We'll talk tonight," he said, "but I'm very upset with you, Shanay."

Tears began to appear in Shay's eyes. What did he want from her? "You're upset because I did my job and didn't let the Tribune or any of our other competitors get the story out before we got it out? Is that why you're upset?"

345

"I'm upset that you would believe I'd betray you like that. I'm upset because you didn't come to me first and let me know what you had. I wouldn't have run to some damn competitor of yours. But I would have devised a strategy for handling the onslaught. This story of yours is going to set off a bomb in this town, a firestorm, Shay, and like always I'm un-fucking-prepared! I expected it from Paige and that *got*damn Brady Beast. I never expected it from you!"

He stared at her longer, and then headed for the shower.

The headline was bold: **New Evidence Exonerates Glazer. Pam Ansley Under Fire**.

John stood behind his desk staring, once again, at that newspaper Pamela Ansley had just tossed onto his desk. She stood there, tall, leggy, blonde and attractive, and shook her head. She was so angry she could hardly contain herself. Craig Yannick was also in the office, along with Wayne Peete. And they, too, felt blindsided.

"How could she do this to you?" Yannick was asking John. "After all you did for her, after how you stood up for her, how could she do this to you?"

"She was doing her job, Cap," Peete said, but it angered Pam.

"How can you defend that bitch?" she roared. "She didn't even bother to get a comment from me! Nothing. I called the publisher of that so-called newspaper this morning and you know what that butthole told me?" She looked at John when she asked this. "He said the public already knows our side of the story. Now it's Glazer's turn. Glazer's turn, he said. A serial killer's turn!"

"Just hold on, Pam," John said. "Hold on, all right?" Then he looked her in the eye. "And if you call Shanay a bitch again you can get your ass out of my office, I don't care how upset you are."

Pamela exhaled. "I'm sorry," she said. "All right? I didn't mean to disrespect your whatever she is to you."

"My fiancé," he replied and everybody looked at him. Especially Pamela, who, after Blair died, had hoped to make some inroads with John herself. Shanay Turner was long gone to Philly. She thought she stood a chance. But when she approached him about spending the night together, he wouldn't even do that. He wasn't available was what he told her. Wasn't available. As if he was waiting for Shanay to come back. As if a bitch like her was worth waiting for.

"Well, whatever," Pamela said dismissively. "But I'm worried, John. My office has already received death threats. Those civil rights activists are all over television gloating about how we were covering up the truth all along. And I just got word that the judge is already considering a defense motion to dismiss all charges. He's already considering it."

"When is he expected to make his ruling?"

"Tomorrow morning. His office says either the trial

will begin as planned on that day and the defense motion will be denied, or the motion will be granted and all charges will be dismissed. Either way, it all goes down tomorrow morning."

Yannick shook his head. "This is bad, Chief. No matter how we try to dress up this pig, it's bad. We've got to prepare for riots in the streets if that defense motion is denied. Now that those activists have this so-called investigative report of Turner's as proof of what they've been saying all along, they'll expect nothing less than a complete exoneration for Glazer. If the judge denies the defense motion to dismiss, we're screwed. This town could erupt."

"What can we do, Chief?" Peete asked the boss.

John ran his hand across his eyes. "I want you and Kincaid to get over to Hurley, Mississippi, wherever the hell that is, and check out that police chief. Talk to the residents, I understand there's only a handful there. I think there's only something like two or three hundred people in the whole town. See what they know about this character."

"Yes, sir," Peete said, hurrying out.

"And Peete," John added, "tell Kincaid to check out that Channel 9 broadcast that supposedly figures so prominently in why that chief realized he had Glazer in his jail."

"Channel 9 in Mississippi?"

"Apparently, yeah."

"What's there to check out?" Yannick asked.

"I just want to make sure it's true, that some news anchor did indeed mention Glazer's middle name over the last few days. If we can show that the chief is lying about that, it won't be so far-fetched to believe he's lying about the rest of it."

Peete nodded his head and left.

Pamela folded her slender arms. John looked at those arms and then looked into her eyes. "We'll get through this, Pammie, don't worry," he said.

"This is bad, John," she said. "If we can't discredit that police chief's story, then we're screwed just like Craig said. I made it clear, our investigation made it clear that one perp for all thirteen girls. No ands, ifs, or buts about it. Given the info that wasn't released to the public, and the fact that all thirteen were killed in the exact same way, it had to be the same perp. But if it wasn't Glazer on three of the thirteen, and we have no evidence that he had some buddy killer with him, we can kiss our entire case goodbye. And, by the way, probably our entire careers while we're at it."

John shook his head, and then took a seat.

Later that evening Shay leaned back on her sofa and watched the news reports. Her article dominated every one of them. John was in the kitchen, pouring himself a drink. When he came back in, he stood behind the sofa, behind her, and watched too.

Activist Marlon Graham was being interviewed and he was, as expected, praising the decision and blasting Pamela Ansley. "She'll stop at nothing to win," he said to the reporter. "Ever since she became DA she's been nothing but a terror to our community. She and Malone both are the worst possible people to be in the positions they're in. They don't deserve to be in those positions. But thank God for Shay Turner," he said with a smile. "She's our very own wonder woman! She came back to town and turned this town upside down. She uncovered the lies and the deceits and the whole cover-up. She's the hero in all of this. But John Malone and Pamela Ansley are a disgrace to the human race and it's time for them to go!"

Shay changed the channel. But another activist was on the different channel: "Malone didn't investigate," he was declaring. "He didn't track down all of the leads or try to disprove his crazy theories. He made the facts fit his theory. It took a young reporter, Shay Turner, to get to the bottom of this. Miss Turner should be commended for her hard-hitting report. John Malone should be ashamed."

Shay quickly clicked the whole thing off. "What does he know?" she asked and tossed the remote onto the coffee table.

She looked at John. He walked from behind the sofa, one hand in his pants pocket, the other one clutching his glass of wine, and lumbered over to the living room window. He just stood there, his back to Shay, and then he turned halfway toward her and leaned his tired body against the window's side frame. Shay's heart pounded against her chest.

"They're just blowing smoke," she said to him. "They know there's no cover-up or anything like that."

"If the man said there was a cover-up, then there's a cover-up. That's the way it works in this town. You know it and I know it."

"But it's not true."

"What the hell difference does that make, Shanay?"

"I was given evidence and I reported it. That's all that went down here. I don't see what's the big damn deal. The judge will make the call tomorrow morning. I can't help it if those activists are on TV giving me more credit than I deserve. I just reported the evidence that I saw with my own two eyes. The police chief in Hurley showed me the records. He showed me where Glazer was in his jail for those two weeks when three of those victims were killed. He showed it to me. And I reported it."

John was staring at her. "Be careful," he said.

Shay didn't like the way he was staring at her. "Be careful of what?" she asked.

"Of your own ambition. Be careful. The Brady Beast has a way of sucking you in, getting you to be the hero of the community, and then spitting you out if your hero status gets any kind of tarnish. Because it will be

351

tarnished, Shay. Willie Glazer killed those women. All thirteen of them. I intend to prove that he did. If it takes me months and months, I'll prove it. Regardless of what that judge does tomorrow."

"So even in the face of irrefutable evidence, you'll still believe that Glazer killed those women?"

"I'll go to my grave believing it," John said.

Shay frowned. She never dreamed he'd be that kind of cop. "You have no DNA on Glazer, you have nothing but some trumped up confession---"

"It wasn't trumped up!" John yelled, pointing his glass of wine at her, some of it spilling over the brim. "I got that confession myself and I don't trump up anything!" He let out a harsh exhale. Then he chugged down his remaining wine in one swift swoop, as if he wanted it to burn going down, and then sat the empty glass on the side table with a hard clack.

"I've got to get back to the office," he said, as if tired of even arguing about it.

Shay was disappointed. She stood up. "You aren't going to stay for dinner?"

He shook his head, moving toward her. "I can't. I've got to meet with some of those activists that just graced your television screen and once again try to persuade them to work with my men tomorrow to keep the calm."

"You're afraid of a riot if the judge doesn't exonerate Glazer?"

He stood in front of her. "A riot is the least of my

worries. I'm afraid of retaliatory killings. I'm afraid of death threats that have been hurled against Pam Ansley. A riot is the least of my concerns, and it's a major concern too."

A look of distress came into Shay's eyes. "What was I supposed to do, John? I had to report it."

John placed his hands on her arms. He rubbed her arms. Then he looked her in the eyes. "I know you did," he said.

"But that doesn't make it any easier for you," she said. "Does it?"

John smiled a smile so drained of cheer that it crushed Shay. He then pulled her into his big arms. He was scared for his town. Scared for the DA. And terrified for Shanay.

EIGHTEEN

The courtroom was packed the morning the judge was set to make his ruling. Every crime reporter in town, including Shay, sat in great anticipation. Shay, in fact, was given the seat of honor directly behind the defense table, and all of the other reporters kept staring at her. Including Ed Barrington, who was representing the Tribune. *How did she get the big scoop*, his expression appeared to say. But she ignored all of their looks. And then it was time. The judge entered the courtroom. They all stood as he made his entrance.

As Shay stood, she glanced toward the back of the room and saw John standing there. She hadn't heard from him at all after he left her house last night, although she tried to phone him several times. But she understood. The man was busying trying to keep the powder keg from exploding. Which, she prayed, wouldn't happen regardless of the outcome.

She tried to get a read on his expression, but she couldn't. Besides, he wasn't looking at her, anyway, but at Pamela Ansley, whom, Shay also noticed, looked extremely strained.

They all sat back down. The silence in the room was palpable. And then the judge, a small, slight man with a receding hairline, began to speak.

He spoke for nearly twenty minutes, about all of his

354

reservations surrounding this case. No DNA, no eye witnesses. Just a confession. A very detailed confession, yes, but a confession that the accuser now claims he didn't willingly make. The judge even mentioned Shay and her "keen investigative reporting" by name. He agreed with her report that if Glazer was locked up in a Mississippi jail during the commission of three of the crimes, how could he have committed the other crimes? He then went case by case, making clear each time how the prosecution determined that there had to be one perp and one perp alone for all thirteen killings. The judge dismissed any talk of copy cats and partners in crime because the prosecution never presented any evidence to even suggest such theories. He had to go with what he had before him, he said. And what he had was flimsy at best.

But when he finally said that he had reached the conclusion to "drop all charges against Mr. Glazer," the courtroom erupted. The victims' families screamed foul and the defendant's family cried relief. And everybody around the defense table, from the defendant himself and his attorneys, hugged and thanked Shay. And his family hugged her too.

"If it wasn't for you," Glazer's mother said to her, as the crowd pressed her closer to Shay, "they would have locked my boy away forever."

Shay felt as if she'd won the lottery, as she couldn't stop grinning from ear to ear. When she looked over at

Pamela Ansley, however, John was at her side, taking her briefcase, and escorting her out of the courtroom, his hand firmly pressed against her back. Shay's excitement waned, after seeing the two of them together, but the euphoria around her wouldn't keep her down. She looked at Glazer, who had tears streaming down his face, and she felt like the queen of the world.

A queen who was alone that night. John didn't come over and he didn't call. And she wasn't about to call him. She knew he was busy. She knew that many of the townspeople were upset by Glazer's release, believing that a serial killer was on the loose again, and he had to quell their fears. Which, she also knew, was a tall order given that he agreed with them.

So Shay spent the balance of her evening taking in news report after news report that painted her as the real hero of the story. And although Shay never thought of herself as excessively ambitious, it still felt good nonetheless.

But the more she watched TV, the less excited she became. Because it was too much. Because she was being given credit that she knew she didn't deserve. And then there was a quick, close shot on one of the broadcasts, of John with Pamela Ansley as they hurried out of the courthouse. His large hand was still pressed against her back, a fact the cameras made a point of recording, and Shay's heart pounded when she saw it. The microphones were shoved in their faces and the camera was practically pushed up their noses, but they both walked with a dignity and grace that Shay couldn't help but admire. Pamela Ansley was a beautiful woman, and far closer to John's age than Shay was, someone who seemed, she had to admit, perfect for him. Which made Shay wonder if he was not only working to calm the fears of the townspeople, but to calm Pamela Ansley's fears too. Then she dismissed such nonsense.

But she still couldn't get him on the phone. Just his voice mail at home, at work, and on his cell. He obviously wasn't available to talk. Or, she feared, available to talk to her.

She leaned back on her lounger, sipped wine, and tried to recapture that feeling of euphoria she felt when the judge announced Glazer's release. That felt so special then. As if it was the crowning achievement of her entire career. But she couldn't recapture it. She kept seeing John, being there for Pamela, taking care of Pamela, while totally ignoring her. She was a big girl, she could take care of herself, but still. He could have at least given her a call. She had vastly underestimated how strongly he felt about the Glazer case, that was clear to her now, but that still, she felt, didn't give him a license to ignore her.

And she refused to let it give her a license to feel bad about herself. She did her job. The evidence dropped into her lap and she knocked it out of the ballpark. And it was a darn good hit, too, she decided.

357

But even as good as she felt about the job well done, it was still a shock to her when Paige phoned and asked her to come over to the office. It was after six at night, and kind of late to be at the office, but she gladly agreed. The last thing she wanted to do was lounge around her house sulking.

When she parked her VW and walked into the Brady Beast newspaper building, she was pleased to see a group of her colleagues, all of whom had been able to tolerate her new dominance at the paper. They sat around laughing and talking at a big table in the back that consisted of two small tables pushed together, and Paige asked everyone assembled to lift their glasses of beer, soda, juice, or water in a toast. When everyone complied, she stood up.

"As you all know we now have a brand new edition to our staff," Paige said. "She's an investigative reporter of the first caliber who has single-handedly tripled our circulation in just three months on the job. And whose very first day of employment netted her what could only be described as the interview of the year. A long sit down with Willie Glazer. As Marlon Graham, that venerable scion of the English language has called her, we now call her, too: here's to our very own Wonder Woman!"

The reporters laughed as they raised their glasses in toast to Shay. Only until now had Shay heard about this remarkable increase in circulation, which made her feel vindicated too. It was, in fact, a wonderful feeling. If

John could have been there it would have been a remarkable feeling. She even stole away and phoned him again. She left a message on his voice mail, telling him where she was and inviting him over, and then she went back to her festive colleagues.

While she was partying it up at the Beast, however, John's Silverado was flying through the streets of Brady, his inside siren blaring, as he arrived at an abandoned building in the heart of Dodge. He jumped from his truck and hurried to the back of the building. Police cars were already camped out in back, and police tape was being gathered to cordon off the entire building. Yannick came out of the building and met him where the body lay.

John bent down on his haunches and uncovered the body. Young, black woman. Yannick bent down beside him.

"Same m.o.?" John asked his second-in-command.

"One-hundred percent the same, even down to that v-cut in the duct tape that wasn't public knowledge."

John exhaled, his heart ramming against his chest. All he could think of was this poor woman and what her death was going to do to Shay.

He stood up. "Haul his ass in for questioning."

"We're already on it. But seems our boy Glazer is nowhere to be found."

"Ah, geez, don't tell me that, Yannick."

"Wish I didn't have to, but it's a fact."

"Put out a warrant for his arrest, *got*dammit."

"That's been taken care of, too."

Then John saw something in his peripheral vision. He looked and saw what he knew could be gold. "Is that camera live?" he asked.

Yannick looked across the field where John was looking. There was a dry cleaners with a camera installed just above the back awning. It was barely visible. "Don't know," he replied.

"Find out who owns that joint and get him down here now."

"Yes, sir," Yannick said and hurried to take care of it.

John shook his head. "What a mess," he said as he bent down again, not to look at the victim's body again, but to keep from passing out himself.

They were finishing their last round of drinks when Paige got the call. Nobody paid her any attention, least of which Shay, who was listening intensely to another reporter go on and on about the plans she had for her own career. But when Paige hung up, and Shay met her eyes, she knew immediately that something was terribly wrong. "What is it?" she asked her.

"There's been another murder," Paige said and the entire staff fell silent.

"What do you mean?" Shay asked.

"There's been another murder completely fitting the description of the other thirteen murders."

Shay frowned. "But that doesn't make sense. How could---"

"And there's more, Shay," Paige said. "They have a video from a dry cleaners that was across from the crime scene. They have Glazer on tape committing this crime."

Shay leaned back, her heart in her shoe. *What have I done*, she thought inwardly, unable to say another word.

She looked at Paige, but Paige was already hurrying to her office to contact the publisher. Some of the reporters followed Paige.

And when Shay stood up to leave, nobody stopped her. Nobody comforted her and told her not to worry. Nobody told her that everything would be all right.

The hero, their silence seemed to suggest, was now the goat.

Shay grabbed up her purse and keys and headed for the exit. She expected her remaining colleagues to at least tell her something, but they were too stunned, still too busy wondering if their readers would turn on them, to give Shay another thought. Shay's goose was already cooked as far as they was concerned. Because they knew, like Shay knew, that it would be Shay who the public would blame first. It was the blowback that they were concerned about. How, they wondered, would this mess affect them?

And John's words came true. Be careful, he told her. The Brady Beast had a way of eating its' own.

Shay made her way out into the parking lot, ready to

get in her car and make a quick getaway. But she faltered. She kept thinking about a dead woman, about how that woman would still be alive if she would not have wrote that story, and she leaned against her Beetle. She covered her face in shame.

She didn't even hear John's truck drive up. She didn't even hear him hurry across the parking lot to her side. All she knew was that he pulled her into his arms, lifted her into his truck, and took her away from there.

John's heart was hammering as he drove a sobbing Shay home. He knew she would take it hard. He knew as soon as word leaked that that douche bag Glazer had killed another girl that Shay would be devastated. Just as he also knew that that same adoring public, who just hours earlier were singing her praises, would be excoriating her now.

"Where are we going?" she asked him between sniffles, as he drove past the turn that would carry her home.

"To my place," he said. "The press won't look for you there."

Shay looked at him. He looked as if he hadn't slept in days. She looked so wounded to him. "You think the press will be looking for me?' she naively asked him.

"Honey, of course," John said, and then, seeing that distraught look on her face, regretted saying it. He placed her hand in his. "It's okay, babe," he said.

"And you're sure it was Glazer? On the video, I

362

mean?"

He wanted to appease her, he truly did not want to upset her any more than she already was. But there was no way around it tonight. "Yes," he said. "It's him."

Shay looked out of the window of his truck again. And he took her to his home.

Two hours later and they were still seated in his living room. Shay was curled up in a chair, a cup of hot chocolate in her hands, and John was lying prone on the sofa, his suit coat off, knowing that he had to get back to the office.

But he wasn't about to leave her right now.

And then the doorbell rang. "Who could that be?" Shay asked as John got up.

"Probably one of my men," John said, knowing that the Glazer case was unfolding faster than even he could contain. And he was right. He opened the door and Yannick was standing there. He let him in.

Yannick glanced at Shay. He could barely contain his anger.

"What is it?" John asked him.

Yannick exhaled. "We caught Glazer."

"Thank God!" John said, walking in to grab his suit coat. "Where is he?"

"Downtown, waiting for you."

"Good man."

"And there's more," Yannick said as John began

363

putting on his suit coat.

"What is it?" John asked, and both John and Shay looked at Yannick.

"That Channel 9 broadcaster never mentioned Glazer's middle name, they didn't even know Glazer's middle name."

John began pulling down the sleeve beneath his suit coat, his heart pounding. "But why would that police chief lie like that?"

"To save his cousin's hide," Yannick said.

Shay's heart dropped. "His cousin?" she said.

"They are distant cousins," Yannick said, "and Glazer's mother begged him to help them. It took them weeks to concoct this scheme about the middle name. Glazer and this cop were both named after some other relative named Cletis. So they knew they could begin there. Claim that's how he remembered Glazer because they had the same odd name."

"Geez," John said, rubbing down his hair, looking at Shay's reaction.

"Chief Cobbler," Yannick continued, "cooked his own books to make it look like Glazer was in his jail cell, and then he contacted the one newspaper they knew would give him the benefit of the doubt."

"The Brady Beast," John said.

"There ya' go," Yannick said. Shay could hardly believe her ears. "When this police chief found out that his cousin Willie Glazer was on film killing another girl, he

364

was mortified. When we contacted him, he was ready to talk. He broke down and admitted everything. That fool actually thought Glazer was innocent, that's why he agreed to help him. He never dreamed any kin of his could be a murderer."

John shook his head. "Haul his ass in too," he said. "His lies helped to spring Glazer and now another young lady has been killed."

"Yes, sir," Yannick said.

Then John looked at Shay. "You go on back to the station, Yan," he said to his captain, "I'm on my way."

Yannick glanced at Shay, his anger still showing. "Sure thing, boss," he said, and left.

John walked up to Shay's chair and bent down, his hands on either side of the arms. "I don't want you sitting up here worrying yourself to death, now Shay," he said. "What happened has happened and there's nothing we can do about it."

Shay nodded her head. "I know," she said. "But it just feels so out of control now. I never once thought we were releasing a serial killer, I never once thought that. I just took that police chief's word for it and---"

"And gave him the benefit of the doubt," John said.

A tear dropped from Shay's eye that she quickly wiped away. "He saw me coming a mile away," she said. "Me and my delusions of grandeur."

John rubbed her cheek and then pulled her into his arms. "Stop beating yourself up. What's done is done.

You didn't kill that girl, Glazer did. You weren't guilty of lying, that police chief was. And you didn't release Glazer to kill again. The judge did that."

"But my story---"

"Was a story based on what you were told. You reported it. Everything else was out of your hands."

Shay knew John was trying to make her feel better. She knew he was trying to make her see the light. But all she saw was darkness, and her part in it. Her oversized part in it.

John kissed her on the lips, warned her again not to obsess on it, told her that he'd be back as soon as he could get back, and left.

Shay had promised to keep it together before he left, but as soon as the door closed, she fell apart.

The tears came and wouldn't leave. John had refused to let her watch the news while he was there, but she knew she had to know. Who was the girl? What happened to her? He wouldn't discuss the details with her, but she had to know.

She turned on the television. She had to wait until the eleven o clock news before she got any information. And it dominated the news. The girl, young, pretty, was named Naomi Barkley. Unlike the others, she wasn't a prostitute, just a random girl walking home from her job at a twenty-four hour convenience store. Glazer was in an alleyway as she passed, had grabbed her, forced her behind the abandoned building, and then strangled and raped her. Just like all the others, he raped her after he had strangled her. She was only nineteen.

Shay's heart sank when a picture of the girl appeared. It sank further when the parents, who were on the scene, spoke to the cameras. Although the father was too devastated to be angry, the mother was outraged. "She did it," she angrily proclaimed. "That reporter, that Shay Turner is responsible for all of this! They got them to release this killer and now my baby's dead. Now my baby's gone. And Shay Turner's running 'round like some big shot. My child's dead and gone and she's running around like she did something big. This ain't right. Ain't nobody nowhere gonna tell me this is right!"

Shay turned off the television. She couldn't take it. Because every word that woman spoke was nothing but the truth. She went into John's bedroom, laid across his bed, and tried with all she had to fall asleep. If only she could sleep.

But sleep wouldn't come. For a full hour she just lay there, thinking about nothing but Glazer and that girl. And then she went back up front. Turned on those late night news talk shows. And listened to the agony of the mother, to the anger of other citizens, as the news of Glazer's new crime dominated local TV.

It would be another hour of this, as if Shay was determined to punish herself, until even the castigation of the news wasn't punishment enough. And suddenly she

367

felt as if she had to leave. She couldn't stay here another second longer. John had given her keys, to his house, his truck, and his Porsche months ago, so she used what she had.

She composed a note, taped it to his front door, and ran. She jumped into his Porsche, her heart hammering, and drove away. She had to get away. She couldn't stay here anymore.

Not long after her decampment, John arrived back home. He wasn't aware that his Porsche, which was normally in the garage, had been taken by Shay until he got out of his truck and made his way to the front door. And he saw her note.

I need time away. Will call. Shay.

That was it. Those seven little words. And John was devastated. He began shaking his head. No, he decided. Not again. He wasn't losing her again!

He jumped into his truck, drove with sirens blaring to her house, hoping that she would have stopped there to at least grab some clothes.

But she had apparently already come and gone.

Then he remembered that her car was still at the Brady Beast. And knowing Shay, she would have preferred her own car if she was leaving town.

He drove, again with his sirens blaring, to the Brady Beast. He was hoping against hope that he was right; that she had made this one additional stop. He began to pray.

And that was when he saw her. She was getting out of his Porsche and going toward her Beetle. John swerved his truck behind her Beetle, effectively blocking it in, and jumped out.

Shay was surprised to see him. She had expected to make a clean getaway.

John placed his hands on her arms.

"I just need a little time," she said with a plea in her voice.

"No, Shay," John said with pain in his. "The last time you needed a little time you stayed away from me for two years. Not this time. I can't take that. If you go, I go. We go together. If you stay, I stay. We stay together. We're in this together, Shay. I let you get away from me before. It cost me two years of sleepless nights. I can't let that happen again."

Shanay tried to smile through her tears. "It hurt so much, John. It hurt so much!"

"I know, baby," John said, pulling her into his arms. "But that's why you have to stay. We'll face this together. Understood?"

Shay closed her eyes and embraced him too. "Understood," she said, although her heart was still breaking, although she really didn't understand any of it

EPILOGUE

The waves crushed against the rocks and John walked along the winding shore in his Bermuda shorts, sandals, and shades. Shay was just ahead of him, picking up seashells, running and grabbing them as if she was a kid in a candy store. John couldn't stop smiling as he watched her. She'd been through so much, but she was still standing. And was still able, he was pleased to realize, to embrace the good, bad, and ugly of life with gusto.

It was a month after that craziness with Glazer. The Mississippi police chief, Glazer's cousin, was fired from his small-town post. The judge who released Glazer and threw out the prosecution's case, resigned under tremendous public pressure. Paige Kent, the senior editor of the Brady Beast, was supposedly called away on a "family emergency" and took an indefinite leave of absence. Presumably until the public outcry calmed down. The young community activists who were spearheading the release Glazer campaign found themselves with dwindling followers after the video of Glazer killing that girl was released. The only career, in fact, left unscathed was Shay's. Not because they didn't want to excoriate her too. They did. But John wouldn't allow it.

He fought for Shay. He even met privately with the

publisher, just the two of them, and reminded him that he knew all about that questionable land deal he made a few years back with those equally questionable out-of-town investors. That deal, John reminded the publisher, could come back to bite him in the ass. The publisher agreed that he wouldn't want that kind of bite, and Shay kept her job. Shay assumed it was because of the ultimate fairness of the Brady Beast brass. John never bothered to disabuse her of that belief.

Shay kept her job, but more importantly than that, John thought, as she started running back to him in her string bikini and that flowing pink sarong around her waist, she kept her spirit too. And her youthful vigor. And her faith in her fellow man.

"Aren't they gorgeous?" she said to him, showing him the handful of shells she'd collected. "They're smooth and rough. They're beautiful and odd looking. There's just something different about each one of them, isn't it?"

"They're odd, all right," John said, taking one of them from her hand and examining it. "I'll give you that. They're certainly different."

"Like us?" Shay asked with a smile.

John smiled too, his blue eyes blazing with joy behind his dark shades. He looked at her with such love in those eyes. "Yes," he said, heartfelt. "Exactly like us."

"I'm going to go and find more," Shay said excitedly, ready to run off again. But John grabbed her by the hand

and pulled her back.

"Hold on," he said. "Not so fast."

He pulled her to him, his arms around her narrow waist. "I want to spend a little quality time with you first."

"You're spending quality time with me."

"Not here," he said. "But upstairs. In our cozy little room."

Shay inwardly smiled. She knew exactly what he meant. "Why, John Malone," she said in her best southern accent, "what do you take me for?"

"Why, Shanay Malone," he replied in his worst southern accent, "I take you for my wife. And my wife and I are here, in Hawaii, on our wonderful honeymoon. I intend to spend a good deal of this honeymoon getting some honey." Shay laughed. "I intend to spend quality time with my brand new wife, in our bed, fucking her brains out."

Shay smiled as her entire body shivered in delight. She remembered last night, when they first arrived in Hawaii, and how her brains were still recovering from the last time he spent "quality time" with her.

"Well, excuse me, Mr. Malone," she said, "but I came here to enjoy the beautiful beaches, and collect the gorgeous seashells. I didn't come here to fuck."

John almost laughed. "Well, Mrs. Malone," he said, pulling her closer, kissing her in quick kisses, "I came here to see the beautiful beaches, to collect the gorgeous seashells, and to fuck my wife silly. Now you have two

372

minutes to decide. Me, in bed, with you, right now, or you and your seashells alone on this beach."

Shay dropped those seashells so fast they slammed into the sand. They both laughed and then began running, hand in hand, toward their magnificent beachfront hotel. They were in love, throbbing with desire, and finally, at least for right now, as free as birds.

ABOUT THE AUTHOR

Katherine Cachitorie is the bestselling author of numerous novels, including Loving The Head Man, Some Came Desperate: A Love Saga, and When We Get Married.

Visit www.austinbrookpublishing.com for more information on all of her titles.

22333404R00216

Made in the USA
Lexington, KY
23 April 2013